WINGS OF FIRE

WINGS OF FIRE

MOON RISING

by

TUI T. SUTHERLAND

SCHOLASTIC INC.

This book was originally published in hardcover by Scholastic Press in 2015.

ISBN 978-0-545-68536-8

Text copyright © 2015 by Tui T. Sutherland
Map and border design © 2015 by Mike Schley
Dragon illustrations © 2015 by Joy Ang

25 24   21 22/0

Printed in the U.S.A.   40
This edition first printing, January 2016
Book design by Phil Falco

For all the FanWings and everyone
who reads these books — I hope you
love the new dragonets as much
as I love you guys!

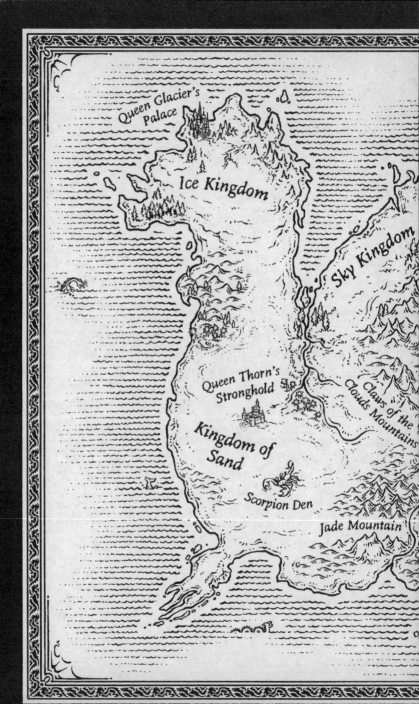

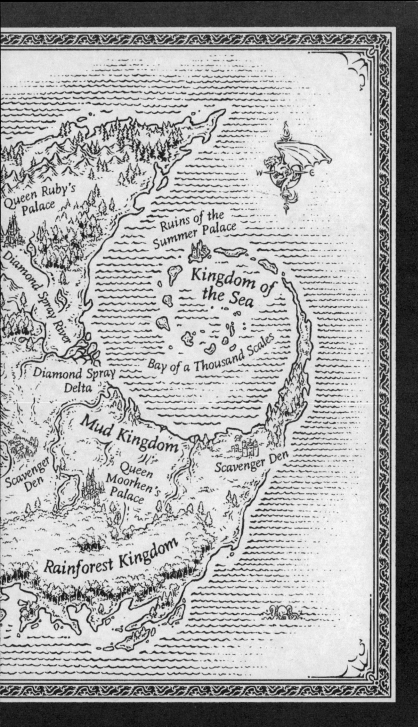

Queen Ruby's
Palace

Diamond Spray River

Ruins of the
Summer Palace

Kingdom of
the Sea

W N E S

Bay of a Thousand Scales

Diamond Spray
Delta

Mud Kingdom

Scavenger
Den

Queen
Moorhen's
Palace

Scavenger Den

Rainforest Kingdom

Ice Kingdom

Kingdom

A GUIDE TO THE
DRAGONS

Sand

Scorpion Den

Jade Mountain

Queen Ruby's Palace

Ruins of the Summer Palace

Scales

OF PYRRHIA

UPDATED AND EDITED BY
STARFLIGHT OF THE NIGHTWINGS

Scavenger Den

Queen Moorhen's Palace

Scavenger De

Rainforest Kingdom

WELCOME TO THE JADE MOUNTAIN ACADEMY!

At this school, you will be learning side by side with dragons from all the other tribes, so we wanted to give you some basic information that may be useful as you get to know one another.

You have been assigned to a winglet with six other dragons; the winglet groups are listed on the following page.

Thank you for being a part of this school. You are the hope of Pyrrhia's future. You are the dragons who can bring lasting peace to this world.

WE WISH YOU ALL THE POWER OF WINGS OF FIRE!

JADE WINGLET

IceWing: Winter
MudWing: Umber
NightWing: Moonwatcher
RainWing: Kinkajou
SandWing: Qibli
SeaWing: Turtle
SkyWing: Carnelian

GOLD WINGLET

IceWing: Icicle
MudWing: Sora
NightWing: Bigtail
RainWing: Tamarin
SandWing: Onyx
SeaWing: Pike
SkyWing: Flame

SILVER WINGLET

IceWing: Changbai
MudWing: Sepia
NightWing: Fearless
RainWing: Boto
SandWing: Ostrich
SeaWing: Anemone
SkyWing: Thrush

COPPER WINGLET

IceWing: Alba
MudWing: Marsh
NightWing: Mindreader
RainWing: Coconut
SandWing: Pronghorn
SeaWing: Snail
SkyWing: Peregrine

QUARTZ WINGLET

IceWing: Ermine
MudWing: Newt
NightWing: Mightyclaws
RainWing: Siamang
SandWing: Arid
SeaWing: Barracuda
SkyWing: Garnet

SANDWINGS

Description: pale gold or white scales the color of desert sand; poisonous barbed tail; forked black tongues

Abilities: can survive a long time without water, poison enemies with the tips of their tails like scorpions, bury themselves for camouflage in the desert sand, breathe fire

Queen: since the end of the War of SandWing Succession, Queen Thorn

Students at Jade Mountain: Arid, Onyx, Ostrich, Pronghorn, Qibli

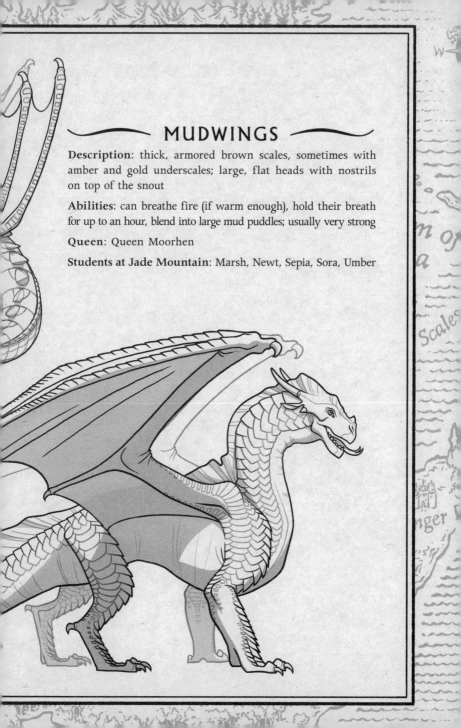

MUDWINGS

Description: thick, armored brown scales, sometimes with amber and gold underscales; large, flat heads with nostrils on top of the snout

Abilities: can breathe fire (if warm enough), hold their breath for up to an hour, blend into large mud puddles; usually very strong

Queen: Queen Moorhen

Students at Jade Mountain: Marsh, Newt, Sepia, Sora, Umber

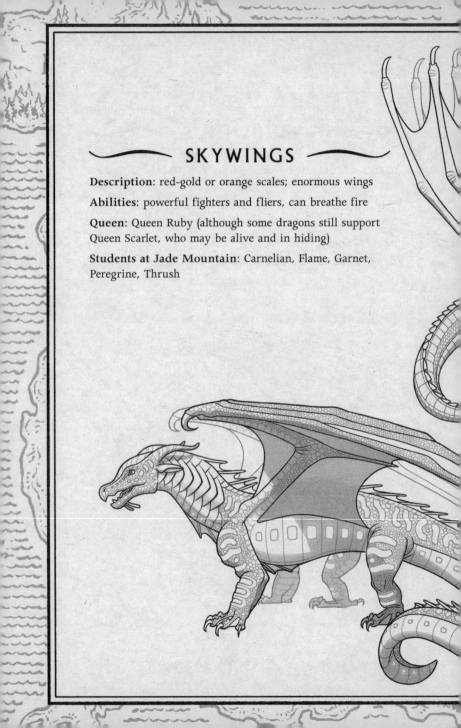

SKYWINGS

Description: red-gold or orange scales; enormous wings

Abilities: powerful fighters and fliers, can breathe fire

Queen: Queen Ruby (although some dragons still support Queen Scarlet, who may be alive and in hiding)

Students at Jade Mountain: Carnelian, Flame, Garnet, Peregrine, Thrush

SEAWINGS

Description: blue or green or aquamarine scales; webs between their claws; gills on their necks; glow-in-the-dark stripes on their tails/snouts/underbellies

Abilities: can breathe underwater, see in the dark, create huge waves with one splash of their powerful tails; excellent swimmers

Queen: Queen Coral

Students at Jade Mountain: Anemone, Barracuda, Pike, Snail, Turtle

ICEWINGS

Description: silvery scales like the moon or pale blue like ice; ridged claws to grip the ice; forked blue tongues; tails narrow to a whip-thin end

Abilities: can withstand subzero temperatures and bright light, exhale a deadly frostbreath

Queen: Queen Glacier

Students at Jade Mountain: Alba, Changbai, Ermine, Icicle, Winter

RAINWINGS

Description: scales constantly shift colors, usually bright like birds of paradise; prehensile tails

Abilities: can camouflage their scales to blend into their surroundings; shoot a deadly venom from their fangs

Queen: Queen Glory

Students at Jade Mountain: Boto, Coconut, Kinkajou, Siamang, Tamarin

NIGHTWINGS

Description: purplish-black scales and scattered silver scales on the underside of their wings, like a night sky full of stars; forked black tongues

Abilities: can breathe fire, disappear into dark shadows; once known for reading minds and foretelling the future, but no longer.

Queen: Queen Glory (see recent scrolls on the NightWing Exodus and the RainWing Royal Challenge)

Students at Jade Mountain: Bigtail, Fearless, Mightyclaws, Mindreader, Moonwatcher

THE
JADE MOUNTAIN
PROPHECY

Beware the darkness of dragons,
Beware the stalker of dreams,
Beware the talons of power and fire,
Beware one who is not what she seems.

Something is coming to shake the earth,
Something is coming to scorch the ground.
Jade Mountain will fall beneath thunder and ice
Unless the lost city of night can be found.

PROLOGUE

Four Years Ago . . .

The volcano was restless, and so were the dragons in the NightWing fortress.

Secretkeeper felt the mountain rumble under her talons as she hurried through the stone halls. There were too many dragons awake — too many witnesses who might wonder where she was going in the middle of the night. She kept her head down, but she felt the curious looks sliding under her scales with each dragon she passed.

How many of them knew what tonight should have been? Did anyone remember?

She didn't need to count days to know. Her bones ached with knowing. It was like a voice in her head screaming, *Tonight! It's hatching! Hurry! Don't get caught! Hurry!*

Because if it happened and she wasn't there . . .

She imagined hungry panthers prowling the undergrowth, dangerous crocodiles with gleaming teeth, or unpredictable curious idiot dragons who might do anything with a mysterious abandoned egg.

But she couldn't run, not with other NightWings still awake and watching her. Why tonight, of all nights? Usually everyone in the tribe slept like sloths from dusk to dawn.

Just before she reached the ledge, she passed Mastermind and Farsight. Mastermind gave her a hard stare. *He knows*, she thought with a stab of panic.

But it was Farsight who stopped and spoke to her. "Oh, Secretkeeper, poor dear," she said, folding her wings.

Secretkeeper winced; her name had never sounded more appropriate. Sometimes she wondered if her name had made her this way — if she was unconsciously trying to live up to it with the biggest, most unforgivable secret a NightWing could have.

"The egg you lost was due to hatch tonight, wasn't it? Are you all right?" Farsight went on. "Do you want someone to sit with you?"

NO! Secretkeeper curled her claws in and shook her head. "I'm fine," she said. "Just . . . going to get some air."

"Do you want company?" Farsight asked. Behind her, Mastermind frowned irritably. "I know it's not the same, but when Morrowseer took my egg —"

Secretkeeper could only think of one way to stop her, and it was harsh, but she had to, because she *had* to go, *right now*.

"It's not the same at all!" she snapped, shooting a burst of flame out her nose. "You have *two* surviving dragonets, and one of them is off on the continent being pampered and overfed and worshipped by the Talons of Peace. So don't try to act like you understand me!"

Farsight recoiled as if Secretkeeper had bitten her. Mastermind looked startled, perhaps a bit impressed . . . maybe a little suspicious. Secretkeeper whirled and fled up the corridor before either of them could say anything else.

I'll apologize tomorrow. She'll forgive me. Farsight is like that.

She took a running leap off the ledge and soared down toward the black sand beach. Behind her, the volcano rumbled again; the dark clouds overhead glowed with an ominous red light. The air was heavy and suffocating, smelling of death and rotten eggs and burning rocks. Secretkeeper swooped low over the red-gold lava river, the brightest spot on the island, and then veered toward the cave.

Only one guard tonight. Nobody really believed any of the rainforest dragons would find their secret tunnel. The guards were often asleep when she came, and Secretkeeper had frequently been able to sneak past without waking them.

But not tonight. Preyhunter was sitting out on the ledge overlooking the beach, watching the volcano and fidgeting nervously.

"Do you think it'll be tonight?" he asked her as she landed beside him. It took her a frightening, disoriented moment to realize he hadn't guessed her secret. He probably didn't even remember that she'd lost her egg — she was only one of many dragons who had in the last few years after all. He was talking about the volcano.

"No," Secretkeeper said, looking back at the hulking shape that loomed over all their lives. "It can't be. Mastermind said we have more time before it erupts."

Preyhunter snorted. "Right. And I'll remember why we trust him any minute now."

She knew what he meant. If Mastermind was wrong . . . well, that was why she'd made her choice, wasn't it? That was the whole reason for her dangerous secret.

"Where are you going at this hour?" Preyhunter asked, eyeing her up and down. "Shouldn't you have backup for night hunting?"

"I'll be all right," Secretkeeper said. "I just — can't sleep and I thought — maybe I'd bring back a sloth or a boar for Greatness to give the queen. . . ."

"Ah." Preyhunter nodded slyly. "Keeping the queen happy. Always a good idea. Right, see you soon, then."

Secretkeeper edged past him, her heart pounding. She bolted through the cave and into the tunnel that led to the rainforest. *Hurry! Hurry! It's happening now! You have to be there!*

She fell through into the clearest, most brightly lit night she'd ever seen in the rainforest. The worst luck; she'd have to hope that no RainWings were out for a moonlit stroll tonight. Even through the thick canopy of the treetops overhead, she could see that two of the three moons were full.

Just like they were the night I left her here.

Secretkeeper stopped. Her heart seemed to be doing some kind of painful aerial loops in her chest.

Her. Suddenly she just knew. She was certain. It would be female.

She flew through the trees, following the small signs she'd left for herself. There wasn't time to travel quietly and cautiously. If a RainWing heard and followed her . . . well, it wouldn't be a good night for that RainWing.

Plunging down, down toward the fallen tree, the artful pile of leaves, the curving ferns. Finally she was here, finally —

Her egg was gone.

Secretkeeper scrabbled frantically in the dark hollow. It couldn't be, it couldn't be gone. One black egg in the darkest hiding place in this gigantic rainforest — who could have found it? Where did they take it?

I should have kept her with me.

I shouldn't have lied to my tribe.

I only wanted to protect her from that island — from the smoke and the smell and the rules and the misery, and from the constant fear that the earth will swallow us in fire at any moment.

And now she's gone.

This is my punishment for deceiving everyone.

She whirled around, hissing, and her eye caught on something.

Not far away there was a clearing — a clearing where the moons broke through the trees and illuminated the forest floor.

In the center of the moonbeams was her egg.

At least, it had to be her egg — but it wasn't black anymore. The last time she'd been able to sneak out and check on it, three days ago, it had been ebony black, like every NightWing egg. Now it was an eerie silver color, as polished and glimmering as if a piece of full moon had fallen from the sky.

Secretkeeper approached it warily. Was this a trick? Was someone watching, waiting to catch her? *Mastermind? Greatness?*

Or was there something wrong with her egg?

Five starburst-shaped cracks already marked the smooth curve of the silver shell.

Secretkeeper circled it, inhaling the scents around it. *How did it roll over here? Why did it change color?*

There were no clues in the mossy hollow where the egg now lay, bathed in moonlight.

The egg rocked suddenly, and a long crack splintered across the top of it. Secretkeeper felt a burst of panic.

Was she supposed to help somehow? Should she crack the shell herself? Or try to keep the egg warm?

She'd never seen a hatching before. There were so few hatchings on the NightWing island, and hardly anyone was allowed to attend them, for fear of contaminating the precious new dragonets.

If she hadn't lied to everyone — about having stomach cramps during a hunt in the rainforest, about the egg coming out cracked, about burying the pieces alone — if she'd had her egg on the island, then she would probably have gotten to see a hatching in the last year. There had only been one, a dragonet called Mightyclaws. An expecting dragon would have been welcome to see how a hatching worked.

But not a dragon who'd lost an egg. There were several dragons on the island whose eggs had cracked before they hatched, and it was considered a kindness to keep them apart from the healthy eggs and dragonets.

So Secretkeeper had no idea what to do. She'd never heard of an egg turning silver. Had she done something wrong when she laid the egg all alone?

Had she hidden it in a place that was bad for it? Maybe she was supposed to be turning it every night or something like that. Maybe she'd already ruined the dragonet's life before it even hatched.

And what would happen now? What if her dragonet was broken? After all the lying and worrying, she wasn't sure she could survive if there was something wrong.

I will love her anyway, she thought fiercely, hoping that was true.

Secretkeeper brushed away tears, trying to focus. No matter what, there was a living dragonet in that egg trying to get out. She crouched and gently wrapped her talons around the eggshell.

The shell instantly splintered into a thousand pieces, showering the ground with glittering shards.

Sitting in between Secretkeeper's claws, blinking, was a tiny black dragonet.

"Oh!" Secretkeeper gasped.

The dragonet looked up, up, up at her mother's head and wings towering over her. She squeaked once, softly, and then stood up and shook herself, unfurling her own small wings.

Secretkeeper stared at her in awe. She was perfect, perfect in every way. Her scales gleamed as though they'd been polished; her claws were miniature curved crescents; her tail was the most perfect tail Secretkeeper had ever seen. She already looked healthier than every NightWing Secretkeeper knew, and that was enough — that was *exactly* why Secretkeeper had risked so much.

She wished she could share this moment with the dragonet's father . . . but he couldn't be trusted. He would almost certainly tell the tribe and insist she be raised on the island. If that meant he would never learn he had a daughter, then too bad.

The dragonet tilted her head back to stare up at the two full moons. Their silvery light reflected in her eyes, and Secretkeeper realized there was one odd thing about her. A silver scale shone on the outside corner of each eye, like a teardrop about to fall. Odd, but beautiful.

Her small talons reached toward the moons, as if she wanted to pull them out of the sky and roll them around.

Secretkeeper picked her up, feeling large and unwieldy with something so small and delicate. She lifted the dragonet up to see the moons and then brought her in close, cuddling her to her chest.

"I'm your mother, little one," she whispered. "I'm going to call you Moonwatcher. You're going to have the happiest life any dragon has ever had, and you're going to live forever and ever, and the volcano will never have you."

Moonwatcher squeaked again and leaned into her mother's warmth.

Secretkeeper let go of the worrying and the guilt. She stopped thinking about what had happened or what was going to happen. She was right where she needed to be.

A long, quiet time passed, and then . . .

"SECRETKEEPER!" a voice bellowed from the treetops.

Secretkeeper jolted awake. Her dragonet was curled in the curve of her wing, sleeping soundly. They were both brightly lit by the full moons overhead. And someone was shouting her name through the rainforest.

Preyhunter! she thought. *Idiot!* What if the RainWings heard him?

Then she came fully awake and realized what would happen if he found her like this — with a secret NightWing dragonet. Moonwatcher would be taken straight back to the island, and Secretkeeper would be punished for lying about her. She wasn't sure how, but she knew anything that involved being separated from Moonwatcher would be unbearable.

"Moonwatcher," she whispered urgently. The dragonet opened sleepy eyes. "We have to hide you."

"Awrk?" her daughter answered.

"Come here." Secretkeeper scooped her up and hurried back into the darker shadows of the forest.

Moonwatcher squeaked sadly and reached for the moonlight again. "No, you can't go out there. You have to stay hidden, do you understand? You must not let any dragon find you except Mommy."

Secretkeeper crouched beside her hollow, where the fallen log and thick ferns created a hidden space. She tucked Moonwatcher into the shadows and started pulling foliage over her to conceal her.

"Rrrrk?" Moonwatcher asked. She reached out and caught one of her mother's claws in her small front talons. "Arrwrk?"

"No, I can't stay," Secretkeeper said. "I'm sorry. You'll be safer if I go." Terrifying images flashed through her head — NightWing hunters finding Moonwatcher by accident, or RainWings stumbling on her and taking her back to their own village. She couldn't, she *mustn't* be seen by any other dragons. What had Secretkeeper been thinking? Hiding an egg was one thing — hiding a dragonet who could move and squeak and call for help was quite another. How could Moonwatcher possibly understand something like this?

"I'll be back as soon as I can," Secretkeeper promised. "Please, please don't leave this spot until I come. All right?"

She realized that Moonwatcher was staring intently into her eyes — almost as if she was reading the images flashing through her mother's mind.

Is it possible? The scrolls say NightWings once had mind reading powers . . . but I thought that was just the lie we tell the rest of the tribes so they'll fear us.

If it was ever true, it certainly hasn't been for the last several generations.

Still, there was something about the way Moonwatcher was looking at her. . . .

Not quite knowing what she was doing, Secretkeeper put her front talons gently on either side of Moonwatcher's head and whispered, "Stay secret. Stay hidden. Stay safe." She thought as hard as she could about the dangers of the rainforest, and especially the dangers of other dragons. She pictured Moonwatcher curling into the ferns and not moving until her mother returned.

Moonwatcher blinked and then nodded, slowly. She backed into the hollow and scratched leaves around herself.

"SECRETKEEPER!" Preyhunter shouted again. He sounded chillingly close.

"See you soon, little one," Secretkeeper whispered. Her claws wanted to clutch the earth, to stay right here with her dragonet and never ever leave. It was harder than anything she'd ever had to do before, but she made herself turn and fly off into the trees. The tears came, and she let them. Perhaps if he saw her crying, Preyhunter would be too embarrassed to grill her about where she'd been for so long and why she was coming back with no prey.

Her wingbeats faded into the darkness, replaced by the chirping of crickets, the scurrying of lizards, and the stranger, more unidentifiable noises of the rainforest at night. Somewhere not too far away, a jaguar roared.

Several moments passed.

"Awrk?" said a small voice from the fern hollow.

Nobody answered her.

"Awrk?" she said again, softly.

She was alone, with the shadows firmly wrapped around her and no company except the frightening pictures her mother had left trailing through her mind.

Two hours old, and all she knew so far was that the world was a dangerous, terrifying place without her mother.

"Awrk?" Moonwatcher tried again.

Rainforest noises. The small drip-drop of rain starting to fall.

A long pause. And then, barely a whisper:

"Mommy?"

Ice Kingdom

Sky Kingdom

Queen Thorn's
Stronghold

Claws of the
Clouds Mountains

Kingdom of
Sand

Scorpion Den

Jade Mountain

PART ONE

WELCOME TO
JADE MOUNTAIN

CHAPTER 1

"I don't want you to leave me here," Moon said. She fit perfectly under her mother's wing, as if that spot had been shaped by the universe just for her. Like a sign: This is where you should be. Stay here for always.

Certainly do not let your mother abandon you on a windy mountaintop positively swarming with strange dragons.

They'd found a spot under a tree where they could watch the main arrival area for the school, which perhaps hadn't been the best idea, as now Moon was fairly sure she'd seen about a thousand different kinds of dragon, all of them entirely too loud. She shied away as two MudWings galloped past her, shouting and laughing. They looked so *big*. And *rowdy*. How was she supposed to learn anything when she might get trampled at any moment by her fellow students?

And what if they hated her? She wouldn't even have to do anything wrong (although that seemed awfully likely to happen anyway). They'd hate her just for being a NightWing;

everybody did, except the NightWings, who hated her for not being enough of a NightWing.

"I really, really don't want to stay here," Moon said again.

"I know," her mother said kindly. "But you have to. And it'll be good for you. I think you'll like it better than the NightWing village, you'll see." *At least Jade Mountain won't be full of NightWings,* her mind went on.

"I like being wherever you are," Moon said. "And I don't mind the other NightWings that much."

"Most of them are awful and you know it," Secretkeeper pointed out. They were both thinking of the stares, the whispers, the open jealousy and hostility when Secretkeeper brought her healthy, well-fed dragonet back into the tribe. That was six months ago, after the volcano destroyed their island and all the NightWings had moved into the rainforest. Queen Glory had officially forgiven her for breaking tribe rules, but that didn't mean anyone else had. "Here you'll be with much nicer dragons. Like Sunny and Starflight. Remember you met them and liked them?"

"I want to be with you," Moon replied simply. It wasn't fair, to finally be given all the time she wanted with her mother — to be with her every moment of the day, instead of stolen hours a few times a week — and then to have it all taken away again.

"I'll visit," her mother promised. "You'll see me all the time. And you'll make friends here, I'm sure you will." *Well, I hope you will, my weird little diamond.*

"I'm not a weird little diamond," Moon protested.

Secretkeeper crouched and put her face right in front of Moon's. "You need to stop doing that, remember?" she whispered. "If you only hear it in your head, don't respond. No one can know about your curse. Everybody thinks NightWings don't have powers anymore — they won't know what to do with you if they find out." *And how will you make friends that way,* her mind worried, *if you keep guessing their thoughts and making them uncomfortable?* "Or they might not believe you, and then they'll hate you for lying. So don't let them find out, all right?"

"I know," Moon answered. "Stay secret. Stay hidden. Stay safe." All the years of pretending to have mind reading powers had made the NightWings truly fear the idea of any dragon reading *their* minds.

She paused. "So isn't this really dangerous? What if I make a mistake here, with all these different kinds of dragons around?"

"You won't. You'll be careful," Secretkeeper said firmly. "I know it's terrible to be the way you are, but if you keep it a secret, you can have a normal life. No one needs to know that you're not a normal dragon. Understand? Are you ready to go inside?"

"Not yet," Moon said. "Can we watch for a little longer?"

Secretkeeper sighed. "Sure." *She's so nervous all the time. I'm sure I was never that nervous when I was a dragonet.*

Moon frowned up at her mother. She was glad the mind

listening only went one way, but sometimes, like now, she wished her own mind could shout back, *Don't you think maybe there's a reason I'm like this?*

"Oh, look," Secretkeeper said obliviously, her eyes lighting up. She pointed to the sky, where blue and green wings were sailing down toward them. "SeaWings! Do you see the one with the ropes of pearls? I think that's their queen!"

"Queen Coral," Moon recited. One thing she *could* do — that didn't involve being stared at by other dragons or accidentally saying the wrong thing — was study, and so she'd done a lot of that to prepare for Jade Mountain Academy. "Those two must be her daughters, since she never lets them out of her sight. I don't know who the other one is."

"Remember not to show off," her mother said. "I mean, thank you for telling me, but the other dragons might not like you if you always know all the answers."

Moon stared down at her claws. It was pretty clear from Secretkeeper's thoughts that her mother was a lot more worried about whether other dragons would like Moon than she was about whether Moon would like them. That, in fact, didn't seem to be among her concerns at all.

A deep blue SeaWing came barreling out of the entrance cave as the other SeaWings landed. "You came!" she called happily. Her wings flared out and wrapped around the older daughter, who was a pale white-pink, like the inside of seashells. The smaller daughter, who had to be less than a year old, bounced around their hug, yelping and trying to get in. She was attached to the queen by a long harness, which kept getting tangled under her talons and tripping her.

"I'm really not sure about this," Queen Coral said in a rumbly voice. She was the same shade of blue as the SeaWing who was now being tackled by the little dragonet. In fact, Moon guessed they might be mother and daughter.

Oh, I'm a snail-brain, she realized. *That must be Tsunami.* The famous SeaWing princess from the prophecy had been in the rainforest for a while, but Moon hadn't met her before Tsunami left to work on getting the Jade Mountain Academy ready.

"It'll be great," Tsunami promised the queen. "I'll take care of Anemone, I promise." She grinned at her sister.

"Me too, me too!" yelled the small dragonet. "I want to go to school, too!" She pounced on her harness and wrestled it to the ground, growling at it.

"You are much too young," Coral said sternly. She tugged the little princess upright. "I can't risk anything happening to you, especially while Anemone is this far away."

"Maybe next year, Auklet," Tsunami said. The little dragon beamed hopefully.

The queen frowned at Tsunami. "And I'm only letting this happen because Anemone has been badgering me about it every day since she got your message about the school. But you can come home *anytime*, you understand? If you feel threatened, or lonely, or overworked, or tired —"

"I'll be fine," Anemone said, wriggling away from her mother's hug.

Moon felt her own wings drooping. Why didn't Secretkeeper want to keep her close like that? Why wasn't *she* getting a speech about coming home the moment she got lonely?

Was it because her mother thought she was cursed? Maybe Secretkeeper really wanted to keep Moon as far away from her as possible. Her thoughts never quite said that, but she'd learned to block some of them over the last four years . . . and she did worry all the time about Moon's mind reading.

Moon wasn't sure she wanted to be normal if it meant grumping around thinking only her own thoughts and mostly all about herself, the way most NightWings did. But her mother seemed very sure that she'd be happier that way. Maybe acting normal was something she could learn here.

"Who's this?" Tsunami asked, turning to the last SeaWing dragonet, who sat behind Queen Coral with a patient expression on his face. He looked about Moon's age, and he was dark green, like an emerald hidden in a cave, with flashes of brighter green underscales and hints of gold in his eyes. He was a little plump, with a sweet extra curve to his snout and upper arms, and his webbed talons were splayed out like he was worried the wind would shove him off the mountain. Unlike Anemone and Auklet, he was not adorned with pearls and jewels; his only accessory was a kind of gold armband studded with glittering black rocks.

"This is one of your brothers," Queen Coral said. "He heard about this and really wanted to come, too. Which one are you again?"

"Turtle," he said, shooting Tsunami a friendly smile.

"*One* of my brothers?" Tsunami echoed. "I didn't realize — I mean, I guess I knew the male eggs were surviving every time your female eggs were destroyed by the Orca statue — but I didn't even think about having brothers."

"There are about thirty of us," Turtle said with a shrug.

"THIRTY?" Tsunami shouted. "I have THIRTY BROTHERS?"

"Well, thirty-two," he said. His gaze caught Moon watching, and he wrinkled his snout in an amused way.

"Why didn't you mention this before?" Tsunami demanded, whipping toward her mother.

"Who cares about them?" Coral asked. "They can't inherit the throne."

Moon tilted her head at Turtle, expecting a reaction, and realized she wasn't hearing any thoughts from him. Nothing at all; just a quiet hum, almost a soothing blankness.

That was strange. Moon had only met a few dragons who could block her reading at all, and then only sometimes, and they didn't even seem to know they could do it. A couple of NightWings had prickly mental shields around some of their secrets, but Queen Glory was the best at it. The RainWing queen clearly wasn't intentionally shielding her thoughts from mind readers, but whenever she got uncomfortable, some kind of instinctive wall went up around her mind. She did the same thing with her scales, keeping them from showing her emotions.

It was unsettling, but in a way that always made Moon really curious. What were they hiding? Was their shielding ability something they inherited or something they instinctively developed?

Turtle wasn't like Glory or those NightWings, though; his mind didn't feel like a thorny wall radiating *I've got secrets, keep out*. It was just . . . serenely still. How was he hiding his thoughts so absolutely? He looked so placid and ordinary.

On the other talon, one thing Moon had been able to figure out so far was that nobody was ordinary on the inside.

Tsunami rolled her eyes. "Well, *I'm* happy to meet you, Turtle," she said. "And I'm glad you're joining our school so I can get to know you better."

"I want to see everything before I leave," said Queen Coral. Moon caught twin threads of annoyance from Tsunami and Anemone, but Tsunami just nodded.

"Of course. Come inside."

As the SeaWings disappeared into the cave, Turtle looked back at Moon one more time, and Moon suddenly had a dizzy, tilting feeling that the mountain was sliding down toward her. Darkness flashed before her eyes, and then a strange image, in bits and pieces like a puzzle whirling together.

A beach.

Sunlight.

And Turtle pinning Anemone to the sand as the white-pink dragon writhed in pain.

Then it was gone, and when she blinked, so was the SeaWing family.

CHAPTER 2

Moon shivered. *What was that?*

But she knew. She'd known since she read the scrolls that said, "NightWing powers include mind reading and visions of the future." That was where her nightmares came from — the future.

What she didn't know was whether the visions were inevitable, or how to interpret them, or what in Pyrrhia to do about them, since, as far as she could tell, she was the first NightWing in hundreds of years to have the legendary powers of the tribe.

Lucky me.

And if the other NightWings wouldn't be able to handle mind reading, she was pretty sure visions from the future weren't going to go over well either. She hadn't even told her mother about those. One curse was bad enough.

Turtle hadn't looked sinister at all, despite the weird blankness of his mind. And she knew quite a lot about sinister vibes after living with the NightWings for the last few months. But perhaps any dragon could become dangerous as they got older (although . . . he hadn't looked much older or bigger in the vision). Or perhaps he was simply much better at hiding his true nature than any other dragon she'd met before.

"Wow. A real queen," Secretkeeper said. "I've never seen one before."

"You see Queen Glory all the time," Moon pointed out, only half listening.

"Queen Glory is barely older than you are," Secretkeeper answered. "I mean a *real* queen, someone who's ruled her tribe for years and years."

Moon studied her mother sideways. Many of the NightWings harbored bitter thoughts about having a RainWing for their queen now, but she didn't think her mother was one of the grumblers.

"All right," her mother said, suddenly and briskly. "That's enough hiding in shadows and 'observing.' Time for you to go find your cave."

Already? Moon was seized with a horribly familiar feeling of terror. "Alone? Aren't you coming inside?"

"This will be good for you," her mother said. *I hope. Remember, Secretkeeper: Be strong. Just turn and fly away.* "I love you, and I will see you soon."

Secretkeeper took a step back, averting her face, and Moon glimpsed a thought track her mother had been carefully burying: *Oh, I hope this is the right thing. What am I doing? How do I know if this will be good for her?*

Moon's heart leaped. *She doesn't want to leave me!* she realized with a surge of hope. But her mother was already hugging her and whispering hurried good-byes in her ear.

"Wait," Moon said desperately. "What if I came next year instead? What if —"

"Trust me, moonbud," her mother said, cupping Moon's snout in her front talons. "You will love it here. Just keep your curse hidden, and you'll be fine. Act normal, no matter what happens. And write to me soon! Good-bye!"

A moment later, Secretkeeper was just a dark shape winging away through the threadbare clouds, taking Moon's heart away with her.

Moon stayed under the tree for a while, decidedly *not* crying, and watched more students arrive. There weren't actually a thousand, she knew. There were only thirty-five students, and it was a privilege to be one of the first few invited to attend. Which made *Why me?* an even more mysterious question.

Well, then, she thought, when she couldn't put it off anymore. *Imagine this is the rainforest, and you're hungry, and your mother's been gone for three days, and you can smell a bunch of bananas inside the cave. If I could be brave enough to feed myself when I had to, I can be brave enough to walk into a school and find the place I'm supposed to be.*

She shook back her wings, waited for a moment when all was quiet on the landing ledge, and darted forward into the yawning mouth of the entrance cave.

"Hello!" a voice accosted her loudly, while Moon's eyes were still adjusting to the dimmer light inside. "Welcome to the Great Hall of Jade Mountain! Let me guess — you're Moonwatcher, aren't you? I'm tremendously good at guessing. In fact, one might even say I'm *mysteriously* good at it." The welcoming dragon, whose scales were midnight black, lowered her voice. "Almost as though I'm . . . *reading your mind*, eh?"

Moon stared at the NightWing in fright. Had she been discovered already? Before even saying a word? *What will Mother say?*

"Just kidding," said the older NightWing. "MAAAAYBE. I'm Fatespeaker. I'm not a teacher like the others; I'm just helping wherever I can. Here's your welcome scroll and your map." She thrust two scrolls into Moon's talons. "Hey, look, you have silver scales next to your eyes just like I do! Yours are bigger and sparklier, though. It is Moonwatcher, right?"

"Yes. Um. Moon." Now she recognized this NightWing, which she should have been able to do from her first thought. She only knew two NightWings apart from her mother who didn't radiate gloom and anxiety. Starflight had a more thoughtful energy, while Fatespeaker's hopefulness poured out of her like overenthusiastic sunlight. Moon had seen the two of them from afar in the NightWing village several times, although they both had chosen to live with the RainWings instead.

She glanced around, wondering hopefully if Starflight was nearby. He was the NightWing from the false prophecy, and he'd been blinded when the volcano exploded. Usually Fatespeaker was with him, guiding him — but not today.

The enormous entrance cave looked as though it could fit four hundred dragons comfortably, with room for more to soar overhead. Sunlight poured in, illuminating the craggy walls and rippled ceiling, where cascades of golden-brown stalactites hung down, some of them reaching all the way to the floor to form twisted columns.

Hanging against the back wall was a huge bronze gong with three flying dragons carved into it. A banner woven of green vines had been strung from one massive stalactite to another in the center of the cave, with letters spelled out in giant purple-and-white flowers: Welcome, students!

Two tunnel openings yawned along the left wall of the cave; two more on the right. Next to each one, a map was posted showing where the tunnels went. The whole cave was busy with bustling dragons: families saying good-bye, friends saying hello, a few dragons carrying around prey or scrolls.

But Moon didn't see Sunny or Starflight anywhere, to her disappointment. Her mother was right; they had been kind to her, and Moon liked them. She particularly liked that, for the most part, their thoughts matched what they said and did.

"Moon, Moon, Moon," Fatespeaker muttered, rolling a scroll between her claws on the floor and scanning it closely.

"Ah, here you are. Second tunnel on the left, fifth cave on the right." She flicked her tail and grinned at Moon. "You're going to love your clawmates."

Apparently I'm going to love all sorts of things, Moon thought, and then she noticed what Fatespeaker had said. "Clawmates?" she echoed. "What are those?"

"The dragons you're sharing a cave with," Fatespeaker said brightly. Moon's wings shivered involuntarily, all the way out to her wingtips. *Sharing a cave? All the time?*

"Oooo, here come some IceWings!" Fatespeaker cried. "Want to stick around and meet them?"

"N-no thanks," Moon stammered. She hurried to the second tunnel on the left, and as she turned into it, she heard a whoosh of wings and felt a cold chill sweep through the cave. She peeked back around the corner and saw two haughty-looking ice dragons pace inside, frowning. No, she definitely did not want to meet them now or, in fact, ever.

"Fifth cave on the right," Moon murmured to herself, moving on. The tunnel wound in a curving shape, like a slithering tail, down into the mountain. Overhead, grass-green and butterfly-blue and hibiscus-yellow glass globes hung from a wire strung along the ceiling, each of them glowing with fire so the walls were lit with color. It didn't feel like she was going underground; it felt more like the sunlit canopy of the rainforest.

Moon had been picturing dark gray tunnels and cramped stone caves, but now that she thought about it, she realized

Sunny wouldn't have wanted her school to be anything like the gloomy caves under the mountain where the prophecy dragonets grew up.

Soon the tunnel straightened out, and Moon could see small cave openings all along either side. This must be the corridor of sleeping caves; she could sense that some of them had two or three dragonets inside already. Each cave she passed seemed to be bristling with chatter and wings and claws and spiky thoughts that clamored for space in her head.

Father said they have a library. I'm going to learn to read! Oh, I hope I'm not the only one who can't read yet. That would be so embarrassing.

What do they eat up in the mountains? We'd better get seagulls sometimes. And soon. Gosh, I'm hungry. Would anyone be mad at me if I went looking for seagulls?

I wonder where the prophecy dragonets are. I wonder if they'll notice me!

So cold here. I miss the desert.

They really expect me to share a cave with a RainWing?

Moon scrunched her eyes shut, trying to hold back the headache. This was what it had been like when she first joined the NightWing village. After the peace and quiet of solitary life in the rainforest, all those voices in her head had been a horrible shock, especially when they were all so resentful and hostile.

They still echoed in there, even though the NightWings were too far away now for her to actually hear them: *It's not fair; Secretkeeper should be punished; I bet she thinks she's bet-ter than us; imagine getting to eat* every *day; that dragonet doesn't know anything about our tribe or what we went through living on the volcano; how can she ever be one of us?*

She had a feeling — perhaps more of a wishful hope — that there should be a way to block out all the voices, but of course there was no one who could teach her how to do that.

Mostly she'd dealt with the NightWing noise by escaping to the tallest tree or farthest waterfall, but where could she go here? She'd be stuck in classes, or trapped in a cave with her "clawmates." Her brain would always be full of the din of other dragons.

I'll figure it out. I'll make *this work.*

Or I'll run back to the rainforest and deal with Mother's disappointment.

Moon opened her eyes again and fixed her gaze on the fifth cave. She squeezed past a pair of chatting SandWings who were taking up most of the tunnel, and one of them stared at her intently with his obsidian-black eyes.

NightWing flashed through his head. *Thorn doesn't like them; we just sent a couple back to Glory as her prisoners; we have no idea what they can do in battle yet, especially if it's true they really have no powers after all. Needs further study. She's kind of cool-looking, with those silver scales by her eyes. Seems nervous. Twitching her wings back to look smaller than she is. Up to something, or shy?*

Moon tried not to look back at him as she went by; she tried to seem unobtrusive and harmless and part of the shadows.

Her sleeping cave had a few stalactites hanging over the doorway like jagged teeth. She ducked inside and found more fire-lit glass globes strung across the ceiling in here: one green, one a fiery red-gold, and one yellow. Two more globes, unlit, rested on ledges on either side of the door, and there was another at her level on the far side of the cave. She picked each one up and breathed a small flame onto the candles inside to set them alight, then surveyed the space nervously.

It was nicer than she'd expected. The doorway made up one wall, and a sleeping spot had been arranged along each of the other three walls. One of these was a bare rock ledge, another was a pile of rainforest leaves and mosses, and the third was a woven green hammock ingeniously suspended from the roof.

Moon hesitated. It seemed as if the beds had been deliberately designed with different dragons in mind, but she wasn't sure which one was meant for her. She knew which one she wanted . . . but how would someone else have guessed what she'd like?

Maybe she should wait for her clawmates and see what they wanted. *I wish I could have a private cave. Maybe if I asked Starflight really nicely . . .*

She noticed that there were also five mahogany scroll racks arranged around the cave, about the height of her fore-leg, each polished until they were as smooth as her scales. There was an empty one next to each bed and one on either side of the door.

She took a closer look and realized with a jump of happiness that the ones by the door were filled with scrolls. A little sign above these two said: Free reading — hope you like them!

Moon slid her welcome scroll and her map scroll into one of the empty racks, then wrapped her tail around her back talons and started going through the scrolls by the door. It was a mix of all the kinds of things that interested her — history, adventure stories, ancient legends, encyclopedias of all the plants and animals in each tribe's territory.

Suddenly she remembered Starflight finding her with a scroll one day. He'd quizzed her on what she liked to read. *If he chose these for me . . . he must have really been listening.*

She noticed that there weren't any of the recent scrolls about the dragonets of the prophecy and their "Epic Quest to End the War of SandWing Succession." She guessed with a smile that whoever had selected these (Starflight? Sunny? Glory?) found those particular scrolls rather embarrassing.

She also found one early-reader scroll that must have been written for tiny dragonets, with giant letters and a guide to the alphabet. This seemed so out of place that she sat and puzzled over it for a minute.

Is this for one of my clawmates? Am I going to be living with a one-year-old? Her mother had mentioned that the academy would take dragonets of various ages, so maybe it was possible, although it seemed weird.

Out of nowhere, Moon felt a sudden burst of angry energy like a spear driving through her skull. She crumpled forward, clutching her head, as shouts and roars echoed in the hall.

"Get your fish-smelling tail away from me —" *I've faced bigger SeaWings than him in battle if he's trying to start something!*

"Don't you dare blow smoke in my face —" *She could be one of the SkyWings who destroyed our Summer Palace!*

"Ow," Moon whispered. "Ow. Ow. Ow." The headache was so blistering, she considered running into the rock wall to knock herself out.

And then, very softly, under all the yelling, she heard . . . *Aha. There you are.*

Moon's head snapped up, and she winced as another bolt of pain crackled through it. This voice — it was unlike anything she'd ever heard before. It sounded crisp and clear and right in her ear, as if it was talking *to* her.

I am talking to you.

Instinctive fear whipped through Moon's veins, paralyzing her. All of her mother's nightmare scenarios started playing again in her head: *Don't trust anyone new, don't trust anything unusual, don't let anyone know what you can do, stay secret, stay hidden, stay safe.*

Three moons, said the voice. *Aren't you a jumpy one.*

"Who are you?" Moon whispered.

Who are you? it answered back, and then, as if the speaker had plucked the answer from her thoughts, *Hello, Moonwatcher.*

Another telepath — how was that possible? Moon tried to push back. She imagined reaching out with her talons, trying to grab on to the voice and open up what was happening in the mind behind it.

It's as if you've had no training at all. The voice chuckled. *How old are you?* Again, the pause, and this time Moon thought furiously of as many different numbers as she could: *95! 76! 12!*

Four already and that's all you can do?

"Who are you?" Moon demanded. "How are you doing that?"

You really have no idea, the voice mused with a hint of puzzlement. *Hmmm. Fascinating. Let me think about that.*

She listened, pressing her temples to hold the headache at bay, but the voice didn't come back.

"Are you still there?" she whispered.

No response.

Did I imagine it? Maybe I imagined it. Maybe the headache and all the noise out there just confused me. Or maybe mind reading is finally driving me crazy. She shook her head and blinked. *But if it was a real mind reader, maybe they could teach me how to use my powers.*

Or expose me to everyone, now that they know who I am, while I have no idea who they are.

Moon drew her wings around her with an anxious shiver.

"Hey now, hey there. Stop, stop, stop," a real voice called in the hallway, interrupting the squabble.

Clay! clamored several voices at once in Moon's head. *It's him, it's really him! Oooo, he's even cuter in real life. Oooo, look at his heroic limp. Oooo, I think he looked at me!*

Moon poked her head out of her cave and saw the large sloping back of the prophecy MudWing. Clay was gently holding apart a writhing SeaWing and a hissing SkyWing.

"It's only the first day, folks," he said genially. "Nothing to be so grumpy about already. You're probably both just hungry. Carnelian, take a deep breath and see me later. Pike, walk with me." He spread his wing over the SeaWing's shoulder and firmly guided him away down the tunnel.

The SkyWing watched them go with narrow eyes, growling to herself. Then, to Moon's alarm, she swung around and marched right into Moon's cave. Without saying a word, she threw herself onto the rock-ledge bed, folded her large scarlet wings forward over her eyes, and proceeded to stew in sullen silence.

One of my clawmates, Moon realized. *Yay.*

She blinked at the SkyWing for a moment, wondering if she should say something. Her heart was beating fast and the headache was still there, receding slowly toward the back of her skull. She cleared her throat, swallowed, opened her mouth . . . and then gave up and turned back to the scrolls.

Several minutes later, a whirlwind burst into the cave, nearly trampling Moon with bright yellow talons.

"Oh my gosh, sorry!" it yelped. "I didn't even see you there! I guess that's a NightWing skill, hiding in shadows, right, ha ha!" *They put me in with a NIGHTWING?* hollered her brain. *Hello, isn't anyone worried about my potential post-traumatic stress?* But the little RainWing didn't drop her enormous smile for a moment. Her scales, too, didn't shift: They stayed a blindingly bright banana yellow dotted with splotches of alarming raspberry pink.

She seized Moon's front talons and pumped them cheerfully up and down.

"Isn't this exciting? I'm so excited I can hardly STAND IT. That's why I'm this color, by the way. I have been trying all morning to turn myself something more dignified and I can't *do* it; my scales are all like, YAY WE'RE REALLY HERE! and will not listen to me."

Moon noticed that there was one spot on the RainWing that wasn't eye-meltingly colorful: a triangle of three small black smudges on her wing that looked like tiny splashes of ink.

"I'm Kinkajou," the RainWing added, beaming.

"You're noisy," the SkyWing observed from under her wings.

"I love this place," Kinkajou said. She let go of Moon and bounced over to the hammock, while her thoughts went, essentially: *Library! Art! Friends!* "Have you explored at all yet? There's the most amazing library — not that I can read yet, but oh my gosh, I'm working on it really hard. And an art cave! It's full of all these colors of paint, like, like, like a couple of RainWings just EMOTED all over it! You guys, we should make amazing paintings and then decorate our cave with them. WOULDN'T THAT BE AMAZING?"

"I might literally die of joy," said the SkyWing flatly.

"You look way healthier than most of the other NightWings," Kinkajou said to Moon, evidently deciding to ignore the SkyWing for the moment. "Your scales are so *shiny*. I'd almost guess you were a RainWing in disguise, but you're not, are you?"

"I didn't grow up on the volcano," Moon said softly. "My mother hid my egg in the rainforest."

"Oh!" Kinkajou said, and her brain went *Aha!* "I've heard of you. Wow, that's a relief. That means you weren't anywhere near the NightWings who locked me up. I mean, I'm all for amnesty and making friends across tribes and forgiving each other and everything, but *seriously*, it was *scary* there, like I thought I might actually die, and so I figured maybe I'd start by making friends with some *other* tribes first and gradually work my way back around to the NightWings, but you're hardly a NightWing at all, so that's OK, then."

Moon winced. "Hardly a NightWing at all" was essentially what she'd been hearing in the NightWings' thoughts about her for months. It was a little brutal to hear someone just say it out loud.

"So what's your name?" Kinkajou asked.

"Moon. I mean, Moonwatcher, but . . . just Moon, really."

"Sure, Moon. And who are you?" Kinkajou asked the SkyWing.

I'm a warrior, the scarlet dragon thought bitterly, keeping her face hidden. *A loyal soldier in Ruby's army, who never did anything to deserve this . . . this punishment of schooling and being forced to live with Ditzy and Mumbles over there.*

Moon hunched her shoulders and looked down at her claws. That wasn't fair. She did *not* mumble.

Kinkajou turned back to Moon, her eyes sparkling. "Ooo, it's a mystery!" she said. "We have to *guess* our third clawmate's name! I'll go first. I bet it's . . . Squelch! What do you think, Squelch is a cute name, right?"

Moon didn't think she ought to smile, given the wave of outrage coming off the SkyWing. "Squelch is a MudWing name, isn't it?" she pointed out.

"True," said Kinkajou. "Maybe her name is Friendly. That would suit her so well."

"That's not a SkyWing name either," Moon said. The red dragon's tail was twitching dangerously.

"Think outside the box, Moon. Look at her! I'm sure she'd *love* to be called Friendly. Let's do that until we find out her real name," Kinkajou said, and then broke down in helpless giggles.

The SkyWing unfolded herself majestically and glared at Kinkajou with her wings spread wide.

"I have fought in *fourteen* battles!" the SkyWing thundered. "No one *giggles* at me! Least of all a RainWing who can't even read and knows nothing about war!" She jumped off her ledge and swept furiously out the door.

There was a pause while Kinkajou got her giggles under control. "Ouch," she said. "But mostly fair. Although I think being imprisoned and experimented on by NightWings and then injured during a royal challenge should give me *some* battle credit, don't you?"

"I — I think Clay said her name is Carnelian, maybe?" Moon offered.

"Oh, that's pretty," Kinkajou said. "Do you mind if I take the hammock, by the way?"

Moon shook her head. "The moss bed is all right with me."

"That's what you slept on while you were growing up on the rainforest floor, right?" Kinkajou guessed, nodding. "This will be so great! We can bond over how much we miss papayas and adorable sloths! But I don't miss anything yet; it's too fabulous here. Come see the library!"

"Oh," Moon said nervously, "I — I think I'll stay here for a bit longer — I need to just, um, um —"

"Nonsense," Kinkajou said. She poked one of Moon's wings with her own. "We're in a new place! This is really exciting! I want to show you everything!"

Oh, I hope she's not boring, Kinkajou's mind whispered. *I don't mind shy; I can handle shy, but please don't be boring.*

Moon straightened her shoulders and folded her wings back. It meant trampling down her terror, but she absolutely did not want to seem *boring* to her first possible chance at a friend here.

"All right, let's go," she said, taking a deep breath.

"Yay!" Kinkajou cried. She bounded out the door and Moon followed.

As she stepped into the hallway, she heard it again . . . that bell of a voice in her mind.

Oh, Moonwatcher, my new favorite dragon. This dragonet with her brain full of bubbles is not your only possibility. I believe you and I are destined for a great friendship.

Moon shivered. Was it real?

Was there a dragon somewhere reaching out to her? If so, how? And who was it? Another student? Was it a fellow NightWing, mysteriously hatched with the tribe's long-lost powers, just like her?

How could she hide from someone who knew exactly what she was?

I can help you, the voice whispered. *And better yet . . . you can help me.*

— CHAPTER 3 —

Moon couldn't handle a mystery mind-voice and a new school full of noisy dragons all at the same time. She shoved her worries about the voice to the back of her head and tried instead to wrestle with the exhausting energy radiating off Kinkajou.

"Where are we going?" Moon asked the RainWing as they headed along the tunnel, past all the sleeping caves, away from the Great Hall. She wondered if she should have brought her school map.

"Today is an exploring day," Kinkajou said with authority. "They want every day to be kind of an exploring day. That's the idea of the school — find out what you're interested in and explore it."

I'm interested in going back to my mother, Moon thought. *Can I explore that?*

"They?" she echoed instead.

"The dragonets of destiny," Kinkajou said. "Although they don't want anyone to call them that anymore, but what are we supposed to call them? The 'founders of the school' makes sense, too, I guess, but that makes them sound like they're perfectly ancient, like old slabs of rock way under the mountain. I'm really good friends with them," she confided as streaks of dark purple shot through her scales. "Especially Queen Glory, we're practically best friends. They knew I wouldn't be able to read the announcements everywhere — I mean, not yet! — so Sunny and Clay explained their whole plan to me ahead of time."

Announcements? Moon paused to look around and saw a small rectangular board made of dark rock hanging under one of the torches. A note was written on it in chalk:

Welcome to the Jade Mountain Academy!

Feel free to explore the whole school today (and every day!). Everything is for you. Food is available in the prey center. (Talk to Clay if you'd like to sign up for a hunting party!) Please come see any of us anytime with questions or requests or worries or anything.

More information about tomorrow will be posted tonight. Small group-discussion classes will begin in the morning.

Have a wonderful day!

"What's a small group-discussion class?" Moon wondered.

"It's exactly what it sounds like," Kinkajou said. "Come on, come on!" She tugged on Moon's wing impatiently, and the physical contact flooded Moon with Kinkajou's radiant excitement.

Kinkajou bounded up a side corridor lined with hanging scrolls; as she followed, Moon saw that each scroll had a quote on it. She didn't have time to read them all, but she saw "Knowledge is a flame in the darkness" and "The claws of war are no match for the wings of wisdom." At the end they turned into a space full of iridescent green sunlight.

It was like stepping into a dream. Scrolls were everywhere, simply everywhere, in cubbyholes along all the walls and more racks and cylinders around the cave. Every corner had a spot to curl up and read in: sometimes a rock ledge, sometimes a pile of moss or an arrangement of carpets. Only one reader was in there: a quiet-looking MudWing with a scroll curled on some reeds. She didn't look up as they came in; the only image Moon got from her mind was something like ripples on a mud puddle.

Sunbeams filtered down through skylights in the roof and windows along one wall. Each of the holes was covered with something thin enough to let the light through but strong enough to keep the wind and weather out. Moon tilted her head back and studied the closest one: emerald green, with traces of veins branching through it.

"Leaves," she whispered.

"Sunny and Glory got them in the rainforest," Kinkajou said proudly. "We use them sometimes as roofs for our RainWing houses. Aren't they perfect for library windows? Hi, Starflight!" She bounded over to a circular wooden desk in the center that was labeled LIBRARIAN. A dark head popped up from behind the desk.

"Hey, Kinkajou." The blind NightWing leaned forward with a smile as Kinkajou brushed his claws with hers. "Is that Moon with you?"

"Hi," Moon said shyly. There was nothing ever hurtful in Starflight's thoughts. His brain was always busy, busy, busy, but he never thought of her as "not a real NightWing" or "dangerous and untrustworthy." He was like her, an outsider in his own tribe. And he liked scrolls, too. She could hear the back of his mind ticking through all the things he still needed to do to get the library completely ready.

But he smiled in the direction of her voice. "Here's your library stamp," he said, sliding something out from under the desk. "I thought you might come by today."

"Library stamp?" Moon echoed curiously, taking it from him. It was a small rectangle of wood, as long as two claws, with her name carved backward in raised letters on one side.

"We're testing out a system," he said. "I'll show you." He brushed his talons over a row of scrolls lined up under the desk. Moon spotted a name carved at the wooden end of each one, arranged alphabetically. Starflight touched them lightly until he felt hers, which he pulled out and partially unrolled. The scroll was completely blank.

"When you want to borrow a scroll," he said, "you bring it up to me here. Each one has a unique carved stamp on the end, like these do. I'll stamp your name scroll with that end to show that you checked it out, and then when you bring it back, we stamp your card over the first image to show that it's been returned. Does that make sense?"

"I think so," Moon said. She turned the stamp over in her claws. She'd never had anything that was really her own before.

"Can she have a pouch to keep it in?" Kinkajou asked.

"Of course." Starflight fumbled under the desk again for a few minutes, then pulled out a soft black leather pouch on a silver chain. Moon slipped the stamp inside the pouch and put the chain over her neck. It felt like her very first treasure.

"Thank you," she said.

"Let me know if I can help you find anything," he said. She heard a flurry of worried *what-if*s start up in his mind, circling a well-worn track of anxiety about how to be a blind librarian. She also heard him firmly beat those worries back. He smiled in her direction again. "I've been practicing to get the whole space memorized."

Moon wondered how she could ask for what she really needed. *Do you have any scrolls about ominous voices in your head?*

"Sora, are you still here?" Starflight asked, raising his voice a little.

The MudWing by the windows lifted her head and nodded.

"He can't see you," Kinkajou reminded her in a loud whisper. "Yes, she's still here."

"Sorry," the brown dragon said softly.

"It's all right," Starflight said. The twinge of sadness in his thoughts didn't spill into his voice. "Sora, this is Kinkajou and Moon. Sora is one of Clay's sisters."

"Ooooo," Kinkajou said. "How does it feel to be related to someone famous? Probably a bit like being best friends with a queen," she answered herself, grinning ridiculously. "Which I am, just incidentally, so, I mean, I totally get it."

Sora's smile was shy, and now Moon could sense tremors of anxiety in her that felt an awful lot like Moon's own fears. Clay's sister was as nervous about being here as Moon was.

It was sort of reassuring, actually, to find someone as scared as she was.

"Nice to meet you," Moon said. *Maybe she could be my friend, too. Maybe Mother was right . . . Maybe I will meet dragons I like here.*

"You too," Sora nearly whispered, rolling her scroll between her talons.

"Let's go to the music wing next," Kinkajou said. "Or, oooooo, I heard there's an old GHOST living somewhere in Jade Mountain! Maybe we can find him!"

Moon's ears twitched. A ghost? Was she hearing the voice of a ghost? That would be . . . unsettling.

"You're talking about Stonemover," Starflight said, "and he's not a ghost. He's Sunny's father, and he's a perfectly nice old NightWing who's lived here for ages. He sleeps a lot and doesn't need little dragonets sneaking up on him or pouncing on his tail to find out if he's real. He does like company, though, so if you're interested in a polite conversation with him, I can tell you how to find him."

"Polite conversation, YAWN," Kinkajou said with a shrug of her wings. "You should tell everyone he's a ghost. That would be much more exciting!"

Not a ghost, but a real NightWing, Moon thought. *Maybe he's the one who can talk in my head.* She'd have to ask Starflight for directions later, if she could work up the courage.

"Are you hungry, Moon?" Kinkajou barreled on. "I might be hungry. We could find the prey center. I haven't done that yet. Which way to the prey center, Starflight?"

He touched his desk lightly, as if orienting himself, and then pointed at one of the three corridors that led away from the library.

"Sora, you want to come?" Kinkajou asked before Moon could think to invite the dragonet herself.

The MudWing shook her head quickly and buried her nose in her scroll again.

"All right. See you soon!" Kinkajou called over her shoulder as they left.

This passageway slanted back down and, Moon thought, out toward the open air. They passed a couple of branches, but Kinkajou barely glanced down them before continuing straight. After a few minutes, Moon caught the scent of living prey up ahead — and the jumble of several voices, both real-world and inside her head. *Uh-oh.*

It was even worse than it sounded. The prey center was total chaos, the opposite of the serene, well-ordered library. It was a mammoth cave open to the air on one side, looking out over a mossy, boulder-strewn slope, towering cliffs, and faraway peaks. There was a low wall of rocks built across the bottom of the opening — useless against dragons, of course, but perfect for keeping prey trapped inside. A fast-flowing river swept along the wall opposite the opening, disappearing through an archway into the next cave.

And there was prey *all over the place.* Shaggy, bleating sheep blundered helplessly under the dragons' talons, yelling in panic. Several speckled-brown chickens, quail, and pheasants were racing around the floor, periodically bursting skyward in an explosion of feathers and squawks. In one corner, a fat black bear was squaring off with a dragonet twice its size, growling.

Worse still, the cave was filled with shouting dragons. Most of them were MudWing, SandWing, and SkyWing dragonets who were gleefully trying to corner the rampaging chickens. They bellowed instructions at one another, yowled when the pheasants dodged them, and shrieked hilariously whenever birds nearly flew up their snouts. At the same time, their minds were all shouting, worrying, planning, reacting, and it felt to Moon like a hundred dragons talking at once.

Clay, meanwhile, was standing on a tall boulder in the middle of the cave, trying to shout over all the noise.

"Everyone stop moving!" he bellowed. "Especially you, chickens! CHICKENS, GIVE UP! WE'RE GOING TO EAT YOU! THERE'S NOTHING YOU CAN DO ABOUT IT! STOP RUNNING AWAY RIGHT NOW!"

"SQUAAAAAAAAAAAAAAAAAAAAAAAAWK!" the chickens shrilled back.

Kinkajou spotted a small mountain of fruit piled near the river and darted over to it. Another RainWing dragonet was there, picking through the options, and Kinkajou shouted something cheerful at him.

Moon hesitated, wishing she could sink right into the mountain and disappear. She was hungry, but it was so loud and horribly overwhelming in here. Maybe she could sneak back to her cave and wait to eat until the middle of the night. Surely it would be quieter then.

But Kinkajou spotted her as she tried to sidle away. The RainWing flapped her wings wildly, beckoning, and finally Moon had to duck her head and sprint over, hoping not to get hit by any chicken parts on her way.

"Moon, this is my friend Coconut," Kinkajou said. *Thought he was my friend* shimmered through her mind, and Moon had a moment to wonder if Kinkajou did have a dark, bitter side after all, before Kinkajou added blithely, "At least, I *thought* he was my friend until I got abducted by bad guys for three weeks and he didn't even *notice* I was gone." She poked him pointedly with her tail.

"Hmmm? Didn't I say I was sorry about that?" Coconut mumbled around a mouthful of papaya. His scales were a kind of quiet lavender blue and his eyes were sleepy. "Or did I? Something like that."

"Mostly you say, 'Hm, what?' every time I bring it up," Kinkajou said. She turned to Moon. "I'm going to learn to read *eons* before he does."

"Why is that?" Coconut asked mildly.

"Because I'm smart and you're not," Kinkajou pointed out. "That was *implied*, Coconut. It was subtext."

"Right," he said, not in the least offended, perhaps because he only seemed to be partially following the conversation. "The mangoes are pretty good," he said to Moon. "I was told to eat them first because they're all ripe. I like bananas better but mangoes are fine. I don't particularly like coconut, though."

"Ironically," Kinkajou said.

"What?" he said.

"See?" she said to Moon, grinning.

Moon nodded, unable to speak through the cacophony inside and outside her ears. At least Coconut's thoughts were slow and meaningless, although she thought she might go mad if she had to listen to them all day long. He passed her three mangoes, and she sliced them open with her claws, the way she'd taught herself to do when she was alone in the rainforest during one of her mother's longer absences.

"Whewf," said a voice behind her. Moon jumped and nearly dropped her mangoes in the river.

"It's just me," Clay said to her kindly. "I'm glad you found Kinkajou. I thought you two would be a good match."

You did? Moon thought with bewilderment. She couldn't see anything in common between herself and the bubbly RainWing.

Clay shooed a chicken away from the fruit and glanced around the tumultuous cave. "So," he said, "my plan hasn't exactly gone as . . . planned."

"Clay, this place is MADNESS," Kinkajou said with a laugh.

"I know," he said ruefully. "We'll try something different tomorrow. I thought it would be fun to bring in live prey and let everyone chase it around. That's what we did in our cave sometimes, growing up, when the guardians wanted us to practice hunting but wouldn't let us go outside. But I guess it was a little more manageable with five dragonets than thirty-five." He wrinkled his snout at the nearest panicking sheep.

Kinkajou shook her head. "I say anyone who is gross enough to eat something that's alive and wriggling deserves to get pecked. You should take those dragons out hunting with you and leave the rest of us here to enjoy our quiet sensible fruit in peace."

"That's a good idea," Clay said. "In the meanwhile, maybe I'll get Tsunami and see if she can help me calm things down." He gave Moon another reassuring smile and hurried out of the prey center.

Moon heard the words *quiet* and *peace* and *calm* as if from a long way away. Through the raucous noise of the dragon minds around her, she could sense something running toward the cave — something like a small thread of pure terror, so tiny it could be blown away in a breeze, but so intense she couldn't miss it, even in the howling gale of emotions in the prey center.

Who is that, and why is their mind so strange? There were no words to go along with the emotions, and there was something fuzzy about it. Could it be a really young dragonet?

She lifted her head and turned to watch for it — but as she did, a vast icicle of cold fury stabbed through her brain and she staggered back, crushing the mangoes in her talons with an involuntary convulsion. Bright yellow-orange pulp splattered all over Kinkajou and Coconut and the rocks around them.

Kinkajou let out a startled yelp, but before Moon could apologize or even get speech back under her control, a louder commotion erupted near one of the tunnels.

"Catch it!"

"Mine! I claim it! Mine!"

"It went that way!"

All the MudWings and SkyWings abandoned the chickens at once and bolted over to that side of the cave. Moon felt the thread of fear twist higher and brighter, as if it had been set on fire.

And then a small shape shot between the dragons and came pelting across the cave, dodging sheep and chickens, and Moon saw what everyone was chasing.

A scavenger!

She'd read about them and seen drawings, but she'd never encountered a real scavenger before. She'd never given them much thought. Apart from stealing the SandWing treasure and killing Queen Oasis twenty years ago, they were just creatures who happened to live on the same planet as the dragons.

But suddenly this one was right here and blazing in her mind as brightly as any dragon. She saw it spot the sheep and chickens, including the ones that had been caught and half eaten already, and she saw it stumble as a bolt of despair went through it.

Why can I feel the scavenger's fear, but nothing from the sheep or the chickens? she wondered. *Aren't they the same?*

The icy anger she'd felt before swept into the cave like an avenging blizzard: an IceWing, pale blue as a frozen ocean, with glittering scales like overlapping chips of ice. He stormed through the yelling crowd of dragonets who were still trying to find the scavenger underfoot, and Moon realized he was chasing the little animal as well.

The scavenger didn't stand a chance. He'd fled into the worst possible place. Someone in the prey center was definitely going to catch him and eat him, and Moon would have to feel his awful terror *as it happened*.

She couldn't watch it die — she couldn't let that happen to something so scared, so helpless and alive and alone and clearly aware of what was about to happen to it.

Moon bolted over to the scavenger, cut it off as it tried to dodge around her, darted left to block its retreat, and deftly snatched it up in her claws.

"It's all right," she whispered to it. "I'm not going to hurt you." It did no good. The scavenger's heartbreaking fear buzzed even more clearly in her mind now that she was holding it. It put its little paws over its head and curled into a ball between her talons.

Silence slowly spread across the cave. Moon looked up and found the IceWing only inches away, glaring at her with dark blue eyes.

NightWing, he thought with a flash of vicious hatred that made her wince. He hissed slowly, exhaling a hint of deadly frostbreath into the air between them.

"You have ten seconds to give me back my scavenger," he snarled, "before I slice your face off."

CHAPTER 4

So much for keeping my head down and staying inconspicuous, Moon thought, feeling the eyes and thoughts of every dragon in the cave on her.

The IceWing was frighteningly beautiful, with horns like deadly icicles and sharp spikes at the end of his whip-thin tail. His gaze pinned her down like a spear.

Never seen one look like that before, she heard him think. *Didn't know they had silver scales anywhere except under their wings. Those ones by her eyes are remarkable . . . and she looks like she's . . . listening to something.* A brief wave of curiosity shivered through his thoughts, and then was abruptly buried in a landslide of anger and self-loathing. *What am I thinking? NightWings killed him, and I hate them all,* all *of them.*

Moon tore her eyes away from his, wishing she could shut her powers off. She could have known from his expression that he hated her. She didn't need to see the layers of how complicated his feelings were. *Who did we kill? Someone he loved, obviously.* She found it easy to believe the NightWings she knew deserved his hatred. *I wish I could be someone else, someone he would give half a chance.*

"Five seconds," he snarled.

"No," Moon said, forcing the word out past the scavenger's terror and the sharp edges of the IceWing's anger.

"That is *my* scavenger," he hissed. "My idiot clawmate let it out, but it is *mine* and I did not bring it all the way here to see it eaten by a lying, smoke-breathing NightWing." He took a step closer, and Moon felt the cold coming off his scales. "I could freeze you one part at a time — first your horns, then snap them off. Then your tail — freeze it and snap it off. Then your claws, and your wings . . . Should I go on?"

Moon closed her talons around the scavenger and brought her wings forward to wrap around it, too. It was impossible to focus her thoughts; the IceWing's mind was so bright, like the sun dazzling off a glacier. In between his threats were images of another IceWing, laughing and shouting in the snow, then the same dragon surrounded by SkyWings in a mountain forest.

She couldn't follow the threads — if that was the dragon he mourned, how did he get killed by NightWings if he was captured by SkyWings? If the IceWing wanted to eat this scavenger, why had he brought it "all the way here"? If he hated Moon so much, how could he also be noticing how gently she held the scavenger?

Say something, she yelled at herself, but already she

couldn't remember what he'd said and what she'd only seen inside his mind.

"Hey, calm down, all right?" A SandWing shoved his way through the watching crowd and stepped between Moon and the IceWing. Moon recognized him as the dragon she'd made eye contact with outside her cave. The one who had noticed how nervous she was.

"No one is getting sliced up or frozen and snapped apart," he said to the IceWing. "What is wrong with you? Did you even try just asking nicely?" He turned to Moon. "Hey. I'm the idiot clawmate, although most dragons call me Qibli. My intimidating acquaintance here is Winter. What's your name?"

He had a gold earring in one ear with a warm orange amber teardrop hanging from it. A few dark brown freckles stood out on his nose, which also bore a small zigzagging scar; the rest of him was a light sandy color. His poisonous barbed tail was tucked neatly into a safe spiral, although it kept twitching in Winter's direction.

He looked like a normal SandWing, but he didn't think like one — or like any dragon she'd met before. Brushing against Qibli's mind was like stepping into a speeding river. He was almost unconsciously scanning the cave as he spoke to her, assessing threats and deciding which dragons were the most dangerous. (She was not on the list.) While he was focusing on defusing Winter's tension and negotiating with Moon, he was also checking escape routes and noting who wore the most jewelry. A small part of his brain was even clocking a chicken in his peripheral vision that he thought might scurry close enough for him to catch.

This did not help clear her mind at all.

They were waiting for an answer from her — to what question? Her name?

"Moon," she managed to whisper.

"Moon what?" the IceWing snapped.

Moon what? She didn't understand the question. The scavenger was moving between her claws, and his fear now had streaks of confusion in it, which was muddling up Moon's head as well. Not to mention the crowd of watching dragons and their excited mind clamor: *Maybe they'll fight! I wonder what scavengers taste like! Why isn't she saying anything? I can't believe she took his scavenger! I bet if he slices her face off, he'll totally get expelled!*

"Moon what?" Winter nearly shouted. "Come on, NightWing. We know your names are all lies. So what's yours? Moondestroyer? Mooneater? Mooncrusher?"

"Winter, you need to seriously cool down!" Qibli yelled. He shot a grin at Moon. "Get it? Because he's an IceWing? I know, I'm hilarious."

"It's Moonwatcher," said Kinkajou, coming up behind Moon. She twined her tail around Moon's. Moon knew that the RainWing was trying to be reassuring and supportive, but the effect was that Kinkajou's thoughts were suddenly as loud as thunder, clashing up against the scavenger's small hot spark of terror.

An IceWing! He's so glittery! And fierce and dangerous! Plus a heroic SandWing! So much drama already! I love school! I love it, I love it!

"Moonwatcher," Winter muttered, deflating a little. There was something shivery about hearing him say her name, but Moon couldn't tell if that was just because Kinkajou was having starry-eyed sparklethoughts about him all over her brain.

"Listen," Qibli said. "This is my fault. I wanted a closer look, so I opened the cage, and that thing was halfway down the tunnel before we could even sneeze. But I promise you the scavenger does belong to Winter, so we're asking you nicely: Please don't eat it."

"Get your teeth anywhere near Bandit and you will lose them," Winter snarled.

"You are not at all clear on the concept of 'asking nicely,' are you?" Qibli said to him.

"Bandit?" Moon echoed. *Who names their dinner? Or keeps it in a cage?* She had a sinking feeling that she had terribly misread this situation. Why, why, in all the furious jumbled thoughts inside Winter's head, hadn't she seen anything about him *not* wanting to eat the scavenger?

"Indeed," Qibli said. "The scavenger with the silly name is Winter's pet. Nobody told *me* we could bring pets here, but I guess the nephew of the IceWing queen gets some special privileges. And if you didn't know he was Queen Glacier's nephew, don't worry, he'd have told you sometime in the next five minutes."

"I only mentioned it," Winter said irately, "because it seems entirely obvious to me that the niece and nephew of the IceWing queen should each be given a private cave, so I wanted you to know we wouldn't have to be claw-mates for very long, as there has *clearly* been some kind of mistake."

"Here's hoping," Qibli said. "So? Moon? Can we catch you a sheep or something instead?" Another million thoughts flashed through his head in the space of two heartbeats. *What do NightWings like? Never trained for bargaining with a NightWing. Can't be too different from other dragons, right? Start with food, but she doesn't look like a dragon who thinks about prey a lot. Not treasure either. Scrolls? She has a cool, scrollish look about her. What can we offer? If she eats him, Winter will be furious. Maybe I can get him a new scavenger.*

"I wasn't going to eat him," she blurted quickly, before she could get lost again in all the tracks of thoughts around her. "I didn't want anyone to eat him. Nobody can eat him, not ever."

Winter tilted his head curiously at her, and she felt his fury thaw a little. "That is exactly how I feel about it."

"Great," Qibli said. "Weird, but great. We're all on the same roll of the scroll, then." He looked expectantly at Moon.

She tried to block him out so she could listen to Winter's thoughts for a moment. It seemed to be true: He was keeping the scavenger as a pet and would violently dismember anyone who tried to eat it. She didn't think the scavenger understood that — he seemed as terrified of Winter as all the other dragons — but at least he'd be safer in Winter's cage than anywhere else in the academy.

She carefully unwound her tail from Kinkajou's and lifted the little creature into Winter's talons. His claws brushed against hers as she did and she flinched, both at the cold and at the furious turmoil of guilt and self-loathing inside him.

"Ew," Winter protested, peering at the scavenger. "You got him all sticky."

Moon realized that her claws were still covered in crushed mango, and she'd gotten bits of it all over Winter's pet. "Sorry," she said softly. "I just . . ."

"She was just saving him," Kinkajou pointed out. "You could actually say thank you."

"Hmmm," Winter said. Moon sensed Clay approaching along one of the tunnels, along with someone whose mind was warm and nearly as excited as Kinkajou's. *Sunny,* she guessed with relief. She really needed to *not* be the center of attention anymore.

Winter took his pet over to the river and dunked him in, prompting several shocked squeaking noises from Bandit. *What does she know about scavengers?* Moon heard him think. *I wonder if she can figure out what's wrong with Bandit. Not that I would ever ask a NightWing for anything.*

"He's hungry," Moon blurted, and immediately wanted to bite her tongue off.

Winter gave her a cold look. "No, he isn't. I offered him a piece of desert rat this morning on the way here, and a bit of walrus the day before that, but he didn't eat either of them." He lifted the dripping-wet scavenger up and inspected him narrowly. The little creature had flopped over and curled into a ball again, shivering. "In fact, he hasn't eaten since Queen Glacier caught him and gave him to me four days ago. I gather that scavengers eat fairly infrequently."

"Or maybe it hates you and is trying to starve itself to death," Qibli offered helpfully.

Winter frowned. "Scavengers don't do that." *Do they?* "He drinks water when I give it to him."

"Have you — um —" Moon faltered as he turned his scowl on her.

"Have I *what*?" he snapped.

Sunny's warm scales brushed against Moon's as the SandWing came hurrying in. "Hello," she said brightly. She was smaller than Winter and Qibli, not much bigger than Moon and Kinkajou. Moon liked the way her mind felt, all hopeful and determined. "What's all the excitement?"

Behind them, Clay started shooing the watching crowd away. Moon could hear them grumbling about wanting to eat the scavenger or wishing there had been a bigger fight, both aloud and in their heads.

"Fatespeaker told me you brought a pet," Sunny said, turning to Winter. "Is that it? Aw, I met a couple just about that size once."

Winter arched his long neck and looked down his nose at her. "Queen Glacier said I could have him if I agreed to come here," he said challengingly. "If you say I can't keep him, I'm going home."

"But you definitely can't have it there," Sunny pointed out in a reasonable voice. "A scavenger couldn't possibly survive the cold in Glacier's palace."

"Well —" Winter hesitated, clearly ruffled by the logic of this. "I don't care. I'll figure out a way. I'm keeping him, that's my point."

"I don't mind if you do, but remember, pets can be a lot of work," Sunny said. "Especially a new pet you're still getting used to. You should ask Starflight if he has any scrolls on the care and feeding of scavengers."

"I'm sure I can manage," Winter said. He started shaking Bandit to get the excess water off. The little scavenger yelped and tried to hang on to one of the dragon's claws. Moon's talons twitched. She wished she were brave enough to grab Bandit back and hold him more carefully.

"There's an awful lot we don't know about scavengers," Sunny said. "Maybe your winglet can study him. And we'll tell everyone there's a no-eating-scavengers policy, but you still have to take care of him and keep him safe." Sunny shifted her wings, and Moon caught the worries going through her mind. *Did that sound bossy enough? Or too bossy? Will anyone ever take me seriously as the boss of anything?*

"No one would dare hurt *my* scavenger," said Winter. "Not if they know he belongs to me. Perhaps I should get him a collar and a label of some sort."

"Belongs to the nephew of Queen Glacier," Qibli suggested with a straight face. Winter nodded thoughtfully, then shot him a suspicious look.

"But," Sunny went on, "is it all right with *you*, Qibli? It'll be in the cave you're sharing, so you have to say yes, too. Otherwise, perhaps we can switch you to a different cave, if we can find someone who won't mind the scavenger."

Winter cleared his throat importantly. "Perhaps you have forgotten that Queen Glacier is my aunt," he said, as though Sunny might be too dim to know such basic facts about the world. "My sister is her niece and therefore in line for the throne. Obviously we should each have a private cave."

"That would defeat the purpose," Sunny said cheerfully. "Living together is part of the school's mission of getting to know each other. Believe me, the SeaWing queen's daughter is here, and she's sharing a cave, too." *With a lot less grumbling about it, I might add,* her mind observed, but she kept that to herself. "Besides, we haven't expanded far enough into the mountain for everyone to have their own cave."

"I don't mind," Qibli said. "I mean, I don't mind the *scavenger*. His owner is the one I might be allergic to."

Moon tilted her head at Qibli. Sunny had given him an easy way to get out of sharing Winter's cave, but he wasn't taking it. He actually wanted to be Winter's clawmate, although she couldn't see why. It wasn't quite that Qibli liked him, but it was a little bit that Qibli wanted Winter to like *him*, and he also kept thinking of a pair of big bad-tempered SandWings (his brother and sister?) in comparison to Winter. In addition, he seemed to be teasing Winter on purpose, as a kind of maneuver to make friends with him. All she could really figure out was that Qibli was more than a little complicated on the inside.

"Don't cause trouble," Sunny reprimanded him, sweeping one of her wings up to stop Winter from lunging at his clawmate.

"I'm not!" Qibli protested innocently. "Someone should probably mention that the scavenger's not going to last very long, though. It looks like it's wilting. Hey, what if it has some kind of disease or something?"

"It doesn't!" Winter growled. He held Bandit up and poked him gently with one claw. Bandit whimpered and flopped to the side. *Don't die!* Winter thought in a panic. He glanced around and caught Moon's eyes again. She tried to look away, but he was already leaning toward her urgently.

"What were you going to say before?" he demanded. "About feeding Bandit?"

"I — I just — I think I read somewhere that they prefer to cook their meat — is all," she stammered. "Have you given him anything besides raw meat?"

"If he's hungry, he should eat anything," Winter said grumpily.

"I think she's right," Sunny said. "I have a —" She paused, and her mind went, *Friend? Former jailer? Dragon who nearly got me killed?* She settled for, "I know someone who kept a scavenger for years, and I think he cooked all her meat for her."

"Well, how am *I* supposed to cook anything for him?" Winter demanded angrily. IceWings had frostbreath instead of fire — Moon knew all he could do was freeze the scavenger's food.

"Someone will help you," Sunny said. "That's one of the many great things about making friends from other tribes."

Ha, Winter thought bitterly.

I would help you, Moon thought, *if you'd let me.*

"You could give him fruit instead," Kinkajou suggested. "Here." She scampered over to the fruit pile and came back with a talonful of berries and a banana.

"Fruit?" Winter said, wrinkling his snout. "Disgusting."

Kinkajou took a blueberry, which was about the size of one of the scavenger's paws, and poked Bandit's nose with it. "Here you go," she said. "Mmmm, blueberry. Eat that."

Bandit blinked and rubbed away the blue juice on his face. He glanced up at Winter, then over at Kinkajou, then reached out and took the blueberry in both his paws. He stared at it for a moment, then bit into it.

He's relieved, Moon realized. *And wary, but too hungry to care.*

"Ha," Kinkajou said, giving the scavenger another blueberry. "See? Moon was right. He's hungry."

Moon shivered as both Winter and Qibli turned to stare at her. Winter's eyes were even more suspicious than before.

"How did you know that?" he demanded.

Oh, Mother, Moon thought anxiously. *It's only my first day, and I'm already making mistakes all over the place. How am I supposed to hide what I can do, with this many dragons watching me and so many ways to mess up?*

"Just a guess," she said softly.

"Lucky guess," said Qibli, and although his tone was friendly, she could hear the chords of wariness echoing in his mind, too. *She's smarter than she wants us to know. Watch out for NightWings, that's what Thorn said. Never trust them. She looks too pretty to be evil . . . but what is she hiding?*

Moon took a step back, and then another. "I — I have to go." She whirled and hurried out of the prey center cave, feeling everyone watching as though their eyes were crawling right inside her scales. Unspoken whispers swirled through her head: *What's wrong with her? Weirdest dragon I've ever seen. Don't understand why she didn't just eat it. Hope she's not in my group.*

And threading through all of it, the pure, icy chill of Winter's last thought:

I thought they said the NightWings couldn't read minds after all.

So why does it seem like she read mine?

CHAPTER 5

Moon hid in her cave for the rest of the day. She pretended to be asleep when her clawmates came back, even though Kinkajou hopefully rustled around and dropped several scrolls in an effort to wake her up. The RainWing's mind was buzzing with how much she wanted to talk about Winter and Qibli and the scavenger, which was exactly what Moon wanted to avoid.

Eventually Kinkajou went off to find someone named Tamarin, Carnelian curled up on her ledge, and Moon fell asleep for real.

The nightmare came immediately this time. Ever since the comet six months ago, she'd had the same awful recurring dream, although the details sometimes changed.

A roaring avalanche crushed dragonets in its path. Lightning split the sky as thunder rolled through the jagged peaks. Dragons screamed in terror and died all around her, their death spasms shuddering through her mind.

That's Jade Mountain, she realized for the first time, watching the earth shake and crack open, the fang-shaped peaks crumbling into a slide of deadly boulders. *Jade Mountain is falling.*

She couldn't move. She couldn't speak, couldn't call for help, couldn't warn the dying dragons. She could only stand and watch as pain pounded through her head and the world was destroyed right under her claws.

This can't be real.

It's just a nightmare. It's just everything I worry about and everything Mother worries about and now probably everything all the dragons around me worry about, all rolled into my head and exploding.

Not a vision.

Not a prophecy.

Not the future.

Please, it can't *be the future.*

A SandWing on fire, screaming. Cracks appearing all along Jade Mountain, opening right under the talons of dragons and swallowing them into the ground. A dragon who looked like Kinkajou, but white with fear, shrieking as falling rocks crushed her tail.

Wake up! Moon screamed at herself.

"Talons and teeth, you poor little dragonet." A huge shape suddenly loomed beside her, as if another mountain had materialized out of the ground. She had a lightning-fast impression of silver and black, and then vast talons closed around her claws and she was suddenly yanked out of the nightmare into darkness.

Cool, still, peaceful darkness. Darkness with no voices in her head, nothing burning or collapsing, no noise or catastrophe or panicking. It was, in fact, the first silence she'd found since arriving at Jade Mountain. She wanted to rest in it forever.

Moon took a deep breath, and then another, and gradually her heart slowed down.

This was still a dream, she knew. Someone — the other telepath — had lifted her out of the nightmare, but she was still asleep. He'd brought her mind somewhere quiet, and she guessed he was waiting nearby.

After a long, long while, there was a voice in the dark, softly. "You are a mess."

Moon hunched her wings forward and wrapped them around herself. She whispered, "I know."

"Someone should be punished for letting you get this way," the voice growled.

"No one knows I'm like this," she said, shaking her head. She hesitated. "Thank you. For . . . that, what you . . ."

"You should be able to do that yourself," he said. She thought it was a "he"; it was hard to tell sometimes from a dragon's internal voice. She could sense nothing else about the speaker; when he was silent, it was as though there was nothing there.

It was sort of creepy, a voice with nothing behind it. She couldn't sense any emotions or thoughts. There was just emptiness, as blank as the dark walls around her. Was this how ordinary dragons felt every day? That everyone else was just a face and noise on a completely opaque backdrop? And all you could know about someone was what they chose to show and tell you?

"Why can't you do anything?" he asked. "Shield your thoughts? Silence the voices? By all the moons, why has nobody trained you to step outside your visions?"

"That wasn't a vision," she said quickly. "It was just a nightmare."

"Really," he said, sounding amused. "That's your opinion?"

She didn't want to talk about the possible future destruction of Jade Mountain. "Who trained you?" she asked.

"My father," he said.

"Oh," said Moon. She'd never met her father, and Secretkeeper didn't want to talk about him. All she would ever say was that he'd died when the volcano erupted. Moon had only learned his name by reading it in her mother's mind: Morrowseer. "That sounds nice."

Now he was definitely amused. "You wouldn't say so if you'd ever known my father. What volcano?"

"I — I didn't —" Moon fumbled for an answer. He'd just plucked that information out of her passing thought. "Please don't do that."

"Do what? Ah, invade your privacy? Rummage through your memories? That would be intrusive of me, wouldn't it? But isn't it what you do to other dragons every moment of the day?"

"Not on purpose!" Moon cried, horrified. "I don't want to! I wish I could stop myself. I know it's a curse and it's terrible hearing what everyone is thinking all the time. And I don't want to know the future, especially if — especially if it's — like *that*." She turned, spreading one wing into the darkness, and hit solid rock. She spread her claws and reached out, realizing she was surrounded by rock on all sides.

"Don't wish to be ordinary, Moonwatcher," said the voice in the dark. "Why would you ever wish for that? Your powers are a gift, don't you know that?"

She brushed her talons along the rough crevices of the wall beside her. *A gift?* "Not according to my mother."

"How strange," he mused. "I've never met anyone who would call our powers a curse. Other powers, yes, but not ours."

"She says everyone will hate me if they find out what I can do," Moon said. "Not that they like me very much to start with."

"Why does it matter if they hate you?" he asked. "You're better than they are. You can do amazing things. Although you could do *more* amazing things if you'd had any training. Right now you're a little pathetic."

"Thanks very much," Moon said, flicking her wings back.

"See?" he said. "Just then you felt angry at me; perhaps you could even hate me a little bit. But you still want to talk to me. Because of my power, you're drawn to me. The same will be true for you. Once they know what you can do, dragons will *need* you. You'll be able to do anything you want."

What if I want to have friends? Dragons who aren't scared of me?

"I'll be your friend," he said, answering her thought as if she'd spoken aloud. "I'm not even remotely scared of you." She suspected he was joking, but it was hard to tell. "Besides, dragons who are scared of you can be very useful. Tell me, would you really give up your powers if you could?"

Moon thought about everything her mother had always told her. And then she thought about being able to see inside everyone, and she thought about the time her visions had saved her from a falling tree, and she thought about what it would be like for her mind to really be empty and quiet all the time, the way it was now.

"No," she admitted finally. "I don't want to be . . . like other dragons. I just want them to not mind that I'm different, if that makes sense. I want to stop being scared — of being found out, of what my visions mean, of other dragons, of everything."

"I think I can help you with that," he said.

"Who are you?" she asked again.

There was a long pause. "You really don't know," he said, as if he finally believed it.

"How would I?" She tried pushing back with her mind, trying to get beyond the blank wall of nothing that went with the voice. But she didn't know how, and she couldn't find anything there at all. "Are you another student? Or a teacher? Why haven't I heard you before?" She touched the rock with one of her talons. "Can we meet in real life? I have so many questions."

"How can you not know about me?" he asked. "I can't find any mention of me in your mind anywhere."

There was a very long, thoughtful silence.

"You must be another NightWing, right?" Moon guessed. "But then why wouldn't you have spoken to me before, when we were all back in the village? Or are you Stonemover, the dragon Starflight told us about?"

There were only five NightWing students at the school, including her. She tried to think about who else had been sent here. Mindreader? That would be funny, if her name were actually true, but Moon had seen into her mind and didn't think so. Mightyclaws? Fearless? Or there was one other NightWing dragonet, a couple of years older, who she hadn't met before because his parents hated Secretkeeper and avoided her. It could be him.

Or Fatespeaker . . . but Fatespeaker hadn't had anything like this in her wide-open mind either.

"The NightWings are in the rainforest now," the voice mused instead of answering her question. "Interesting. I can't reach that far. But I don't know any of those dragons, so more time has passed than I realized."

Moon touched her head, puzzled. Was he not from the tribe? Was he not a NightWing at all? "More time has passed since what?" she asked.

"What year is it, Moonwatcher?"

She breathed a plume of fire into the dark. Nothing but rock around her. No other dragons in sight.

"How long since the Scorching?" he asked. "Surely this is something you've learned from one of your beloved scrolls."

Moon knew he'd just get the answer from her brain anyway. "Five thousand and twelve years," she answered.

A pause.

"What?" he roared.

And then suddenly, with a wrenching twist in her stomach, Moonwatcher woke up.

She lay there on the moss for a moment, feeling as if she'd been dropped from a great height. And plunged into a vat of noise, because even in the middle of the night, minds were buzzing all around her. Carnelian's dreams were belligerent and blood-soaked. Kinkajou's were sunny and colorful, but with a hint of anxiety around the edges that her waking mind normally wouldn't allow in.

What just happened? Are you still there? She tried reaching out to the mystery voice, but there was no answer.

Along the passage, she could sense four dragonets still awake, each in a different cave, their brains circling nervously.

Was one of them the voice who'd been talking to her? It didn't seem like it; they were all preoccupied with their own troubles, and none of them were thinking about her at all.

Moon recognized one of them as Sora. The MudWing was doing some kind of breathing ritual where she imagined mud pouring over all her fears, burying them, so all Moon could see was ripples. Another dragonet was reading, but couldn't concentrate on the words; he kept thinking, *Everyone will know I don't belong here*.

Of the sleepers, several of their dreams echoed with images from the war, a few of them nearly as bad as Moon's nightmare.

She stretched her mind until she found Winter and Qibli's cave by the little spark the scavenger gave off, even in his sleep. The IceWing was deep in a sleep without dreams, but Qibli's dreams were worried in an odd way and seemed to involve other SandWings throwing snakes at him.

All right, so if it wasn't one of the students in the sleeping caves, it had to be one of the older dragons. Maybe it was time to try to find Stonemover. If she could track down his cave on her own, she could ask if he was the voice in her head.

She stepped over to the doorway as quietly as she could, but her tail bumped one of the scroll racks and it rattled across the floor. Kinkajou made a sleepy noise of protest. In her dream, Carnelian growled and whirled around to face a new attacker.

Moon held her breath until they were still, and then she picked up her map of the academy, whisked into the hallway, and turned to head deeper into the mountain. Her guess was that Stonemover lived on the far side, probably as far from the school as he could get so he wouldn't be disturbed. She chose the quietest, darkest paths, breathing out small plumes of flame to study the map as she went. Stonemover's cave wasn't marked, but there were notes on the map about areas to avoid: "passage too narrow for dragons down this way" or "swarms of bats here."

As the voices from the school grew quieter, she listened intently for anything else — a different mind, or the sound of dragon claws. She knew the other mind reader could shield his thoughts from her, but perhaps if he was distracted, or she caught him unguarded, or if she managed to get closer to him . . . well, maybe something would filter through.

And then, in a dark tunnel with a low roof, to her surprise, she did hear someone.

Lost another scale today, I think. And she didn't come. But then, why would she?

That was followed by a long sound, like a mental sigh — and then she heard the echo of a real sigh reverberate off the walls around her. It came from a branch of the tunnel off to her right. She ducked her head and climbed up the passageway.

This mind's thoughts were very, very slow, as if they were boulders being pushed up a hill. *Hungry again. Nothing I can do about that.*

Moon hesitated. He didn't sound like the dragon she'd been talking to, but she'd come this far.

She heard scales scraping against stone. Cautiously she crept around the next corner . . . and there he was.

A huge dragon lay stretched out against the cave wall with his eyes half closed. A torch flickered from a post near his head. His scales were shades of gray and black, and he looked weighted down, almost more like a statue than a real dragon.

But real black eyes opened to stare at her as she came in.

"Hello," she whispered.

"Hrmmm," he said. There was no flash of recognition in his eyes. Surely if this were the dragon in her head, he'd know who she was.

"Are you — are you Stonemover?" she asked.

He exhaled slowly. Without lifting his head, he answered, "Unfortunately, yes."

"I'm Moonwatcher," she said.

"My first visitor from the academy," he rasped. "Apart from Sunny, of course. She said I might have other dragons to talk to from time to time. But there has been no one so far. Not even Sunny today."

"It's only the first day," Moon explained. "I'm sure someone else will be along soon. And it was probably a really busy day for Sunny."

"Hrmmmmm," he said again.

There was a long pause, and Moon couldn't help thinking that for a dragon who supposedly longed for company, he certainly had very little to say. He didn't even have very much to *think*. His mind was slowly revolving back around to how hungry he was.

She couldn't ask him if he'd been talking to her in her head. If it wasn't him — and she was fairly sure now that it wasn't — then she'd be giving herself away. But maybe she could try a more roundabout approach.

"You must know a lot about NightWings," she said.

"Because I'm so old?" he creaked. "I suppose. Compared to you, I certainly am."

"Oh — no, I just — I mean, I was wondering if there were any mind readers in your generation," Moon said.

He let out a kind of grunt that might have been a chuckle. "Ah, no. No, the mind readers are all gone, for many, many moons now. There are always young dragons who hope the legendary gifts will reappear. But we are far better off without them. That kind of power . . . will ruin your life."

Moon shivered. That was the same thing her mother had always said. But this dragon was different. He knew what he was talking about, because now she could see his own curse in his mind.

He was an animus dragon. A miserable one who wished he had never been hatched; a dragon whose power had stolen his one love, his hope for a family, his home, and, in the end, his very scales, which were turning to stone around him.

What she couldn't see was how — she couldn't see all the steps and choices that had brought him here. What if she chose differently? Was it possible to have powers and not lose everything else? The mind reader who'd been speaking to her seemed to think so. If she could find him — if she could learn from him, maybe she could avoid Stonemover's fate. He certainly seemed like a better role model than this poor dragon.

"I'm sorry," she said. "I should get back. It was . . . nice to meet you."

"You too," he said with another sigh.

It took Moon a while to find her way back; she was relieved when she finally saw the light of the sleeping caves up ahead. And she hadn't been gone as long as she'd thought; the same four dragons were still awake, and Carnelian was deep in the same dream, now battling an IceWing.

As she approached her sleeping cave, something tugged insistently at her mind. Someone's dream, perhaps — but as she let herself follow it, suddenly she found she was listening to a conversation, as clear as parrots shrieking in the rainforest:

I see how you benefit from this plan, but I'm not hearing any guarantees for me. Killing is easy enough, but if I kill them, how do I know you'll tell me the truth? And what happens to him if they catch me?

They won't catch you, said a deeper, more slithery voice. *Just do it. Do this for me, and I'll give you the one thing you want most.*

Moon froze, staring around the deserted hallway.

What was *that*?

It wasn't the mind reader's voice — not the one Moon was starting to think of as her friend. These voices were close by, and the conversation was happening between minds, not out loud.

How could that be possible? Were there even more telepaths here?

And . . . why were they talking about killing?

Moon closed her eyes and tried to listen as hard as she could. But now she couldn't separate out the conversation she was looking for; it had either ended or faded back into the confusing, rolling sounds of the dreams around her.

Her eyes popped open.

That's the answer.

A dreamvisitor.

Someone had been using a dreamvisitor to talk to one of the dragonets at the school.

And whoever it was . . . was planning a murder.

CHAPTER 6

"It's MORNING!" Kinkajou sang, pouncing on Moon's tail. "Isn't that WONDERFUL?"

Moon blinked hazily at the RainWing, who was now more pink than yellow, but altogether still too bright. She felt as if she'd only just fallen back to sleep.

"It is the opposite of wonderful," Carnelian observed grouchily. She flung her wings over her head.

"We get to meet our winglet today!" Kinkajou cried. "Isn't that exciting?" She nudged Moon's tail with her own and then plunked herself down on the moss beside her, giving off so much delighted energy that Moon felt both contagiously uplifted by it and exhausted at the same time.

"What does that mean, our winglet?" she asked, hoping perhaps she could fall back to sleep while Kinkajou explained. She missed the feeling of her mother's scales at her back while she slept. She wondered if her mother missed her, too.

"Oh, it's the best idea," Kinkajou said. "I mean, all right, I was a little worried about it at first because I was, like, ACK that means I'll have to make friends with a NIGHTWING, but now that I know it's you, there's nothing more to worry about, because you're just lovely and not in the business of kidnapping or experimenting on dragons after all. Right?" She poked Moon's shoulder.

"Right," Moon agreed. "What?"

"We've been organized into five winglets — get it? It's not a whole wing of dragons, just a smaller group, so, a winglet. Five groups of seven dragonets, with one dragon from each tribe. We're in the Jade Winglet; my friend Tamarin is in the Gold Winglet. The idea is that we'll work with the other six dragonets and get to be friends with them and then we'll totally understand all the tribes and nobody will ever want to go to war ever again. It's brilliant, I love it. I can't wait to meet our SeaWing, they sound so weird. Let's go, let's go, let's go!"

Kinkajou seized Moon's tail and tried to drag her to the door.

"All right, I'm coming," Moon protested, wriggling free. She rubbed her eyes as Kinkajou bounced ahead to the door.

And then, with a horrible jolt, she remembered what she'd heard the night before.

If I kill them . . .

Moon shivered from wings to tail. If someone at the school was planning a murder, she had to tell Sunny or Starflight. But she couldn't — not without revealing her own secret.

But I have to warn them, don't I?

Her mother's favorite rule rang in her head. *Stay secret, stay hidden, stay safe.*

And what if I'm wrong? Maybe it was just a dream. My dream, or someone else's.

But it had definitely felt like two voices talking to each other.

What good is having this power if I can't do anything about what I hear?

"I have to go to the library," Moon said. She didn't know enough about dreamvisitors. All she knew was that there were three of them, created by an animus dragon thousands of years ago. She knew they were sapphires, and she knew any dragon who held one could walk in another dragon's dreams and sometimes communicate with the dreamer that way.

But she didn't know who had them now. The scroll she'd read said they were lost centuries ago. Maybe if she could figure out where they were, she could find a way to warn Starflight and the others without giving away her own power.

"You can't go to the library *now*," Kinkajou said. She held up one of the little boards with a message chalked on it. "We have our first class with our winglet this morning."

The sound of the bronze metal gong being struck reverberated through the halls — *BONG! BONG! BONG!* — three times.

"That's the first warning," Kinkajou said. "Come on, Carnelian!" She grabbed a scroll from one of the racks by the door and threw it at the SkyWing's head. "We have to figure out where our meeting cave is."

Carnelian unfolded her wings with a majestic scowl and flowed off the rock ledge like a wrathful waterfall. She stalked past Kinkajou and Moon without a word and turned left, clearing a path through the milling dragonets with the force of her glare.

"Does that mean she knows where we're going?" Kinkajou asked Moon.

Moon spread her wings with a confused shrug.

"Well, one way to find out!" Kinkajou bounded after the SkyWing.

Moon hesitated. She didn't want to be late for her very first class, although getting to the library to research dream-visitors seemed more important. But her teacher and clawmates were waiting . . . and she could always go to the library after class . . . and maybe she'd find a way to ask about dream-visitors during the discussion.

Reluctantly she followed Kinkajou, keeping her head down to avoid the looks from the dragons around her. That didn't help to block out their thoughts, though. The ones who noticed her definitely remembered the scene from the prey center — there were echoing murmurs of *Oh, there's the weird NightWing who doesn't talk* and *She's the one who tried to steal that IceWing's scavenger* and *Seems stuck-up like all the other NightWings, doesn't want to make friends with anyone.*

After a minute she realized, though, that most of the drag-onets were too busy worrying about their first class to pay much attention to her. *What will they think of me?* was the prevailing whisper in all their minds. *Will anyone like me? What if I say something stupid?*

She didn't catch any thoughts about strange dreams or murder plots, although it was hard to tell through all the noise.

Carnelian went through the Great Hall — where Fatespeaker was sitting proudly with a mallet next to the bronze gong — and chose a tunnel on the opposite side, slanting up. To Moon's surprise, this passageway was lined with plants: some with pale green heart-shaped leaves growing out of cracks in the rock, others with vigorous bundles of dark purple leaves, sprouting from small pots of dirt. Green vines covered the ceiling, winding around the green and yellow globe lights, with long blue flowers hanging down like dragon tails. A rivulet of silvery water trickled down the center of the tunnel, carving a small groove in the stone.

As they went higher, the air felt more damp, until finally they ended up in a cave swarming with vines that was open to the sky on one side. Water cascaded down the back wall like a moving, bubbling tapestry, pouring into a small pool that fed into the stream in the tunnel.

Tsunami sat on the ledge with the morning sun shining behind her, grinning at them as they came in. Her royal blue scales looked as if they were made of melted sky.

About time, she thought. Her tail shifted, rustling the trails of leaves that spilled across the floor and out onto the mountainside. *My own fault for getting up at the crack of dawn, but really it's time to get started, let's GO!*

Moon ducked her head. There was something about the SeaWing that made her nervous, and it was only partly the fact that her thoughts were so *loud*.

BONG! BONG! went the gong, only twice this time.

"Hello!" Tsunami said. "Welcome to your first class. Nice work finding the right cave. Carnelian, Kinkajou, and Moonwatcher, right? Oh, be impressed, I've been practicing so hard to memorize all of you. Thirty-five new names! Easy as cows for Starflight, but a whole lot trickier for me and Clay, believe me. I mean, it helps that I knew some of you before, of course."

"Like ME!" Kinkajou trilled.

Tail kisser, Carnelian thought grumpily.

Someone moved in the tunnel behind Moon and she turned to see a smallish MudWing coming into the cave with a SeaWing close behind him. She didn't recognize the MudWing, but the SeaWing —

"Turtle!" Tsunami said enthusiastically. "Oh, good, I asked to be given your winglet first. Hey, everyone, this is my brother. Can you believe I have a brother? Or a million brothers, apparently, but I'm just assuming this one's the best, since he's here right now." She slung one wing over his shoulders and gave him a toothy grin.

Turtle smiled back at her. "It's true, I am."

Moon studied the green SeaWing dragonet, remembering the vision she'd had when she first saw him — the vision of him attacking Anemone. Could *he* be the one from the dream last night? Was someone trying to convince him to kill his sisters?

She tried cautiously to reach into his mind, which she didn't exactly know how to do; it was like trying to listen harder in one direction. Most dragons were constantly broadcasting their thoughts and feelings, but Turtle still had that odd quiet around him, as though his brain were wrapped in blankets. It was almost peaceful, leaning into his thoughts, but also a little terrifying, because Moon had absolutely no idea what was going on in there.

Is there any chance he's the voice in my head? Are there any SeaWing telepaths? If he can shield his thoughts, maybe he can send them, too. . . . Mystery voice? Are you Turtle?

He caught her staring at him and smiled, but there was no clear answer in his expression.

"This is my clawmate Umber," Turtle said, turning to the little brown MudWing.

"Oh!" Kinkajou said. "Clay's brother!"

Sora's brother, Moon thought, and realized she'd been hoping Sora would be in their winglet.

"That's right," Umber said. His mind rippled with warmth and anticipation in a way that matched Kinkajou's. Moon could also sense relief — almost an ongoing, permanent state of relief that seemed to have to do with not being at war anymore.

"Ooo, the Jade Winglet is so cool," Kinkajou said happily. "I wonder who we'll get for our IceWing and SandWing. Does Sunny have any sisters?"

But Moon could now sense the last two dragonets coming up the tunnel, and her heart dropped.

"Actually," Tsunami said, "after yesterday, we decided to switch a couple of dragons around, since you guys seemed like a good match." She flicked her tail at Winter and Qibli as they stepped into the cave. "You've already met, you're all interested in scavengers — we think you'll fit well together."

BONG! went the warning bell one final time.

Moon stared into Winter's cold blue eyes and felt as if ice was traveling across her scales to her wingtips. How could she hide from him if they were constantly in class together?

It's her, he thought, and an echo came from Qibli's mind as well: *It's her.*

Now I can keep an eye on her, thought one.

Now I can figure her out, thought the other. *Did she just get more tense as we came in? Is it Winter she's worried about, or both of us? She looks a little scared of everyone. But also like she can take care of herself, if everyone would just leave her alone. She likes that RainWing, though, her clawmate, the one who's all heart. I wonder if I can get her to like me.*

I'll find out why she knows so much about scavengers, Winter thought. *I'll find out everything about her.*

I could protect her. Would she want that? Qibli wondered. *It's what I do best. It's what I've done for Thorn since I was three. She said I need to find something else to do with myself, that I'm wasting my potential and she has enough dragons to protect her. As if I trust any of them. Wonder what Thorn would think of Moon. Is she a threat? Or the kind of dragonet the Outclaws are sworn to protect? Why haven't I figured her out yet?*

And then, more softly, but chiming from somewhere inside both of them: *I wonder what she thinks of me.*

She didn't know. She wasn't sure quite what she thought of either of them; she kind of wanted to hide from them but she also wanted to keep listening. It was hard, actually, to have any thoughts of her own when so many others were crowding in all at once. From across the cave, Kinkajou was brimming with *Eeee! The ominous handsome glittery brooding IceWing!* Umber thought quietly, *Wow. He's gorgeous.* And Carnelian sat down with her wings folded and scowled at her talons: *Bah. I hate everyone. All of these dragons would be useless in battle.*

Moon found herself edging a little closer to Turtle, who was like a small island of peace in the middle of the crosscurrents. Eight dragons in one small cave, all thinking at the same time. How was she going to get through this?

"Let's go around and introduce ourselves," Tsunami said. "I mean, maybe it's unnecessary, but that's what Sunny said to do. And then she said I probably wouldn't listen to her anyway, so I am *proving her wrong*, so there. I'm Tsunami, if anyone didn't know. I was going to give myself a title like Commander of Recruitment, but then for some reason everyone voted that I would be terrible at recruiting, whatever *that* is all about, so they made me Head of School instead. So I'm pretty much the boss. And I'm running your first small group-discussion class, which was Glory's big idea, so I figure we'll figure it out together. Any questions?"

"Yeah," said Carnelian. "Are we stuck with this group?"

"That's not quite how I would put it," said Tsunami. "But yes."

"What if we would *prefer* to be in a group with other IceWings?" Winter asked. "Such as my sister?"

"That's not how the winglets are set up," Tsunami said. "But you'll be in some bigger group classes with her and have plenty of time to make other friends as well."

"I love our winglet," Kinkajou volunteered.

"When do we eat?" Umber asked. "Just kidding. Pretending to be Clay." He grinned, then shot a look at Qibli. *Did he think that was funny? I hope that was funny. Did I sound like an idiot?*

Oh, it's Qibli he noticed, Moon realized, *not Winter.* It was impossible to ignore how handsome Winter was, especially with Kinkajou thinking about it all the time. But it was true that Qibli was good-looking, too, in a warmer way, now that she looked. His thoughts were so distractingly fascinating that she hadn't noticed it before.

"Ha! Actually I brought food," Tsunami said. She cleared aside a tangle of vines and revealed a carved stone bowl full of fish, which she set in the middle of the floor. "Help yourselves."

"Awesome," said Turtle.

"Yyyyyyyuck," said Kinkajou. "I'll wait and have a banana later, thanks."

Moon took a step toward the fish, but so did Winter, and she jumped back to stay out of his way. He gave her a curious look. *She's frightened of me. Mother would be so proud.* He turned away, skewering a fish on one of his claws. *I guess I did threaten to slice off her face.*

"Here," Qibli said, taking a fish and handing it to Moon. She could feel the heat rising from his sand-yellow scales as she accepted it.

"Thanks," she said. He smiled crookedly at her, thinking rushing, busy thoughts about what else he could do to get her to like him, and trying to fit her into a pattern of other dragons he'd known before. She had never met a dragon who had so many thoughts a minute. Consciously he was thinking about her; unconsciously he was observing that Carnelian was the most battle-scarred and probably the most unpredictable dragon in the cave, so he was angling his tail toward her, just as a precaution. And part of him was also remembering what he knew about Tsunami and the kinds of dragons she liked, while yet another part was planning to go out and survey the mountains later.

It was almost like reading a scroll, or maybe like reading five scrolls at once. Moon wished she could escape his attention and just listen to him think for a while.

"Right, introductions," said Tsunami. "Carnelian? Want to go first?"

No, muttered the SkyWing's brain. She heaved a deep sigh. "I'm Carnelian."

There was a pause.

"Anything else?" Tsunami prompted. "What should we know about you? Family, favorite color, anything?"

Carnelian growled, low in her throat. "I'm a loyal subject of Queen Ruby," she said finally. "I'm in the camp that believes Queen Scarlet is dead, and if she isn't, I'd be happy to kill her myself to protect my queen's throne. I'm here because my queen told me to be, although I *should* be training with my battalion and guarding her palace, not eating slimy wet fish with a bunch of spineless dragonets." She frowned at them all for a moment. "And my favorite color is red."

Insecure, Qibli thought, studying Carnelian. *Only comfortable when she's fighting. Worried we'll think she's dumb and that Queen Ruby will find out she's dumb and all her chances of advancing to general one day will be ruined. Is she as stupid as she thinks she is? Have to wait and see.*

Moon blinked at him. None of that was obvious, but it was all there in the less conscious parts of Carnelian's mind. He was right. How could he know all that?

He couldn't be a mind reader, surely, or she'd be able to tell. Had he figured all that out just . . . by noticing?

"All right," said Tsunami. "Good to know. Kinkajou?"

Bright flares of yellow and purple shot across the RainWing's scales. "Oh, sure; I'm Kinkajou, I'm a RainWing, and I've never met any SeaWings or SandWings or IceWings before, I mean, apart from the dragonets of destiny, of course, because I'm really good friends with them. I'm excited to learn how to read and I want to know everything about all your tribes and I think this school is the best idea in the world. And *my* favorite color is yellow!"

"Of course it is," Carnelian said.

Should I tell them about being a NightWing prisoner? Kinkajou wondered. *No, that's a little grim for first impressions.*

"Your turn," Kinkajou said, bumping Moon's side. A flurry of happy thoughts leaped through her scales into Moon, pushing her past her nervousness.

"I'm Moonwatcher," she said softly, "but please call me Moon." *Or nothing, that would be all right, too. I guess I can't say, "Please don't talk to me at all," can I?* "Um. I grew up in the rainforest." *And I'm a mind reader. And I can see the future, and I'm afraid Turtle might kill his sister, and I'm pretty sure someone is spying on our dreams, and that the whole* mountain might fall on us one day. Also, I miss my mother. "I like scrolls," she finished nervously.

How did she grow up in the rainforest? Winter thought, narrowing his eyes at her, but Tsunami had already turned away and Moon couldn't jump in to explain, in case he guessed that she'd read his mind again. She focused on her talons, avoiding his gaze.

"Me too," said Turtle. "At least, I like scrolls that weren't written by my mother. I've read way too many of those." He rolled his eyes. "I'm Turtle, by the way."

Used to being invisible, Qibli thought, tilting his head at Turtle. *Almost prefers it, but not always. Easygoing. Doesn't want to try hard enough to be noticed. I wonder how much that armband is worth. Don't recognize the kind of stones. He looks like he wants to go back to bed.*

Moon listened intently; she hadn't been able to figure out anything about Turtle at all. Qibli seemed to think the SeaWing was harmless. She wondered what he'd think if she told him about her vision — not that that conversation was ever going to happen.

"I'm Qibli," said the SandWing. "I was one of Thorn's Outclaws before she became queen. My plan is to learn everything as fast as possible and then get back to help her run the Kingdom of Sand."

"I'm sure she's lost without you," Winter said scathingly.

"And I'm sure *you're* perfectly *essential* to the operation of *your* kingdom," Qibli shot back. Winter frowned, and Qibli thought, *Ah, that hit home. I was right; he doesn't think he's worth much to his family, although he would like us all to think differently.*

"And I'm Umber," said Clay's brother. "I think — I think we might have been in a battle together once," he said to Carnelian. "I mean, you look familiar."

"Oh," she said, squinting at him. Her frown softened. "I didn't realize you fought in the war, too." *Where SkyWings and MudWings were on the same side,* she thought quietly. *Maybe I do have allies here.*

"Yeah, with my brothers and sisters — my brother Reed is our leader," he said. "But he said Sora and Marsh and I could come to school now that the war is over, since there's so much we wanted to learn. I miss him and Pheasant, though." Memories flashed through his head, of flying surrounded by other brown dragons, whisking through clouds and turning and diving all together. Marshes, a muddy swamp camp. A large brown dragon cuffed his shoulder affectionately; another one dropped a pig in front of him and waved for him and Sora to share it. All of them laughing around a fire.

"They can visit anytime," Tsunami promised. "They can even camp out and live here if they want. The more the merrier."

"They're working for Queen Moorhen right now," Umber explained. "But maybe one day." His wings drooped a fraction of an inch, and then he pulled them back up.

"Well, *I* am Winter," said Winter.

"Queen Glacier's nephew," Qibli said at the same time as he did. Winter straightened up and glittered dangerously at him.

"Don't you mock me," he said.

"I wouldn't dream of it," Qibli said innocently.

"If you're the Head of School," Winter said to Tsunami, "does that mean you're the dragon to talk to about getting a private cave?"

"Why, yes, I am," Tsunami said. "The answer is no."

"See, I'm your destiny," Qibli said to Winter with a cheerful shrug.

Wish he were my destiny, Umber and Kinkajou thought nearly simultaneously. Moon smothered a giggle and got a pleased look from Qibli.

"Can we get on with the discussion?" Winter asked. "What exactly is the point of this?"

"The point is to talk about anything you want to talk about," Tsunami said. "To find out what dragons from other tribes think, and see things from a new point of view. I'm sure it'll be different when you have this class with Starflight or Clay or Sunny, but I, for one, think you guys should pick the topic."

"All right," Winter said. "I want to talk about NightWing powers."

As far as Moon could hear, no one noticed her expression of terror before she managed to fix her face. Except maybe

Qibli, who thought, *Is she all right? Winter's such a moonlicking crocodile, picking on her for no reason.*

Kinkajou, also, glanced at Moon and thought, *Poor thing, she's not going to enjoy that.*

"Maybe we could talk about the war instead," the RainWing suggested. "I want to know what Queen Thorn is like. You've been inside the SandWing stronghold, haven't you?" she asked Qibli.

"Wait, I'm confused about the NightWings, too," Turtle said before Qibli could answer. "Is it true they don't have powers anymore? Just because they moved to the rainforest?"

"I heard a rumor that they *never* had powers," Carnelian chimed in, suddenly animated. "That they made all of that up and they've been lying to us for thousands of years."

"But what about the dragonet prophecy?" Umber challenged, flicking his tail. "About my brother and his friends ending the war? *That* was clearly real, because look, it came true."

No, it wasn't, Moon thought. *All the NightWings know it was false, because there haven't been any true prophets in the tribe in forever. But they won't admit* that *to anyone outside the tribe.* Not even her; she'd figured it out by reading their minds. *Most of them are furious that the world knows they have no powers.*

"What if they're lying *now* and they secretly *do* have powers but don't want us to know?" Turtle asked.

Moon shivered involuntarily and focused on the fish in her claws.

Oh, snail droppings, Tsunami cursed inside her head. *I told Starflight we'd get asked about this. I never remember our story. And why should I have to lie? To protect the NightWings' precious reputation, or the worthless Talons of Peace? Who cares if the prophecy wasn't real, now that the war is over?*

"It doesn't really matter, right?" she hedged. "The war is over. There are no more prophecies. We can do whatever we want, which includes ignoring the NightWings if we want to. No offense, Moon."

"It *matters* if they were *manipulating* us," Winter hissed. "Do they have powers or not? Or did they when they lived in their secret location? If so, were all of them psychic, or just a few? And how did they lose them?" He shook his head, his icicle-sharp spikes clattering faintly. "There are thousands of dragons who are still terrified of the NightWings — they deserve to know the truth."

Tsunami looked calm, but Moon could hear her squirming on the inside. *I TOTALLY AGREE WITH YOU,* the SeaWing thought.

"Well, nobody's sure what the truth is," she said finally.

"Nobody's sure?" Winter swept one glittering, pale blue wing toward Moon. "We have one right here. This is all about understanding other tribes, isn't it? Can't we ask her?"

Three moons, the horrible force of seven pairs of eyes staring at her — green, amber, black, blue, orange — ranging from curious to hostile with matching tidal waves of emotion behind them. Moon wondered what anyone would do if she bolted from the cave. And maybe flew all the way back to the rainforest without stopping.

"Moon doesn't know anything," Kinkajou jumped in loyally. "She wasn't raised with the other NightWings; her mother hid her in the rainforest. She's been told all the same lies as everyone else."

Moon thought perhaps she loved Kinkajou at that moment more than any other dragon she'd ever known. *Please, please believe her*, she prayed. *Don't ask me any more questions.*

"Oh." Winter gave Moon that look again, the one like she had shifted her scales and turned out to be a different dragon than he'd expected, or possibly a howler monkey and not a dragon at all. *Maybe I don't have to hate her after all,* he thought. *But still . . . a NightWing's a NightWing, and none of them can be trusted.*

Aha, Qibli thought. *That explains some things. She doesn't have the same beaten-down yet insufferably smug aura of the other NightWings. Does she miss the rainforest? Or is she happy to finally be with other dragons? Was she lonely? Must have been alone a lot. Maybe she prefers it. Or maybe she's not used to making friends. I could be her friend. Careful, Qibli. Figure her out first.*

"Look, the important thing is that if the NightWings ever did have powers, they don't anymore," Tsunami said, spreading her wings so the sun shone through her royal pattern of phosphorescent scales. "As long as everyone knows that, the NightWings can't manipulate the other tribes ever again. So just remember that there's no mind reading, and there's definitely no seeing the future. NightWings are not these all-powerful mystery dragons who know everything. And if someone ever tells you you're in a prophecy, tell them to eat their tails. I wish I could have done that to the Talons of Peace a lot sooner."

She wouldn't believe me, Moon realized. *If I went to Tsunami about the voices I heard, or my vision of Jade Mountain collapsing — she'd think I was lying. She doesn't trust NightWings . . . or anyone who tries to tell her what to do, or what her future will be.*

"But —" Winter started to protest.

"Who wants to go hunting?" Tsunami nearly shouted. "I know I do! Great idea, Tsunami! No arguing with the Head of School; off we go!" She shot off the ledge and whooshed away into the clouds.

Carnelian snorted. "I guess that discussion is over," she said.

Moon let herself smile at the fact that fearless, awe-inspiring Tsunami had been the one to bolt, not her.

But her smile faded as Winter paced across the cave and

stopped right in front of her. He studied her with his piercing gaze, almost as if *he* could read *her* mind if he just stared at her long enough. His scales were so bright and so cold, his eyes so weirdly blue and suspicious and angry and sad all at the same time.

"Hey, Winter, leave her alone," Qibli said, sliding up next to Moon. "She's not the enemy."

"Pyrrhia is at peace now," Turtle agreed. "There are no more enemies."

Because the queens signed a peace agreement and accepted Thorn as the new SandWing queen, Winter thought. *But there are some things that cannot be forgiven. That should not be forgiven. And we're supposed to just sit back and let the NightWings get away with it?*

It wasn't her, though, whispered another part of his mind.

But she's still one of them.

"You say you don't know anything," Winter said, settling his wings. "But you know the other NightWings. You can find out the truth and come back to tell us. Right?"

Ha. They'd probably tell an IceWing all their secrets long before they ever trust me, Moon thought. "Um," she said. "Maybe?"

"I want to know everything about their powers," he said. "Were they ever real? How do we know they're gone? What else are they lying to us about?" He cleared his throat. *If I'm scary enough, she'll do what I want,* his mind whispered.

That's what Mother would say. "I mean you. What else are *you* lying to us about?"

"Hey, igloo-face, that's not cool," Qibli barked.

"Yeah, Moon's in our winglet," Kinkajou said, bristling. "We're supposed to support each other."

"I'm with igloo-face," Carnelian said. She stood up and stretched her massive wings, making Umber duck so he wouldn't get whacked in the head. "If we're supposed to get all snuggly with each other, there shouldn't be any more secrets. Let's make her tell us everything." Her orange eyes glared at Moon, and an ominous image flashed through her head of Moon pinned under her talons.

"I wasn't joking!" Tsunami yelled, swooping by outside. "We're going hunting! Come on!"

Carnelian stalked to the ledge and leaped out. Umber glanced at the others — *Poor Moon,* he thought, *but I want to know the truth, too* — and then hurried after her.

Turtle shrugged. "Whatever you guys decide." And a moment later he was gone as well, leaving Moon, Kinkajou, Qibli, and Winter facing off.

I'll fight him if I have to, Qibli was thinking fiercely. *He curls his claws like he relies on his front talons in fighting, so I'll go for his shoulder first, slow him down without doing too much damage. Have to disable his snout to stop his frost-breath, too. Will Moon like it if I fight for her? Or is she the kind of dragon who would rather see me try a peaceful argument first? Kinkajou would like me either way. I like that about her. But I can't even guess about Moon. Doesn't seem like a fighter but she's not scared in a normal way. Hope she stands up to him. She can't let him get away with intimidating her like that.*

On Moon's other side: *It is SO WEIRD that I can't tell what he's feeling by looking at his scales!* Kinkajou thought, watching Winter. *His shiny, shiny, gorgeous scales. Don't get distracted! No being mean to my new best friend, no matter how dazzling you are!*

Moon blinked at Kinkajou, her fear shrinking. New best friend? Did she mean that? Or was Kinkajou the kind of dragon who had a new best friend every two minutes?

Either way, for *these* two minutes, at least, she had backup, even if she hadn't done anything to earn it.

She turned and met Winter's eyes, which felt a little like staring into a glacier. "All right," she said. "But please stop trying to scare me." She hesitated, and then, riding one of Qibli's sharp observations, she added, "You are not as terrifying as you think you are."

He took a surprised step back, his mind whirling.

Nice, Kinkajou thought, grinning. *Take that.*

Knew she was cool, thought Qibli.

Stop liking *her,* Winter ordered himself with an internal growl. *Remember what Father said: They're all liars. Be strong, be vigilant, strike first. Trust nobody. Not even interesting NightWings with silver teardrop scales.*

"Fine," he said. "You find out the truth about NightWing powers . . ."

"And you stop threatening everybody," Kinkajou said.

He paused, and then an unexpected expression creased his face. "Hey, I didn't promise anything about everybody," he said. "Just her. I have an IceWing warrior mystique to maintain, after all, come on." He looked at Moon again, and then he turned and jumped out into the sky, flying after Tsunami and the others.

"I'm probably wrong," Qibli said, "but I *think* my claw-mate just made a joke. Is that possible?" Inside he was thinking, *Yes! I knew that dragon was in there, if I can just drag him out.*

Moon returned his smile.

"You were totally hallucinating," Kinkajou agreed. "Too many smokeberries."

"Are you all right?" Qibli asked Moon.

She nodded. She was more all right than she'd been in months. Mind reading was one thing — one awful thing — when you were surrounded by dragons who hated you, as she had been in the NightWing village. But when you were with dragons who actually liked you, or wanted to like you, for whatever mysterious reason . . . well, she didn't expect it to last (*What happens if they find out the truth about me?*), but for now, it was kind of great.

"What's a smokeberry?" Qibli asked Kinkajou as they started toward the ledge.

"Oh, they're crazy," Kinkajou said. "I had some while the RainWing healers were working on my wing injury. They gave me the wildest hallucinations — flying panthers, quetzals the size of dragons, scavengers with superpowers. You name it, I saw everything."

They soared into the sky. Moon started to follow them, but stopped on the ledge, feeling the wind whip around her. Up in the clear, cloudless sky, her new friends were diving and whirling like flower petals in a rainforest storm, gold and scarlet and green and pale blue.

Don't get too comfortable, little Moon, said the whispering voice softly. *Even mind readers can be taken by surprise when they think they know whom to trust.*

The dragons who like you now are the ones most likely to betray you.

Believe me. I know.

CHAPTER 7

Moon rose through the sky, feeling the paper-soft brush of thin clouds parting around her dark wings. It was quieter up here, but not quiet enough. She wondered how high she'd have to get before she couldn't hear anyone anymore. She wondered if it was possible to get high enough that even her mystery friend couldn't reach her mind.

A furry smell caught her attention, and she spun to study the ground. There — a mountain goat clambering between two rocks, behind a screen of straggly bushes.

Moon glanced around, but Tsunami and most of the others were circling over a glassy lake, looking for fish. The closest dragon to Moon was Qibli, who was trying extremely hard to seem as if he wasn't watching her. Carnelian was within shouting distance, drifting on her vast wings, but Moon wasn't about to do any shouting, and certainly not to get the grumpy SkyWing's attention.

Guess that means this goat is mine, she thought with a tiny bit of glee.

Swooping suddenly into a dive, Moon plummeted down toward the ground. Below her, the goat saw her shadow coming and let out a bleating scream of fear. It scrambled quickly up the rocks and tried to leap into a narrow ravine, where dragons would not be able to follow.

But it wasn't fast enough. Moon twisted in a quick spiral and snatched the goat in midair, whisking it back up into the sky and killing it in one motion with a squeeze of her claws.

"Wow!" Qibli shouted from above her. "How did you *do* that? Carnelian, did you see that?"

The SkyWing flew closer, eyeing the dead goat jealously. "I thought NightWings didn't know how to hunt."

"I thought so, too," Kinkajou chimed in. The RainWing sailed up from a bramble-covered slope. Her snout was stained with dark purple blackberry juice. "Starflight told me they do this thing where they bite their prey and then wait for it to die of infection and then they sniff it out and eat the dead things. It sounds super horrible, like, even worse than regular hunting."

"Gross," Qibli agreed.

"They're not supposed to do that anymore," Moon said. "Glory and Deathbringer are teaching them how to hunt properly. And I just, I, um — taught myself to hunt in the rainforest. . . . Mother was always leaving me alone, so . . . I kind of had to." She held out the goat. "Um — maybe we can share it?"

"Really?" Qibli said. "That would be great. I'm going to need more practice to figure out how to hunt here. The land is all *folded* and squiggly. Too many hiding places. Give me a big flat desert and some half-asleep sunbathing lizards any day."

Moon guessed it wouldn't take him long to master hunting in the mountains. His eyes were darting across the landscape below them and he was storing away observations in neat stacks in his mind. He was also trying to gauge whether she meant it about sharing the goat, and whether she'd like him better if he was self-sufficient or if he accepted her offer with appropriate gratitude.

"I can catch my own food," Carnelian said stiffly. She swung away, broadcasting offended thoughts. Moon winced.

"Nice work, Moon," Tsunami called. "We've caught a few things, too. Let's take all this back to the prey center and eat there." Another SeaWing, this one a blue-green adult dragon with a scar on his side, had joined them with a net, which was now full of squirming fish. He hefted it in his talons and nodded to Tsunami, who tilted her wings and soared back toward Jade Mountain.

The others followed her, one by one, with Moon flapping slowly at the back. The goat was heavy; it smelled of meat and the blood that had left dark red streaks on her claws. But the thought of going back into the prey center was enough to make her lose her appetite. The noise, the memory of everyone staring at her . . . She was tempted to get lost on the way.

If you are always cowering in a cave alone, you'll be wasting your powers completely, the voice muttered.

Easy for you to say, Moon shot back. *Clearly* you *don't get splitting headaches every time you walk into a crowd.*

Why has no one taken care of you? the voice wondered. **Even if the skills are lost, there must be scrolls about coping techniques.**

No one thinks I need scrolls like that, even if they do still exist, Moon pointed out. *If anyone found out what I can do, I'd probably be thrown out of the tribe. I'd definitely be thrown out of school. I'd probably be thrown off the peak of Jade Mountain, or into the ocean. This is not a popular power to have right now, is what I'm trying to say.*

You don't need to be popular if you're powerful. The voice chuckled. Then it stilled for a moment, and added musingly, **Although perhaps a little more popularity would have been helpful in my situation.** Another thoughtful pause. **In any case, listen and perhaps I can help.**

I'm listening.

Imagine the sound of ocean waves.

I've never heard ocean waves, Moon admitted.

What? the voice demanded. **Were you raised under a mountain? Fine, then — some other repetitive, soothing noise.**

Moon caught a wind current and tilted her wings, shifting the goat's weight between her talons. *Would rain work?*

Yes. Exactly. Fill your head with rain.

Moon thought of all the long, lonely days and nights she'd spent hidden in her fern burrow, listening to the rain patter on the leaves all around her. Watching the raindrops slowly drip from the ends of the curled fronds onto her tail. Wishing she could hear the approaching whoosh of her mother's wings instead.

You tragic little dragon, the voice said sympathetically.

I'm not *a tragic little dragon,* Moon protested. *I'm lucky. I didn't have to grow up on the volcano. Mother saved me.*

Mmmmm. She seems to have a lot of opinions about what's best for you, none of which involve finding out your preferences first. Before Moon could defend her mother, he went on. ***Now hold on to that falling rain sound, and then imagine that you're taking each voice you hear and slipping it inside one of the raindrops. Do that as you enter a cave full of dragons, and after a minute all their insignificant mental howling will be drowned in the downpour.***

Moon concentrated for a minute.

The voice chuckled in her mind again. ***Oh, it won't work with mine, dragonet. I'm not so easily submerged. Go try it on that yammering RainWing, or the frenetically intelligent, strangely desperate SandWing.***

Moon wanted to ask what he meant by calling Qibli desperate, but she could see the opening to the prey center below her. Winter and Turtle were already gliding down to the entrance, and beyond them she could see the flash of scales and milling tails; the prey center was as busy today as yesterday, if not more so. She needed to master this new trick right away.

She beat her wings to soar closer to Kinkajou, whose mind was going, *I wonder what we'll do after lunch — oo, maybe reading practice! Or history! Or music! Sunny says the SandWings are a surprisingly musical tribe. Kind of hard to imagine Qibli singing, I must say. Ha ha, imagine Winter singing! I wonder if he can scowl and sing and look darkly handsome and mortally offended all at the same time. Probably. Oh, I have to remember to take Tamarin to where the blackberry bushes are. I hope Glory visits us soon.*

Moon imagined collapsing Kinkajou's thoughts into a raindrop and whisking them into the quiet background storm.

It almost seemed to work, until Kinkajou spotted her, turned pink, and grinned. Her mind went, *MOON! She's so funny. All quiet on the outside but secretly a total fierce-face.*

It is more difficult when the thoughts are specifically about you, the voice in Moon's head pointed out. ***And easier when there are many voices at once. This works best in a crowded room, not so well in a two-dragon conversation. Also, it takes practice.***

I'll practice, Moon vowed. She angled her wings and swooped down toward the prey center, side by side with Kinkajou. The hubbub of thoughts rose up to envelop her.

Totally hungry . . .

Why must I be in the same cave as her?

What did I just eat?

If that MudWing makes ONE MORE grotesque slurping noise —

The dragonets weren't in the war; it's easy for them to talk about forgiveness.

This papaya tastes boring. I guess I normally like papaya. But this one is sort of boring all the way through. Like eating water. Boring water. I wonder when it will be sun time. Maybe I should try a different papaya after this one. But what if the next papaya is boring, too?

That last train of thought was clearly coming from Coconut. Moon seized his thoughts and slid them into the sound of rain in her mind.

It worked! She waited a minute to be sure she couldn't hear him anymore, and then did a delighted flip in the sky before landing outside the cave.

Kinkajou laughed. "You look happy all of a sudden."

"Just figuring something out," Moon said. Coconut and his meaningless thoughts were one thing; they were practically background noise already. She reached out to grab the nearest SeaWing's thoughts — *Webs brought us fish! I could eat his tail, I'm so hungry!* — and tried the same trick.

Her mental voice melted into the noise like just another raindrop.

This is amazing, Moon thought. *Thank you.*

It is the first trick a mind reading dragonet learns, the voice said. **Otherwise they could go mad. You should have had these**

lessons soon after hatching. *It is rather a wonder you're as ten-uously sane as you are.*

Very funny, Moon thought back. *But seriously, I was alone most of the time, so it was never this bad before. Luckily I didn't need to shut out the sloths and toucans.*

She noticed Kinkajou watching her curiously. "Are you all right?" the RainWing asked. "You looked like your head was taking a walk on one of the moons for a minute."

"What does that look like?" Moon asked.

Kinkajou's scales turned purplish-black; she wrinkled her nose and gave the tip of the mountain a glassy-eyed stare.

"Talons and tails," Moon said, giggling, "please tell me I don't really make that face."

"FISH!" shouted several dragons inside the prey center. The SeaWing with the net had dropped it on the cave floor, leaving large silver fish flopping across the stone. A horde of dragons descended on it at once.

Moon and Kinkajou edged past the flapping mass of wings and found a spot near the river where Moon could slice up her goat while Kinkajou raided the fruit pile. *Raindrops,* Moon thought, battling the noise in her head. She took a deep breath. *It's all raindrops.*

She was concentrating so hard that she jumped when Qibli swept up and sat down next to her.

"Sorry," he said, tilting his wings away from her. "You said — the goat, remember? But if you changed your mind, no worries; I can go wrestle for a fish instead." *Another fish, how unappealing. Not sure I'll ever get used to slimy wet sea creatures sliding down my throat. But I don't want her to think I can't feed myself — maybe I'm not that hungry —*

"No, of course, here," Moon said. She used her claws to slice away half of the goat and pushed it toward him.

"I could totally get a fish away from all those dragons," Qibli informed her. "In case you were wondering. If living in the rainforest on your own makes you good at hunting, then let me tell you, being a dragonet in the Scorpion Den with a family who hates you makes you really good at stealing, fighting, scrounging, and tricking dragons into looking the other way while you nab their roasted camels."

"Why did your family hate you?" Moon asked.

"Oh." He looked awkward for a minute. "They sort of hate everyone. It's no big deal."

Moon could sense that it had certainly been a big deal for the first three years of his life, at least. The pace of his conscious thoughts slowed for a moment, and she caught a flash of his mother, a large SandWing with snakelike patterns down her spine, hissing at tiny Qibli and two other, bigger dragonets. She saw his brother and sister beating him and threatening him with their venomous tails, just to steal his talonful of date palms. She saw an old male SandWing, radiating authority, stalking through to inspect them with beady black eyes. She saw little Qibli offering a stolen coconut to his mother, his face hopeful, and she saw him thrown against a wall for weakness instead.

None of that was going to fit in a raindrop.

"I'm sorry," she said to Qibli, and then gasped with sudden pain. She couldn't stop herself from doubling over as a new vision blistered through her mind.

This wasn't a passing memory. Those were always a little blurred and jumbled together with the dragon's other thoughts.

But visions like this, scenes of the future, came bright and clear, even if just for a moment, usually along with a lightning-sharp headache.

In this one, the same old SandWing loomed over Qibli, his snout twisted with hatred. Behind him hulked Qibli's brother and sister, now fully grown and even more menacing, wearing medallions etched with some kind of bird. Qibli curled his tail up dangerously and shouted, "Where is she?" into their sneering faces.

"Hey," she heard his voice saying in the real world. "Whoa. What happened? Moon? Everything all right?"

Moon blinked, shaking the vision away. The pale gray walls of the prey center came back into focus around her. Bright sunlight reached across the floor to glint off Qibli's amber earring; one of his talons was resting lightly on hers, and his mind was spiraling with curiosity and concern.

"Yes, sorry, it's nothing," she said. "I get these headaches. It's gone now. Sorry . . . you were saying, about your family?"

Does she really want to know? Qibli wondered. *Or is she distracting me? Should I be worried? Headaches like that don't sound normal. Thorn took swordleaf root for her headaches; I wonder if I can find some of that for Moon. My family — she doesn't need to know all the horrible details. It's all sand in the wind now anyway.*

He shrugged casually. "I joined the Outclaws when I was three, and Mother was happy to shove me out the door. The best news of my life is that I'll never have to see any of my family ever again."

But that's not true, Moon realized. Not according to her vision. If that was really the future, then Qibli's awful family wasn't done with him yet. What did they want from him? Who was the old male SandWing? And who was the "she" Qibli had been asking about? His mother? Thorn?

I wish I could warn him.

I wish I could save him.

Moon turned back to her lunch with a sigh. If only she lived in a world where dragons weren't afraid of her powers — where she could tell everyone about them without losing her new friends. A world where they'd believe her and wouldn't hate her for what she could do. If only the NightWings hadn't ruined everything with their centuries of lies.

Then I could do some good with everything rattling around in my brain. I could use it to help dragons, couldn't I?

Her mystery voice didn't respond.

I have to go to the library, Moon remembered. *Maybe I can't help Qibli, but if I can find out about the dreamvisitors and figure out whom I heard last night . . . maybe I can still save someone.*

—⁓ CHAPTER 8 ⁓—

"I should go," Moon said to Kinkajou as soon as the RainWing came back from the fruit pile.

"No!" Kinkajou cried. "We're eating together! You haven't even finished your hairy smelly carcass thing! Sit!" She nudged Moon back to sitting. "Just for five minutes," she wheedled.

Moon wanted to argue, but there was a thread of anxiety in Kinkajou's mind — *Don't leave me alone, please stay and be my best friend* — that she couldn't resist.

"Sure, OK," she said, and was rewarded with glowing pink scales.

"Can you tone that down?" Umber asked Kinkajou as he and Turtle joined them, each carrying a fish. "I mean, it's a very exciting color that I can't say I've ever seen before, but it's a little —"

"Bright," suggested Turtle.

"Noticeable?" tried Umber.

"Eyeball-scorching," offered Qibli.

"This happens when I'm happy," Kinkajou said, unruffled. "But if you'd prefer something more sedate —" She turned a vibrant shade of lime green splashed with violet spots. Moon nearly choked on her goat.

"Aaaah!" Qibli yelped, covering his eyes.

"I don't actually know you," Umber said to Kinkajou. "You might be totally serious right now."

"No, I'm just kidding," Kinkajou said with a giggle, bumping Moon's side again. "I can be totally ordinary and boring, don't worry." Her scales shifted again, rippling to the same quiet brown as Umber's, and she gave him a wide-eyed, "see? boring" stare.

"*Boring* hasn't exactly made it onto my list of words to describe you," Moon said.

"Winter!" Kinkajou shouted.

The IceWing paused in the act of sweeping majestically past them. "Yes?" he said frostily to Kinkajou.

"Don't you want to sit with us?" Kinkajou asked. "I mean, since we're your winglet now, and everything." A wave of ice blue shimmered across her scales and then vanished again. Moon tried and failed to stuff all the dreamy thoughts from Kinkajou's head into a raindrop.

Winter looked down his nose at the RainWing. "Absolutely not," he said, and stalked away toward another IceWing perched on a ledge slightly above the rest of the dragons.

"He's so tortured," Kinkajou sighed happily.

"You're a little weird," Moon pointed out.

Kinkajou was about to reply when a hush fell over the cave. They all twisted around and saw Anemone pace slowly through the door with her head held high, followed by a thin, quiet-looking SandWing.

The SeaWing princess, rippled through everyone's minds.

"Oh, thank the moons," Anemone said, spotting the net of fish, her voice clear and high. "I haven't eaten since we left Queen Moorhen's palace yesterday." She stepped delicately around a SandWing who was chewing something on the floor, and surveyed the few small fish that hadn't been claimed yet. A number of MudWings, SeaWings, and SkyWings were clustered nearby, brown and green and red scales side by side as they ate.

"Hmmm. I'd like that one," Anemone said sweetly. She pointed at a giant gray fish with a pale, speckled pink belly. A NightWing — the one Moon didn't know — already had his claws around it and was lifting it to his mouth. He paused and stared at her.

She gazed back innocently, her chin raised.

"Uh," said the NightWing. "This one?"

"That one," said Anemone. "It's my favorite kind."

"This one that I'm eating?" he said.

"You heard her," snapped one of the SeaWings, a skinny grayish-blue dragon whose hostile mental vibrations seemed familiar. Moon thought for a minute, and then guessed that he was the same one Clay had separated from Carnelian in the hallway yesterday. Pike, if she remembered right.

"But . . . I'm eating this one," said the NightWing in a tone of deep confusion.

"Oh, but I would like it very much," said Anemone.

"Anemone —" Tsunami tried to interrupt, stepping forward.

"Don't you know this is the SeaWing princess?" Pike snarled. He shoved himself in the NightWing's face and flexed his webbed talons. "The heir to the throne! Give her the fish. Now."

"Uh —" said the NightWing. *She's not* my *princess, though,* his brain mumbled.

Clay hurried over through the silence that had slowly fallen around Pike, Anemone, and the NightWing. Most of the other dragons were staring at them, except for Coconut, who was deeply focused on a bunch of grapes.

"Hey, this is an understandable mistake," Clay said, gently scooting the NightWing back away from Pike. "We haven't posted any prey center rules yet, but we will. Basically whoever gets their claws on it first, they get to eat it. If we find that doesn't work, we'll revisit the rules in a couple of weeks. But that's how it is right now. All right?"

Pike scowled. "But the princess wants that fish!"

This one's going to be trouble, Moon heard from Clay's mind, clear as day. He sighed.

"I do," Anemone agreed. She looked up at Clay with large blue eyes. "Mother would want me to have it."

"There's lots of other fish," Clay said, "and you're welcome to join us in the evening when we go out to catch more in one of the mountain lakes."

"That'll be fun," Tsunami said, elbowing her sister heartily. "I'll come, too. There are some awesome lakes I want to show you, not far from here."

Anemone blinked. She looked from Clay to Tsunami, and then narrowed her eyes at the NightWing, who was surreptitiously starting to chew on the fish's tail.

So that's how it's going to be? I don't like this at ALL, said her mind, but her mouth said, "Oh. Very well."

Moon wondered if she'd imagined the ghost of a smile that whisked across Turtle's face.

"You can have my fish, princess," Pike said, handing her a dripping salmon that he'd already sliced lengthwise with his claws.

Anemone looked down her nose at it, then shook her head. "I'm not actually that hungry after all. Come on, Ostrich." She swept out of the cave, deliberately avoiding Clay. The SandWing glanced around, thinking disappointed hungry thoughts, but hurried after the princess.

Pike hissed at the NightWing. "You'll pay for this, Bigtail," he snarled. "Nobody disrespects the SeaWing princess."

"Time to cool down, Pike," Tsunami said sternly.

Pike hissed again, but slunk off with his salmon.

Oh, dear, thought Clay. Moon watched him smile at the NightWing as if nothing was wrong, and then give Tsunami a "we should talk about that" look. She rolled her eyes and hurried after her sister.

Umber's whole face lit up as Clay paced over to them. "Hey," Clay said affectionately, nudging his little brother. "Where are Marsh and Sora?"

"Coming over now," Umber said, waving his wings.

Moon sat up and saw Sora approaching with another dragon who looked like her, only more fidgety and nervous. Sora's expression was subdued, but painful anxiety clawed at her insides, all jumbled into scraps of thoughts: *are we safe; miss Reed; I saw her; can't sleep; not safe anywhere; oh, Crane, I wish you were here.* The MudWing took a deep breath and started the same internal ritual Moon had found in her mind the night before. Sora imagined mud slowly pouring over all her worries, leaving only a rippling, peaceful swamp.

She's like me, Moon thought. Everyone here was anxious in some way, but with Sora it ran deeper, all the way to paralyzing fear. She wanted to escape as much as Moon did.

Or at least, the way I wanted to escape yesterday. Now . . . Well, she had to admit now she was wondering if maybe her mother was right. Maybe school wasn't so terrible after all. *Poor Sora. She needs a crazy, enthusiastic clawmate like Kinkajou to take care of her.*

Or maybe I can help her. Maybe because I know how scared

she is — maybe I can make her feel better. Maybe that's one good thing I can do with my powers.

"This is my brother and sister," Umber said. "Marsh is really fast — you should see him fly. And Sora knows everything; she's the only one who ever practiced her reading." He beamed at them both as if they were the most special, perfect dragons in the world.

"Hey," Qibli greeted them, his mouth half full of goat. He looked as though he wasn't particularly paying attention, but a part of him whispered, *That's the MudWing sibling bond. Loyal like the Outclaws are to Thorn, probably more so. Wish I had a brother and sister I liked that much. Actually a brother and sister who didn't actively try to kill me every time they see me would be a dramatic improvement.*

"I'm Moon, remember?" Moon said to Sora, trying to look friendly and nonthreatening. "Would you like some?" She held out a piece of her prey.

Sora gave her a shy smile. "Thank you." She took the goat leg in her claws, tore it in half, and gave the other half to Marsh.

"Who's in your winglet?" Umber asked. "Marsh, you're in the Copper Winglet, right?"

"Yeah. That's my clawmate," Marsh said, nodding over at Coconut.

Ha, Qibli thought. *That's perfect. Put the slowest, least threatening dragon in the world with the most nervous. Not even this twitchy MudWing could be scared of that sloth masquerading as a dragon over there.*

Marsh looked around, twisting his claws in nervous circles. "I don't remember the other names yet."

"That's all right, you'll figure them out. Sora?" Clay prompted his sister. "Anyone really nice?"

She fiddled with the meat in her talons, pulling out tufts of fur. "There's a RainWing in my winglet who seems nice — she's blind."

"Tamarin!" Kinkajou cried. "Oh, you must be in the Gold Winglet. She's my best friend!"

Moon decided not to be hurt by this. She knew Kinkajou would have other best friends. Possibly six more by the end of lunchtime.

"A SandWing named Onyx," Sora said, counting on her claws. "That SeaWing over there, Pike. His clawmates: a NightWing called Bigtail, and a SkyWing with a bad scar across his snout. And my clawmate." She nodded at the far wall, at the IceWing seated on the ledge next to Winter. They were both gazing disdainfully down at the eating dragons. Above them, sharp, twisting stalactites studded the roof of the alcove where they sat, almost as though they were glaring out of a mouth filled with enormous teeth.

"Winter's sister?" Qibli said. "Then you and I are in the same tent, friend. Is she as stuck-up as her brother? Has she mentioned being in line for the IceWing throne yet?"

Sora blinked at the IceWings. Ripples shuddered across the mud puddles in her mind, but she refused to let whatever was under there escape. "Her name is Icicle."

"To be honest," Clay admitted, "from what we'd heard about Icicle, we figured we had to put her in the same cave as the nicest, least offensive dragon we could think of, so there wouldn't be any casualties the first week of school. I hope it's going all right, Sora."

His sister dropped her gaze to her claws. "It's fine," she said.

"Let me know if not," Clay said gently. "It's really important to me that you be happy here."

Sora nodded, thinking of the same brothers and sisters Moon had seen in Umber's mind.

"Don't we have history together next?" Turtle asked. "Our winglet and your winglet together?"

"Do we?" Umber said, delighted.

"I think so," Qibli said. Moon could see that he had the day's schedule memorized, plus a detailed layout of the school map in his head, but he was pretending to still be figuring things out with the rest of them.

"I have to go to the library first," Moon said to Kinkajou. "But I'll catch up to you." She stood up and paused, listening to the uneasy rippling quiet in Sora's mind. "Um . . . do you want to come with me?" she asked Sora.

The MudWing blinked at her in surprise. "I *do*," she said, standing up. As they headed out of the prey center together, Moon could hear the reactions stirring behind them.

That was nice of Moon, Umber thought.

Aw, maybe they'll be friends, went through Clay's mind.

Does she like her better than me? Kinkajou thought forlornly.

My boring little clawmate with a NightWing? came a frigid thought from across the cave. *What's that all about?*

Moon hurried into the stone tunnel, trying hard to think about raindrops. They were halfway to the library before she realized that neither she nor Sora had said a word the whole walk.

"Um," Moon said. "The library is great, isn't it?"

Sora nodded.

"I like the leaf windows," Moon added.

Sora nodded again. "Me too," she whispered.

Is this what I seem like to everyone else? Moon wondered. *Shy and really hard to talk to? Maybe I should try a little harder. It's easy to talk to my mystery friend . . . but I don't have to hide anything from him. I guess I couldn't, even if I wanted to.*

Starflight sat up as they came into the library, setting aside a stone tablet with letters carved into it. "Hello?" he said tentatively.

"It's Moon and Sora," Moon said.

"Oh, hi," he said, relaxing. "Sora, I found that scroll on IceWings for you." He slid a scroll across the desk with his claws.

Sora glanced at Moon, ducked her head, and mumbled something like, "Figuring out my clawmate." She took the scroll and scurried over to her spot by the windows.

"How are you, Moon?" Starflight asked. "How was class this morning?"

Terrifying. "All right — interesting," she said. "Do you have any scrolls about dreamvisitors?"

He tipped his head, frowning a little. "I'm sure we do. Why? You didn't — I mean, you haven't been visited by someone, have you?"

"I'm just curious," Moon said quickly. "Someone mentioned them, um, in class, and I don't know anything about them."

Starflight slid out from behind the desk and started walking along the shelves, touching the carvings here and there. "If you ever do see a strange dragon in your dreams, let me know, all right? Especially if she's a SkyWing." A viciously scary orange dragon wreathed in smoke flashed through his mind.

"A SkyWing?" Moon said alertly. "Why?"

Starflight sighed. "Queen Scarlet — *ex*-Queen Scarlet is out there with a dreamvisitor, and she hates us. I worry sometimes that she'll start scaring our students in their dreams." *And that's far from the worst she could do,* he thought anxiously.

"How did she get her dreamvisitor?" Moon asked.

"We're not entirely sure," Starflight said. He tilted his wings back and scratched his head. "She must have found it while she was imprisoned in Burn's weirdling tower, and Burn must not have known it was there. My theory is that

Scarlet found it in or on this NightWing dragon corpse she disemboweled, somehow."

"Oh," Moon said. "Does anyone know where the other two dreamvisitors are?"

To her surprise, Starflight nodded. "We know one for sure — it's right here in the school. I think Sunny has it this week. She got it from a scavenger, who stole it from the SandWings. And we're pretty sure the other dreamvisitor was lost in the volcano. I found it in the NightWing treasury, but someone stole it from me shortly before the island exploded."

"You don't know who?"

He shook his head, flickers of guilt ricocheting through his mind. "Here." He brushed his talons across a section of the wall, and then chose a scroll and held it out for her. "This should be *The Animus Histories*. It's about several animus-touched objects, but the dreamvisitors definitely have a section in there."

"Thanks," Moon said. Could she have heard Queen Scarlet in someone's dream last night? Another awful thought followed that one. She hesitated — but she had to ask. "Could a dragon ever use a dreamvisitor to talk to someone while they're awake? I mean, like in their heads?"

Now Starflight looked really puzzled. "No, that wouldn't make sense," he said. "The way they're enchanted is to get into dreams, nothing else. Why do you ask?"

"Just a story I heard once," Moon said.

I promise you, little Moon, I am no SkyWing.

Then who ARE you? Moon thought back fiercely.

No answer, of course. She took the scroll over to a ledge by the biggest window and curled up with her back against a tapestry-covered wall.

There were more animus-touched objects than she would have expected, considering there hadn't been that many animus dragons in Pyrrhia's history — at least, as far as anyone knew. She stopped on a spread with a beautiful drawing of a tall, sweeping pavilion, twelve stories high, made of white stone and looking as if it had grown straight out of the water into this perfect shape.

The SeaWing Summer Palace, read the caption. *Made of stone enchanted by Albatross, a SeaWing prince, to grow into a tower he designed.*

That's really pretty, Moon thought, brushing one claw lightly across the drawing. *I wish I could create something like that.* She rolled the scroll to read the longer paragraph on the side.

Albatross was one of the first known animus dragons, hatched over two thousand years ago, before anyone truly understood the limits of this power. He used his animus magic to create many things, including the beautiful Summer Palace pavilion, whose location is known only to SeaWings. But at the time nobody realized the terrible price of using animus powers, and nobody saw that Albatross was slowly going insane.

Not until the Royal SeaWing Massacre.

It was a devastating shock to the entire Kingdom of the Sea when Albatross, who had been hailed as one of the greatest SeaWings of all time, suddenly snapped and tried to murder his entire family. He managed to kill nine dragons, including his sister the queen, his own daughter, and her husband, before someone was able to stop him with a spear to his chest. Among the few who survived were his young grandson, Fathom, and granddaughter, Pearl. Pearl ascended the throne peacefully and ruled for many years. One of her first edicts was to outlaw the use of animus magic anywhere in her kingdom.

Her brother, Fathom, was an animus dragon himself, but after the massacre he refused to ever use his power — except perhaps once. [See: Fathom]

Moon shivered. What an awful story. *I guess there are worse powers than mine in the world.* At least mind reading only made her socially anxious and gave her headaches. She was pretty sure it wasn't turning her homicidal, though.

She found the section on dreamvisitors and studied the drawing of three star-shaped sapphires. Dreamvisitors, read the caption. Enchanted by a NightWing named Darkstalker to allow whichever dragon holds one to walk in any other dragon's dreams.

Moon hadn't realized they were made by a NightWing. She unrolled it to the longer description.

The first known animus dragon in the NightWing tribe, Darkstalker, also had the powers of mind reading and prophecy, making him a truly formidable dragon. He created three dream-visitors so there would be one for him, one for his best friend [see: Fathom], and one for his beloved, a dragon named Clearsight. They were intended to link the three, no matter how far apart they were.

That's sweet, Moon thought. If it were her, who would she give dreamvisitors to? *Mother, of course.* She felt a twinge of sadness and also guilt, that she'd managed not to miss her mother every second she'd been gone. *Who else? Kinkajou?* The idea of Kinkajou flinging rainbows around in Moon's dreams as well as in her waking thoughts was a little alarming.

The answer is no one, really, Moon admitted to herself. She didn't want anyone to see inside her subconscious. If they did, she was sure they'd never trust her again.

Ultimately Darkstalker grew to be too powerful and his ambitions began to terrify the dragons around him. He claimed he'd found a way to make himself immortal. Rumor had it he planned to overthrow the NightWing queen and seize the throne for himself. After he killed his own father with an aspect of animus power that no one had ever seen before, the tribe agreed: He was too danger-ous to be free.

The details of the trap set for Darkstalker are lost to his-tory, but it is certain that he and Clearsight disappeared one night and were probably both killed at the same time. It is also believed that he was ultimately taken down with an animus-touched object created by Fathom — the only time Fathom ever used his power.

Fear of the Darkstalker lingered in the NightWing tribe, however, causing them to move to a new, secret home in case he ever returned. NightWing ghost stories still speak of him, and there are those who believe that one day Darkstalker may yet rise again and come seeking his revenge. . . .

NightWing ghosts, Moon thought, touching the scroll lightly. *Mother never told me any traditional NightWing ghost stories. She had much more effective ways of terrifying me, just by telling me about the volcano and the RainWings and what would happen if another NightWing ever found me in the rainforest.*

She rolled the scroll in either direction, but there was no more information about the dreamvisitors.

Read the section on Fathom, the mystery voice suddenly commanded in her head.

On Fathom? Moon thought, glancing up. Sora shifted slightly, but kept her eyes on the scroll in front of her, drowning her worries under a deluge of words about IceWings. *Why? To find out what he did with his dreamvisitor?*

Just read it, the voice said, and there was an odd vibration to it that she hadn't heard before, like an egg shuddering before it cracked.

What do you know about Fathom that I don't? Moon wondered as she rolled through the scroll. She quickly found the section on Fathom, alongside a giant illustrated question mark.

Grandson of Albatross, the perpetrator of the Royal SeaWing Massacre [see: **Albatross**]. **Fathom** was so traumatized by his family's murder that he swore an oath to his sister, Pearl, the new SeaWing queen, that he would never use his animus magic.

Fathom was sent to the Night Kingdom to befriend and guide a young animus dragon named Darkstalker. The hope was that Fathom's sad story, his caution, and his understandable wariness about their powers would have a positive effect on the ambitious, brilliant NightWing. At first it seemed to work, and they became close friends.

But Darkstalker could not be convinced that his powers were dangerous, and as he used them more and more, Fathom and the other NightWings became afraid of him. Fathom was among the first to sound a warning about his friend, and the stories say he was the one who convinced Clearsight that Darkstalker could not be trusted.

The legend says that Fathom finally agreed to use his power just once: to enchant an object that could stop Darkstalker, since nothing and nobody else could. Whatever the object was, it must have worked, as Darkstalker disappeared and was never seen again.

How sad, Moon thought, studying the picture of a worried-looking SeaWing. *He must have felt awful, doing that to his friend. I wonder what he enchanted.*

There was a deep pause, and Moon could almost have sworn that she felt the mountain tremble slightly under her talons.

It was a bracelet, the voice whispered, soft as leaves falling.

Moon blinked at the scroll. *What?*

A bracelet. A wrist cuff. Enchanted to put me to sleep forever. Since I couldn't die — that story about making myself immortal is true — they had to come up with something else.

Her whole body felt numb, like ice was sweeping across her scales.

I knew it, the voice went on. *I knew when she pulled it out — right before she put it on me, I thought,* Fathom must have touched that. *He broke his sacred oath to his sister, just to betray me. But I wasn't sure until now.*

What are you saying? Moon asked, pressing her claws into the stone below her.

I'm saying, nice to meet you, Moon. My name is Darkstalker.

PART TWO

STAY HIDDEN

━━━ CHAPTER 9 ━━━

"But you *can't* be," Moon whispered, then realized she'd spoken aloud when Sora looked up and blinked at her. She turned toward the wall and thought, *Darkstalker lived over two thousand years ago.*

I know. He sighed. *I've been asleep a long time, apparently. I suspect this bracelet was supposed to keep me that way forever.*

So what happened? Moon asked. *Why are you awake now?*

It's broken, he said. *After two thousand years, almost anything becomes weaker. Something must have jarred it and snapped it off.*

The earthquakes? Moon wondered. *There was a comet six months ago — as it passed by, there were a lot of earthquakes and strange weather.*

That's when I woke up, he said, *so you're probably right.*

Moon hesitated. Six months ago was also when her nightmares had started. The ones about Jade Mountain falling. Was she seeing visions of something that would ultimately be caused by Darkstalker's awakening?

I'm not actually a monster, no matter what the scrolls and ghost stories say, he said. *Can't you tell?*

Where are you? she asked instead of answering.

That, I don't know. Somewhere dark. Covered in stone. I can't move. I can only . . . think. He let out an odd sort of chuckle. *Perhaps you can see why I was so pleased to find you. I can hear others, but no one else can hear me. Makes for a lot of very boring, one-sided conversations.*

She didn't know what else to say. She'd expected . . . well, another dragon like her, someone she could meet and go flying with. She had not expected to be talking to the legendary monster of NightWing nightmares.

I'm not a monster, he said again quietly. *It seems history has painted me that way, but perhaps that's what happens when you disappear before you can tell your own story, and only your enemies are left to finish it. Or your best-friends-turned-enemies, apparently.*

Moon rolled back to the Darkstalker section of the scroll. A handsome dark face stared regally out at her. He had the silver scales in the corners of his eyes, too.

Formidable dragon, Darkstalker said with mild amusement. *I suppose that's true, but it is not my fault I was born with these powers. I think you know something about that.*

I've never plotted to steal any thrones, though, Moon pointed out. *Or killed my father.*

I think you would, if you'd had my father. I saved the tribe from him, Darkstalker argued. *He was a lot worse* than I am. This scroll's version of the story is highly oversimplified. As for being king — why not? Just because we've only ever had queens, does that mean a king is impossible? Why would I have all these gifts if I wasn't supposed to use them to lead and protect the tribe?

It felt as though he'd suddenly seized her mind in an iron grip. Moon winced, touching her head.

Listen, Darkstalker said. *I could see the future, but not just any future —* all *the possible futures. Do you understand what that means? I could have guided the tribe along the best path, to safety and glory and power and everything else. At each crossroad, I would have known the right thing to do. I loved my tribe, Moonwatcher. I would have been the best ruler they'd ever had. I know it; I* saw *the futures where I was king, benevolent and beloved, married to Clearsight with six little dragonets of our own. Those were possible. They could have happened, if anyone had had faith in me.*

He paused, then went on. *She saw them, too. Clearsight had the gift of prophecy, as strong as mine. She knew those futures existed . . . but she also saw the ones where I turned toward evil, destroying instead of protecting. She didn't believe me that I could avoid those paths.*

In the end, I guess she didn't believe in me at all.

I wonder what happened to her.

There was another really long pause.

This is going to sound weird, Moon offered, *but I kind of want to give you a hug right now.*

Darkstalker barked a laugh.

How did she surprise you, then? Moon asked. *If you could see all these futures — how did she trick you with the bracelet?*

I had too much faith in her, he said. *I saw the possibility that she would betray me in more than one future — but further down the line. I didn't want to believe it, so I never studied those paths, just as she was supposed to stop looking down my darker paths as well. Up until the last moment, even with visions of blackness pressing against me, I still thought I could change her mind — that I could talk her into trusting me so we could fly into our bright, perfect future.*

He made a kind of growl, but Moon couldn't tell what was behind it — bitterness, revenge, despair? Loneliness?

I never saw any of this back then, though, he said. *I suppose prophecy doesn't extend two thousand years forward, not even for me.*

So you don't know what happens next? Moon said.

All I can see is darkness, he said softly. *All I can do is hope.*

Hope for what?

Hope for someone to set me free. You, specifically.

Moon jumped up, dropping the *Animus Histories* scroll. Starflight turned his head toward her, and Sora blinked up in surprise.

"Sorry," Moon said. "Just — had a thought." *How can I set you free?* she cried. *I'm nobody. We have no idea where you are. And you're — you're —*

The most dangerous dragon in Pyrrhia history? Darkstalker said drily. *You shouldn't believe everything you read, Moon.*

Even if I did agree to do it, Moon thought, *which I'm not saying I will . . . how could I?*

There's something I need, he said.

"Moon!" Kinkajou called, sticking her head into the library. "Didn't you hear the three gongs? We have to get to history class! Sora, you too!"

Sora scrambled to her feet, dropped her scroll with a clatter, and fumbled around trying to roll it back up. Moon picked up the *Animus Histories,* wondering if she could skip class somehow. She kind of wanted to keep talking to Darkstalker, which would be hard to do in a cave full of dragons all thinking at the top of their brains.

"Hi, Starflight! I'm superexcited," Kinkajou said. "I don't know *anything* about history. I have a *million* questions for Webs. Like, what's the Scorching, and is it true there used to be scavengers everywhere, and who started the Talons of Peace, and what's the big IceWing tragedy from the past, and —"

A scream of terror suddenly echoed through the tunnels.

"Help!" somebody shrieked. More screams and the clamor of running dragons joined the tumult. "The SkyWing! She's here to kill us all!"

—— CHAPTER 10 ——

Queen Scarlet shot through Starflight's mind as he leaped over the desk. *She's come for us.*

"Find somewhere to hide," he cried to Moon, Kinkajou, and Sora. He stumbled forward, talons outstretched. "Don't let her see you." *Which way to the Great Hall?* he thought frantically. *I have to get there. I have to protect them.*

"Who?" Kinkajou yelped. "Who are we hiding from?"

Sora curled into a ball on the reeds, trembling. Horrible images were lurching up from the mud puddle in her brain: dragons on fire, dragons screaming, spears bristling, a little brown dragon bleeding from her neck as she plummeted to the ground.

Moon clutched her head. The images weren't just coming from Sora; all over the school, dragonets who'd been in the war were hearing the alarm and having awful flashbacks. She could hardly think straight through all the violence reeling around in her head.

Raindrops, she tried to think.

That won't work here, Darkstalker said. *Everyone is too panicked. Find the calmest voice and anchor yourself. Focus on it. It'll help if it's someone who knows what's going on.*

Moon closed her eyes and searched rapidly through the tumult around her. Her mind landed, unexpectedly, in Carnelian's.

She won't hurt me, Carnelian was thinking, wary but unafraid. *I wonder if she remembers me.*

So it's not Queen Scarlet, Moon realized. *Or Carnelian would be angrier than that.*

Starflight was already hurrying away to the Great Hall, his wings brushing the rock walls on either side, his talons reaching forward anxiously.

Moon started after him.

"Aren't we hiding?" Kinkajou asked.

"Is that what you want to do?" Moon asked.

"No!" Kinkajou said, flaring green and purple and white and yellow in dizzying spirals. "I thought that's what *you* would want to do. But chasing after him to see what's happening is MUCH more exciting!" *I love my clawmate!* she thought ecstatically, bounding along beside Moon.

They burst into the hall only a few moments behind Starflight.

A SkyWing stood in the center of the cave, staring wildly around her with eerie blue eyes. Smoke rose from her shimmering metallic-orange scales.

Most students had fled, but Winter and Icicle stood in one of the tunnel entrances, glaring at the SkyWing. Carnelian was there, too, watching curiously. Two other dragons had apparently fainted before they could run away, a SeaWing and a SandWing Moon didn't know.

"Who's there?" Starflight called, his voice shaking. Moon realized that he was trying to look brave, but that he was almost paralyzed with fear. His visions of the former SkyWing queen were intensely replaying over and over, most of them featuring Starflight bleeding in some kind of arena while she laughed.

But the dragon he was afraid of was not the dragon here in front of them. Moon didn't know who this was, or anything about her. Trying to look into the newcomer's mind was like touching an inferno. She couldn't read a single thought in the blaze.

"That's not Queen Scarlet," Moon said, touching his shoulder.

"It's not?" Starflight said. His wings collapsed with relief.

"Peril!" Clay shouted as he hurried into the cave, moving fast despite his limp. "You came!"

Oh, great, Tsunami thought, coming in right behind him.

Peril instinctively shrank away from Clay, but the wall of flames in her mind cooled for a brief moment as she looked at him. Moon caught a stab of fierce, desperate love and guilt, and then the fire swallowed everything coherent again.

Clay didn't seem to notice her pulling away; he took one of Peril's talons and pressed it between his. A sizzling sound and burning smell rose from his scales where they touched, but when he let go, the burn healed over almost instantly.

"When we didn't hear from you, we assumed you weren't coming," Tsunami said.

"I thought I could find her," Peril said, tearing her gaze away from Clay. "But she's nowhere. I don't know where else to look. I'm sorry."

"Don't be," Clay said wholeheartedly. "We're glad you're here."

That's only true for him, Moon thought. *Not remotely for anyone else. Peril's lucky* she *doesn't have mind reading.* Almost every dragon who knew she was here was brimming with hostility, fear, fury, or, in most cases, all three.

"We don't have a group for you," Tsunami said, folding her wings back. "We didn't know you were coming, so there's a SkyWing in each winglet already."

"I don't have to stay," Peril mumbled. She edged back a step, toward the outside.

"But I want you to," Clay said. "If Scarlet's looking for you, too, we'll all be safer together. Don't worry about the winglets, we'll figure it out." He shot Tsunami a frown. *Don't scare her away. She deserves a second chance.*

Tsunami rolled her eyes, but a memory of Peril saving Clay's life kept her from saying the rest of the snappish things in her head. "I'll go ask Sunny where we should put you," she said instead, and swept away.

"She can't stay here!" Winter suddenly barked, stepping forward. He jabbed a claw at Peril. "*That* dragon killed more than twenty IceWing prisoners. She was Queen Scarlet's favorite weapon. It's one thing to force us to work with deceitful NightWings and lowborn SandWings, but a straight-up murderer? No one is going to stand for this."

"Besides, she's dangerous," his sister pointed out in a smooth, high-pitched voice. "Whether she's still working for Queen Scarlet or . . . not." The tone of her voice made it perfectly clear which of those she believed.

"A lot of dragons have done things they need to be forgiven for," Clay pointed out. Just around the corner, Moon felt Tsunami hear him, pause, and wince. "Especially in the war. The agreement between the queens was amnesty for everyone, no grudges, no revenge."

Easy for him to say, Winter thought bitterly, and the IceWing from the mountains shot through his head again, this time along with the word *brother.* "Fighting in battles, following orders from your general, that's normal warfare," he said. "Killing prisoners while they're chained up, or forcing them to fight a monster — how is that forgivable?"

Peril seemed to be shrinking and burning hotter at the same time. Her weird eyes glowered at Winter through the smoke.

"Even Queen Ruby hasn't agreed to pardon that dragon," Icicle pointed out. "She's been banned from the SkyWing palace, hasn't she?"

"All the more reason to welcome her here," Clay said. "Where starting over and second chances are the whole point." He smiled at Peril again. She lashed her tail and ducked her head. "Come on, let's go see the others," Clay added diplomatically, waving Peril toward the tunnel where Tsunami had disappeared.

Icicle turned to Winter as they left and hissed, "I'll send a messenger to Queen Glacier tonight."

The gong sounded twice, echoing through the tunnels.

"Time for history," Kinkajou said cheerfully. "Come on, Winter!"

Icicle gave him an amused, arch look. *How adorable, a RainWing with a crush on my brother.*

Winter shifted his wings uncomfortably and started after Kinkajou. *She thinks it's funny, but if she knew what I've been feeling — who I've been thinking about . . .* He slammed a wall of ice down over his thoughts, almost hard enough for Moon to feel the vibrations in her own skull.

The history lesson cave was far down inside the mountain, at the intersection of three winding, narrow tunnels. There were fewer of the fire globes along these tunnels; the ones here were shades of orange and blue, and they were interspersed with flickering torches. Moon noticed that Kinkajou edged quickly past the open flames; the RainWing also didn't love the claustrophobic closeness of the walls or how much darker it was this far down.

Inside, the history cave's stone walls were covered in maps, the paper curling up at the edges, with different borders and years written on each one. Stacks of scrolls were piled untidily everywhere, overflowing the wooden racks provided for them.

Webs stood in the center of the cave, waiting for everyone to gather in a circle around him. Moon sensed that he was the one who'd chosen the space, and that he preferred the dimmer, more underground feeling. He was the SeaWing who'd brought the fish in the net, and he was a lot older than the prophecy dragonets. Trails of regret ran underneath all his thoughts, even when he was mostly focused on the lesson he was about to give. Moon wondered why he was here and how he'd gotten the scar on his side.

Moon's winglet filed in, and so did Sora's. As each dragon entered, Moon slipped their minds into the background rainstorm noise, and she felt her wings relax. Even in a cave filled with fifteen dragons, she could be all right. Her head didn't hurt, and she didn't feel overwhelmed or confused. She could think her own thoughts . . . thanks to Darkstalker.

Moon noticed that Icicle and Sora sat on opposite ends of the cave and didn't speak to each other. The other NightWing was the male uninspiringly named Bigtail, the one Pike had growled at; now she realized they were clawmates. She guessed that would be an uncomfortable cave to sleep in tonight. Bigtail glanced at Moon and then quickly away, as if he didn't want to be associated with her. Pike slid past him, glowering, and nearly flicked Bigtail's nose with one of his wings.

She was surprised to see that Carnelian didn't acknowledge the other SkyWing. He had a horrible scar across his snout, as if he'd been in battle, like her. She hesitated for a moment, then let go of that raindrop for a moment to check Carnelian's mind.

Flame, she heard Carnelian scoff, shooting him a glare. *Talons of Peace.*

Oh, that explained it; he'd hidden with the underground peace movement instead of fighting in the war. Moon wondered where he'd gotten that scar, then, but even brushing the surface of his mind gave her a queasy feeling of overflowing rage, so she decided to stay out of it instead.

Kinkajou spotted a small blue-and-gold RainWing and dragged Moon over to her, excited sparks going off in her mind.

"Moon, this is Tamarin. Tamarin, Moon is our new best friend. She's super funny. Moon, can Tamarin touch your face?"

I'm super funny? Moon thought. *In what universe?*

"It's all right, I don't have to," Tamarin said, smiling. Moon saw the pale film across Tamarin's eyes and remembered that the RainWing was blind.

"You can." Moon let her talons touch Tamarin's, and the RainWing brushed her claws gently across Moon's scales, horns, and snout. Moon got a shivering glimpse of a world without sight, of Tamarin's quiet competence and immense concentration.

"Have you figured everything out yet?" Kinkajou asked Tamarin. "She had the rainforest all memorized, but of course this is a whole new place," she added to Moon. "So Queen Glory arranged for her to come early and spend a few days walking all the tunnels. I bet you know Jade Mountain better than anyone now."

"Ha," Tamarin said. "Well, I'm getting used to it. It's useful to have walls, in a way."

"I can't wait for suntime, though," Kinkajou said. "Moon, after this we're going to go sleep in the sun for the rest of the day. Want to join us?"

"Uh — no, thanks," Moon said. She'd seen RainWings doing that before, but it still seemed odd to her.

"Everyone sit!" Webs ordered.

A muscular SandWing a lot older than the others darted into the cave and sat down next to Tamarin. "Hey," she whispered. "Did I miss anything?"

"This is my clawmate Onyx," Tamarin said.

Onyx had very black eyes and little black diamonds embedded between her pale yellow scales all along her wings. She wore a metal amulet around her neck and branching black lines were tattooed on her horns and neck. Her gaze was sharp, studying the others in the cave, and her mind was like shifting sand. Moon tipped her head and realized that Onyx was as hard to read as Turtle. Nothing came from her mind but that same weird quiet fuzz.

How is she doing that? Darkstalker? Can you read Onyx and Turtle? Am I just not powerful enough?

A pause, and then, **No. They are both impenetrable to me as well.**

Really? Are they just really good at shielding?

I'm not sure. I've never seen mental shielding advanced enough to block me, and who would have trained them? But perhaps my powers have grown weaker over time. Or perhaps this kind of shielding evolved over the last two thousand years.

Moon studied Onyx, then glanced across the cave at Turtle. The two dragons had nothing in common that she could see. How could they both be the only dragons immune to mind reading?

"Some of you might know who I am," Webs said, clearing his throat importantly. "For those of you who don't, my name is Webs, and I used to be part of the Talons of Peace. You may have heard of my son, Riptide, who is the new leader of whatever the Talons of Peace is becoming. I was one of the guardians who raised the dragonets of destiny. I taught them the history of Pyrrhia, and now they've asked me to teach it to you. So, we'll start at the beginning, with the Scorching."

"I have a question," Icicle interjected.

"Already?" Webs said, ruffled. "I haven't even begun yet."

"About that SkyWing," Icicle pressed on. "The one who burns everything she touches. Have there been other dragons like that in history? Aren't they terribly dangerous? I mean, even frostbreath doesn't work on her. So how have tribes dealt with dragons like that in the past? Is there a way to kill her?"

"That's . . . rather a gruesome topic for our first day," Webs sputtered.

"*I'd* like to know more about Thorn," Onyx spoke up.

"You mean *Queen* Thorn," Qibli snapped.

"It's unprecedented, right?" asked Onyx, ignoring him. "There's never been a queen in history who wasn't descended from the royal family. Isn't that true?"

"Well, not exactly —" Webs tried.

"Queen Thorn is the best queen the SandWings have ever had," Qibli flared loyally. "If you think you could do better, maybe you should challenge her for the throne."

"But that's my point," Onyx said sharply. "Does this mean now *anyone* could take the throne and become queen? Could that happen in the other tribes, too? I mean, it sounds like asking for chaos and rebellion everywhere. That's all I'm saying."

"Er, but it's rather an unusual — I mean, given the Eye of Onyx — and the situation with the three sisters — this is hardly an appropriate —" Webs flapped his wings around, his mind spinning.

This might be a good chance to get some answers, Darkstalker whispered in Moon's head.

"Are we going to learn about the NightWings?" Moon blurted out. "I mean, historically, like, maybe two thousand years ago? Like, where they lived, or, um —" *Where they buried the Darkstalker? How am I supposed to nonchalantly ask THAT question?*

"We may learn more about the NightWings, but not today," Webs said grumpily. "As NONE of this is RELEVANT to TODAY'S TOPIC, which is the Scorching. Ahem." He gathered up a bunch of scrolls and thrust them at Turtle. "Give these out, one to each dragonet. We'll begin AT THE BEGINNING. That means over five thousand years ago, before there were tribes or kingdoms, back when scavengers swarmed over the whole continent. Unroll your scrolls to the first map, please."

Moon took her scroll from Turtle with a sigh.

It was worth a try, Darkstalker observed.

You said there was something you need, Moon thought.

Yes. If you can find it, and bring it to me, then I could free myself.

Moon thought of the general reaction to Peril. If they were so terrified of *her,* how would everyone react if Moon brought back the creature from their nightmares? Could Darkstalker be trusted any more than Peril? Even if she believed he could be, would anyone else believe it? And wouldn't they all hate her even more than they already did, for being the one to bring him into the light again?

She furrowed her brow. *Wait . . . why can't you use your animus power to free yourself now?* Moon asked him. There were those animus-touched tunnels from the rainforest to other parts of Pyrrhia — couldn't Darkstalker just make one of those and pop out wherever he wanted?

For a long, nervous moment, Moon had the anxious feeling that exactly that might happen: that Darkstalker might suddenly just burst through the wall and appear in the cave right in front of her.

I can't, Darkstalker said finally.

Why not?

He chuckled sadly. *I was too smart for my own good.*

"There are many stories about life before the Scorching," Webs intoned. "After so many thousands of years, it is hard to know which ones to believe."

What do you mean? Moon asked.

I had a truly brilliant idea, he answered. *After what Albatross did — the massacre — we realized that animus magic took a little of your soul every time you used it. So I gathered all of my power and put it in a . . . a vessel. Do you see what I mean? If the power wasn't in me, it couldn't turn me evil. I could use the vessel to cast my animus spells — as many as I wanted — without ever being affected.*

I thought this would prove to Clearsight that she didn't have to worry about me. I would always be myself, and what happened to Albatross would never happen to me.

Of course, that means I need my object of power in order to use it — and of course I didn't have it with me when Clearsight betrayed me. Wherever I am now, it's not here. But if I had it back, I could get myself out. You wouldn't have to do anything except bring it to me.

Please. I need your help, Moon. I just want to be free. After two thousand years . . . can't you imagine? Is that so much to ask?

Moon rolled a corner of the scroll between her claws. Transferring the animus power to an object — that *did* sound like a brilliant idea. Had any other animus ever thought of that?

Maybe Darkstalker was telling the truth. Maybe he wasn't evil, and never would have been.

Bring it to you, she thought, *which would mean finding it and then finding you and also figuring out how to get it to you. Not that simple.*

I'll help you, he promised. *Any way you need. Please don't take away my only hope. Please tell me you'll at least think about it.*

"Most of the pre-Scorching stories would best be described as 'legends' or perhaps even 'fairy tales,'" Webs was droning on. "It is unlikely that scavengers were ever capable of being as organized or advanced as some of these imaginative fictions would have us believe. Stories often change and grow over time."

Like Darkstalker's story? Moon thought. *Everything we know about him was passed down by those who defeated and feared him. Maybe there's more to it.*

But how would I know?

She glanced around the cave — at her winglet, at these new friends who had accepted her so far. If they found out about her powers, would they be afraid of her, the same way Clearsight and Fathom ended up fearing Darkstalker? Would they think she was dangerous or cursed? Was her mother right, that they'd reject her and maybe even want to kill her?

Moon curled her talons in and took a deep breath.

All right, Darkstalker, she promised. *I'll think about it.*

CHAPTER 11

Moon did think about Darkstalker; she thought about him the rest of the day, as she explored the tunnels of the school during Kinkajou's suntime. She ran into a dead end and thought about what it must be like to be trapped in stone forever. She heard the flurries of anxieties swirling around about how dangerous Peril was, and she thought about having powers you can't control, and what you can choose to do with them, or whether what you do with them isn't really up to you in the end.

Eventually, she realized she was going to have to talk to somebody.

Worse, she was going to have to talk to a NightWing. One from the tribe, not Starflight or Fatespeaker.

There were four others at the school. Bigtail wouldn't be any help, even if he knew anything about Darkstalker. Which left Mindreader, Mightyclaws, and Fearless.

She searched the school carefully with her mind until she found one of them alone. Mightyclaws was in the art cave, with no other dragons around.

Was this a good idea? Mightyclaws was one of the more outwardly friendly dragons, but she'd seen darkness and jealousy in his head before. They were close to the same age, and once she'd heard him think, *If my mother had any spine, she'd have hidden* me *in the rainforest*.

She hesitated in the entrance to the art cave. Normally the cave would have been flooded with sunlight, coming through holes in the walls and ceiling, but it was twilight outside now. Art supplies were tucked into every crevice: brushes, all colors of paint, blank scrolls, clay for sculpting, wood and glass and metal and beads, even a loom where someone had already begun a tapestry.

Clever little wooden dragon statues were perched on outcroppings around the walls, with green or blue or orange glass beads for eyes. There were too many to have been made in the last two days, so Moon wondered who had made them — one of the school founders? Over her head, a giant metalwork sculpture made of gleaming copper wire wound across the ceiling, looking like flames. Several clear glass globes were suspended from it, glowing with firelight now that the sun was going down.

A black dragon stood in the middle of the cave, considering an easel with a canvas on it. He was not as thin as he had been when she met him five months ago, but he looked as though he hadn't filled out quite evenly — he had a round belly now, but his face was still lean, with sharp jawbones and deep hollows under his eyes. Even after six months of clean rainforest air and healthy eating, he still had a hint of a rasp to his voice and sometimes his claws shook a little when he reached for something. And he thought about food almost constantly.

Until he was distracted by something — for instance, her. Mightyclaws looked up and narrowed his eyes when he spotted Moon in the doorway.

"Hey," he said, neither welcoming nor hostile. *Never know what to say to her,* muttered his mind.

"Hi," Moon said nervously.

He fiddled with a few small jars of paint on a table beside him, then glanced over at her again.

"You here to paint?" he asked. *Or just stare at me awkwardly?*

"Um — yes," Moon said. This was going to be a disaster. How could she get any answers to her questions if she couldn't even say two words to him? He gestured with one wing to a stack of canvases, and she took one and propped it on an easel not too far from him, but where neither of them could see the other's painting. It felt like it would be too intrusive to stand where she could watch what he was working on.

Moon had never tried painting before. She had no idea where to begin. She ran her claws over the different sizes of paintbrushes — smooth wooden handles, neat bristles ranging from fang-sharp thin to fat as a dragon's ear. After a minute, she chose one somewhere in the middle and brought it back to her canvas along with a few shades of blue and green.

Mightyclaws didn't say anything for a while. He looked as though he was concentrating on his painting, but his thoughts were swooping in all different directions like a disturbed cluster of dragonflies. *No idea what I'm doing. Why does Starflight think this will help me? Would it be weird to go back to the prey center again tonight? Maybe there'll be some sheep left. Three meals in one day; will anyone notice? Or yell at me? Why is Moon here? Maybe Starflight sent her, too. Although she doesn't have any trauma to work through. With her perfect life in the rainforest, always as much as she wanted to eat, no adult dragons yelling at her, no classes on lying, no death smoldering right over her head all the time . . .*

"Do you like it here?" Moon finally said, breaking into his thoughts to try and stem the flow of resentment about her.

It worked; he stopped and twitched his tail, staring at his painting. "I guess." *It's more like the fortress here than the rainforest, except it smells better and there's sunshine. And prey, and dragons of all colors.*

"It's weird being around all the other tribes, isn't it?" Moon tried.

"Definitely," he said. "We were always told to stay away from them unless we were on a mission. Like, to deliver a prophecy or put the fear of NightWings in them. Otherwise, stay away so they don't figure us out."

"That we're ordinary, you mean?" Moon asked.

He flicked his wings with a frown. "NightWings aren't *ordinary*." *Of course she would think so.* "We're more intelligent than any other tribe. We shape the world; other dragons just live in it." She could hear that he was parroting lines he'd heard — over and over again — from older NightWings.

"I mean — I just meant, that we don't have the powers we — say we do — right?" Moon stammered.

"Maybe we don't right *now*," Mightyclaws said. He looked away from her and stabbed his paintbrush into a pot of red paint. "But we did and we might again one day. We should have let everyone keep believing in them. We were well trained; no one would have guessed, if we were careful. Especially after the success of the dragonet prophecy."

"Well trained?" Moon echoed.

"Our classes." Mightyclaws slashed his brush across his canvas. "How to lie, how to develop a convincing prophecy, how to sound like you're reading someone's mind. You missed out on all of that." *Lounging around with sloths, eating bananas all day.* "But we had to trade all our secrets for safety. Now, thanks to Queen Glory and Deathbringer and Sunny and Stonemover, the whole world knows that NightWings have no powers. No one respects us anymore." *The looks the other dragons give me here — like I either ate their favorite scroll or I might suddenly burst into flames, and they don't know which.*

"But is it true?" Moon said hesitantly. "That no one has powers anymore? Not anyone?"

He shook his head, glaring at his painting. *Not in hundreds of years,* he thought. *If the old scrolls were true. If we ever had them in the first place.*

"Why do you think we lost them?" Moon wondered.

Mightyclaws shrugged. He looked as if he was hoping to get out of the conversation by focusing on his canvas. But in his head she heard, *Maybe the volcano sucked it out of us,* and she felt the heavy smoke and heat that lingered in his memory.

They painted for a while in silence.

"Um," Moon said finally. "Do you know anything about the Darkstalker?"

Mightyclaws jumped as if she'd flung paint all over him. "Don't talk about him! Why would you ever talk about him?"

"I just wondered," Moon said, startled. "I thought he was a ghost story."

"No, he's definitely real, and he's definitely coming back to kill us all one day," Mightyclaws said with a shudder. "My father used to tell me about him while he taught me to fly. He'd say, 'Flap harder! Imagine the Darkstalker is chasing you!' or 'If you can't twist into a dive faster than that, the Darkstalker will catch you and rip off your claws and eat your brain!' He told me about how the tribe buried him a long time ago and then ran away to hide, but he's slowly clawing his way out, and one day he'll break free and come to kill us all for revenge."

Moon blinked at him for a minute before she realized she was dripping cerulean paint all over her talons.

Wow, Darkstalker whispered in her head. *I seem to have gotten a lot scarier in the last two thousand years.*

You must have been pretty scary to begin with, Moon observed, *if the whole tribe moved to hide from you even after you'd been defeated.*

Completely unnecessary. A huge overreaction. I killed ONE dragon, who deserved it.

"What did he do?" Moon asked Mightyclaws. "I mean, what was so bad about him?"

Please keep in mind I'll be terribly offended if you believe this scrawny dragonet and his monster fantasies over me.

"He killed, like, twenty dragons," Mightyclaws said. "All at once. With his MIND. He could make anyone do anything he wanted to."

Is that true? Moon demanded, appalled.

I did not kill twenty dragons. Maybe two. On two separate occasions, and I had to. Moon, come on, I promise not to eat anyone's brains.

Mightyclaws was not faking his terror of the Darkstalker, though. A million nightmares from the last few years were replaying in his head. She also saw a game where the young dragonets took turns pretending to be the Darkstalker, hiding for a long time, then bursting out to chase and attack the others. Mightyclaws had never liked that game; it always made his nightmares worse.

"Does anyone know where he's buried?" she asked.

Mightyclaws wrinkled his snout at her. "Of course not. That was thousands of years ago."

"What about the old NightWing kingdom?" she asked. "Where was it?"

"I have no idea," he said. "What's with all the questions?"

"Oh," she said. "I just — I wondered — I mean, you're right, I missed out on all the stuff a NightWing dragonet should know. I thought maybe if I . . . knew more, I'd . . . be more of a NightWing."

Mightyclaws stepped around his easel to look at her canvas. She'd painted (quite badly) an evening sky, twinkling with stars and all three moons, over a quiet rainforest scene of green leaves and crooked trees. He took one look at it and snorted, then grabbed his painting and threw it on the floor at her feet.

It was a painting of the volcano she'd seen so many times in the NightWings' heads. Red-and-gold lava spilled down the sides of the black mountain, and a dark cloud of smoke hung over everything, so you couldn't tell if it was day or night. It took her a minute of looking at it to realize that Mightyclaws had painted hidden eyes and teeth all over the volcano, as if it was watching, waiting to devour someone.

"That's really —" Moon started, wanting to tell him how good it was.

"This," Mightyclaws said. He pointed to her painting, and then to his. "*This* is why you'll never be one of us." *Because everything was awful, and you escaped, and it is not fair.*

He stormed out of the cave before she could respond.

Moon sighed.

What's really not fair, Darkstalker pointed out, **is everyone blaming you for a choice your mother made.**

Moon picked up the volcano painting and propped it carefully back on the easel to dry. She gazed at it for a moment, then suddenly glanced back at her own painting.

The sky . . .

Her heart flipped over.

My egg was laid under two full moons and hatched under two full moons. Her mother had told her the story of the moonlight and the way her egg had turned strangely silver. *Is that why I have powers and no one else does? Do the NightWing powers come from the moons? Maybe that's why they disappeared . . . because there was no moonlight on the volcanic island, and the eggs were all hatched deep inside the caves.*

Darkstalker rumbled inside her head. **Of course our powers come from the moons. One full moon at hatching gives a dragonet either mind reading or prophecy. Two gives them both. Three is so rare. . . . the theory for a while was that perhaps**

the animus powers were a third gift, but we eventually deter-
mined that those are genetic, not moon-given. We think the
third moon makes the first two powers even stronger.

Moon brushed the silver scales by her eyes. *Are these a*
sign of our powers? Because Fatespeaker has them, too.

They should be, but I've seen absolutely everything in that
silly dragon's mind and she's certainly not a mind reader. Nor
a prophet, I believe, although she may have a very weak power.
Perhaps she nearly hatched under the moons, or was sup-
posed to.

The Talons of Peace had her egg, so she wasn't on the vol-
cano, but she probably wasn't out in the moonlight either, Moon
thought. *And they also had Starflight's, but I know for sure he*
hatched underground.

Yes, on a brightest night, with three full moons, Darkstalker
growled. **What a waste. Think of the power he could have had.**

He paused. **But the connection between moonlight and**
NightWing powers was common knowledge in the tribe. How
could everyone have forgotten that, even in two thousand years?
Why would the tribe risk losing all our powers by hatching
their dragonets away from the moonlight?

"I have a guess," Moon whispered.

What?

She put her own painting down in a clear space on the
floor. The blues and greens were too bright, all the lines too
unsure, and the trees looked like blobby mushrooms. She set
it on fire.

"I think . . . it was because of you." She watched the flames for a long moment. "The other NightWings were so afraid of your powers and what you did with them — whatever the truth is, whatever you did — that they stopped having their eggs in the moonlight. They gave up the NightWing powers on purpose, because they wanted to be sure there would never be another Darkstalker. Another you."

He was silent.

Moon wrapped her wings around herself and watched her painting burn to ashes.

CHAPTER 12

"I can't set you free," Moon whispered to the wall that night, after Kinkajou and Carnelian were asleep.

Do I really seem evil to you, Moon?

She buried her nose in a pile of moss, but she knew she couldn't hide the answer from him. *No.*

We don't know what really happened back then, after Clearsight and Fathom tricked me. We can't be sure the tribe ran and hid and gave up their powers because of me. I mean . . . nothing I did was awful enough for that.

Moon rolled onto her back and gazed up at the ceiling. *What about the things they knew you might do, in the future?*

A rumble in her head, like flames building: *Is it fair to judge me for possibly dreadful deeds I never even did? We all might do terrible things. Your friend Turtle might kill his sister. This SkyWing in your cave might smother Kinkajou in her sleep just to shut her up. The IceWings might conspire to murder Peril, or you might let a killer escape, or you might send a friend to certain death.*

What are you talking about? Moon asked. *Do you know what's going to happen? Have you had visions of all those things?* She sat up. *Do you already know if I'm going to free you or not?*

He sighed. **Moon, I told you. With a prophecy gift as advanced as mine, I can see all the possibilities. I see futures where you free me, and futures where I live like this, trapped in the dark, alone, for thousands more years. All your choices spiral off into different futures. The visions you've had are only brief glimpses of the most likely outcomes; you see them about as clearly as you'd see a dark cave with one burst of flame. And they could still all change.**

So you could manipulate me into freeing you, Moon pointed out. *You can see exactly what you need to say to make me say yes.*

A long pause.

That's not fair, Moon. What can I say to that? Anything will sound like a trick to you. But it's not manipulating you if I tell you that what I'm going through now is torture. That's just the truth. This is not what the tribe planned for me; Clearsight would not have wanted this. How can I not tell you these things, if they might convince you?

However, he went on, **I cannot make you do anything. You make your own choices. That, unfortunately, is the essential problem with prophecy. Every dragon has the power to choose their own future.** He let out a low, sad chuckle. **Except me, of course. Ironically.**

You're going to haunt me for the rest of my life if I don't free you, aren't you? Moon asked.

He chuckled again. *I'd argue that this is not so much "haunting" as it is "clinging desperately to my only conversational companion."*

At last Moon fell asleep, straight into another night of dreams about the Jade Mountain Academy collapsing around her and her friends. Now Darkstalker's face from the scroll loomed over the whole nightmare. A warning? A promise?

Was the fall of Jade Mountain something that would happen if she freed Darkstalker — or something that would happen if she *didn't*?

The next afternoon, the Jade Winglet met in the music cave with Anemone's group, the Silver Winglet. Moon could hear the deep warbling sound of didgeridoos as she climbed up the tunnels behind Kinkajou. The sound seemed to swallow her up, reverberating in her bones, and then the dragonets emerged into a vast cave full of echoes.

It was like being inside a singing bowl; the music catapulted around the high, smooth walls like thread winding around and around the assembled dragons.

Moon recognized Anemone's clawmate, the little SandWing named Ostrich, as one of the players. She held a wing-shaped harp and was plucking the strings with her claws. Beside her, Umber was trying to keep up on a hollow stringed instrument as tall as a dragon that boomed in a deep bass register.

"Let's join in!" Kinkajou cried happily, shouting over the music. She seized a pair of gourds that rattled as though they were full of dry seeds, and she tossed Moon a wooden box.

The box was square, as long as Moon's forearm, and looked like it had several metal tongues of different sizes attached to the top of it. A label carved into the side said it was a mbira. When she plucked one of the tongues with her claw, a reverberating, twangy noise came out, and it turned out to be a slightly different noise for each tongue.

She sensed Winter arriving, wrapped in chilly discomfort. Moon couldn't imagine him or Carnelian ever making music. Almost at the same moment as she had that thought, she caught Kinkajou thinking the same thing about her. *Moon — too shy to make music — sad, she's missing out.* The reception was blurry in here, with all the noise happening, and everyone's thoughts were fragmented.

Still, Moon caught enough to understand the gist of it, and she focused her attention back on the mbira, trying to feel determined and stubborn instead of downcast and small.

Soon after that, Qibli came bounding into the cave and straight over to the drums, where he ousted a bewildered-looking SkyWing. As he began to play, Moon managed to stop thinking about Darkstalker for the first time all day.

Qibli drummed with his whole body, like he was dancing and drumming at the same time. His tail thumped a rhythm on a huge bass drum behind him, while his front talons jumped and skipped and bumped from one small drum to another. Anemone grabbed Turtle and started dancing, and after a moment, Kinkajou, the other RainWing, and the other MudWing joined in. The RainWings whirled together, their scales shimmering from color to color in time with the music.

Moon wished she were brave enough to dance, or to drum along with Qibli. *Maybe one day.* Across the cave, he grinned at her, and in his mind she saw an entire drum circle of SandWings around an oasis pool, firelight flickering behind them. No sign of his family there; only trusted friends and a leader who danced along with them. *Outclaws. Thorn. Safety.* The scene melted back into the thundering rhythms.

It was even better than the raindrop trick; here, with the drums echoing off all the walls and swallowing individual thoughts, Moon felt like her head was clear and she didn't have to worry about anything.

It seemed to work for Qibli, too. For once, his mind was moving at about the normal speed of other dragons, absorbed in the pounding below his talons.

Afterward, to Moon's surprise, Winter caught up with her on her way to the library.

"I want you to look at my scavenger," he said brusquely. *Don't make eye contact!* he was shouting at himself inside his head. *Don't think about her! You're a disgrace to the royal IceWing lineage, Winter! Your brother would never have been so weak!*

"Oh," she faltered, "I — I mean, sure, but — I don't really know anything about them."

"Then use your intuition or whatever," he said. *Or . . . whatever,* his mind echoed ominously.

Moon didn't like the sound of that. "I was just, um, going to the library," she said, preparing to add, "so maybe later," but he started talking over her.

"Fine, I'll bring him there." He whisked away before she could protest.

"Oooo," Kinkajou said, pouncing on Moon's tail from behind her. "What did he want? What did he say? Can you believe he initiated a conversation and aren't you so excited?"

"It was nothing," Moon said.

Oh, Moon. Sometimes it's like talking to a tree, Kinkajou's mind sighed.

"Um," Moon said quickly, "just, he's bringing Bandit to the library for me to look at."

"Oh, wow!" Kinkajou said. "He must like you, to be asking for your help, right?"

Moon searched Kinkajou's face and thoughts, but found no jealousy under those words. Kinkajou seemed as delighted by the prospect of witnessing a romance as she was by the idea of being in one; it was all part of the thrilling new drama of school to her.

"Well, no. I'm pretty sure he hates me," Moon pointed out. It was odd, because she thought she, of all dragons, should be able to be *sure* about how another dragon felt about her. But being able to read Winter's mind somehow didn't make him any less confusing. It almost seemed to make things worse, actually, as if she were trapped in a maze of icy mirrors. She wondered if that was how he felt all the time.

Sunny and Fatespeaker were in the library with Starflight; Fatespeaker was reading to him and Sunny was sorting a new bundle of scrolls into neat piles.

"Hi there," Sunny greeted them warmly.

"We have some free time before history, and Moon said she'd help me practice my reading," Kinkajou said, turning her scales the color of old scrolls with black speckles.

"That sounds great," Starflight said. "Did I hear Carnelian with you?"

"Yes," Carnelian muttered behind Moon, making her jump. She hadn't realized the SkyWing was there, which meant the raindrop trick was really working. "Is there any news from Queen Ruby?" *Maybe calling me home? Or at least sending me new battle formations to learn?*

"You got a letter this morning," Fatespeaker said, producing a small scroll from under the desk. She handed it to Carnelian, who inspected the seal suspiciously and then retired to the darkest corner to read it.

Kinkajou had just chosen a scroll called *Journeys in the Ice Kingdom* when Winter came hurrying in, carrying a covered cage. He set it down in front of Moon and whisked the cloth off.

She crouched to peer inside, trying to ignore how furious and resentful he felt about asking for help.

The cage looked a bit like a tall birdcage, but with an elaborate little environment constructed inside of it. There were stairs, a kind of running wheel on the lower level, a nest with tiny blankets piled on it on the upper level, and a swing hanging from the top bars of the cage.

It took Moon a moment to spot Bandit, because he was buried in the heap of blankets on the nest. But as the light filled the cage, a furry head slowly emerged, and then the rest of him, emitting little groans and rubbing his arms.

"Awww, he's *so* cute," Kinkajou said.

Winter snorted.

"Did you build all this?" Moon asked, touching the cage lightly with one claw. It was very detailed; it must have taken a long time and a lot of thought.

He nodded. "All the stuff inside. I thought he'd like it, but he's hardly used any of it — he won't climb on the swing or use the running wheel. Mostly he eats and then goes back to sleep. I thought scavengers were curious and unpredictable, but he's been unbelievably boring." The IceWing gave her a sideways look. "Any suggestions? Is he sick? I've been feeding him fruit, so he's eating fine. Why won't he *do* anything?"

What can I say without making him suspicious? Moon extended one claw through the bars of the cage. The scavenger jumped back, then looked up and seemed to recognize her. Tentatively Bandit stepped forward and put one paw on Moon's talon.

Again, she could sense feelings without words, but strong, complicated feelings. She could feel that he was still afraid, but now there was mostly sadness huge enough to engulf Moon. She felt a sudden immense longing for her mother.

"Maybe —" she started, then hesitated. She didn't like the feeling that Winter was testing her, but she wanted to help the little scavenger.

"Maybe he's depressed," Sunny interjected, coming over to peek inside. "Webs was like that for a while after the Summer Palace attack. He didn't get out of bed for months."

"Oh, poor little Bandit," Kinkajou said.

"Webs is a *dragon*," Winter pointed out. "This is a scavenger. Next you'll be telling me the cows and fish in the prey center are moping."

"Actually my theory is that scavengers are a lot more complicated than we think," Sunny said.

"He could be lonely," Moon said. She blinked at Bandit and withdrew her claw. He sat back down on the blankets, his shoulders slumped.

"That's true!" Sunny said. "Scavengers usually live in packs. Although I met one who was happy with just the company of dragons for a long time, but Flower was kind of special."

"Bandit might be special," Winter huffed.

"He might be delicious," Carnelian muttered from her corner. She was grumpier than ever, because the letter had rejected her official request to be sent back to battle training. "I can think of one good way to find out."

Winter hissed at her. He turned to Moon and growled, "So, what? Should I get *another* scavenger, just to keep this one happy? What if *that* one is depressed, too?"

"Or *you* could make friends with it," Moon suggested, and stopped, startled by her own boldness.

He folded his wings back and drew his head up. "What?"

"Flower and Smolder seemed to really like each other," Sunny said.

"How am I supposed to do that?" Winter demanded. He flung the cover back on the cage. "This is useless," he growled, and stormed back out of the library with it.

Sunny shrugged at Moon. "Don't feel bad; he's just worried about Bandit. *I* thought it was a good idea." She moved back to her pile of scrolls.

Moon curled her tail and wings in. It was true, Winter was worried about Bandit, but he was also mad at her in a kind of general ongoing way with no particular reason behind it.

Kinkajou nudged her shoulder. "Ignore him. He clearly doesn't like hearing good advice. Let's read about IceWings instead and see if they're all that full of themselves." She started unrolling the scroll on one of the low wooden tables. "Glory once told me that IceWings and NightWings have always hated each other, and it goes back to some big tragedy in the IceWings' past, but she didn't know what it was. The scrolls she read were mostly written by NightWings or SeaWings and never talked about the details. I'm so curious, aren't you?"

"Did you try asking Starflight?" Moon asked.

"Yes, but he didn't know either," Kinkajou said. "So I have to learn to read, so I can read all the scrolls ever written about IceWings and figure it out myself."

They worked on the scroll for a while, with Kinkajou puzzling out the words and turning lavender with delight when she got them right. After a while, Moon paused, thinking, and said:

"Winter or Icicle might be able to tell you."

"Ha ha, can you imagine them telling me anything?" Kinkajou said, turning herself a chilly blue. "We don't share IceWing secrets with mere RainWings, haughty sniff."

Moon giggled and Starflight looked up with a smile.

"I'm glad you two are getting along," he said. "We spent a lot of time working out all the clawmates."

"I'm still not sure about all of them," Sunny chimed in, frowning anxiously.

"Like me?" Carnelian asked. She had been pacing along the shelves, pulling out scrolls, glancing at them, and shoving them back in. Now she came stomping over to the desk. "Maybe you could move me to a cave where there's less *talking all the time*."

"Don't be silly," Kinkajou said. "Moon hardly ever talks. She talks more in her *sleep* than she ever does when she's awake."

"I do?" Moon said, horrified.

"Three moons, yes," said Carnelian. "And that's exactly what I mean. It is *so* annoying. One of them talks all day and the other one yammers all night."

Mother, why didn't you ever tell me this? Why didn't you warn me? Why didn't you think that talking in my sleep might put me and my secrets in danger?

"What do I say?" Moon asked nervously.

"All KINDS of fascinating nonsense," Kinkajou said. "Darkness and thunder and talons of doom and who knows what else. You must be reading something really exciting. Can I borrow it when you're done?"

"Um," Moon said, shifting on her talons. "You know, I think I might head to history a little early, if that's all right."

"Why?" Kinkajou asked.

"I just — want to look at the old maps." Now that she said it, it sounded like a good idea. Maybe she'd find a clue about the old Night Kingdom somewhere on there.

Kinkajou wrinkled her nose and turned pale orange. "Spend *more* time in that dank hole? No, thank you. I'll be there when I have to."

I doubt the maps will be helpful, Darkstalker pointed out as Moon headed through the Great Hall.

I know, Moon thought. *NightWings were the ones making*

the maps for hundreds of years, and they made sure to erase any trace of either NightWing kingdom, old or new. Still . . . maybe there's something.

At least you're looking, he said quietly. **Maybe you haven't completely forsaken me yet?**

I don't —

Moon faltered as a flash of light suddenly blistered through her mind, then vanished.

She stopped, blinking and disoriented. She was halfway down the tunnel to the history cave.

Did you do that? she asked.

No. Moon — watch out —

A slow pounding was working its way up her spine, along her neck, to the base of her skull. . . .

A moment later, pain shot through her like a claw brutally stabbing into her eye socket.

She collapsed to the floor, clutching her head, and the vision came.

Roaring flames tearing along the walls of the history cave, swallowing the maps, leaping to the seated dragonets in the space of a breath. Fire blistering along Moon's scales, her own voice screaming. Beside her, Kinkajou shrieking and burning, white amid the smoke. Qibli, Winter, Turtle, all on fire.

Everyone dying.

All of them, dying.

— CHAPTER 13 —

Moon, Darkstalker shouted, perhaps more than once, dragging her back to herself. *Moon, it's not real, you're all right.*

She staggered up and caught herself against the rough stone side of the tunnel.

What do you mean it's not real? she asked. Her heartbeat was too fast, squeezing her chest so she could hardly breathe.

I mean, it could have been, but it won't be, he said. *Whatever that was, it's in the history cave. Stay away from there and —*

The vision returned, fiercer and more agonizing than before.

Now Moon was outside the history cave, and fire was pouring out into the tunnel, along with the screaming, burning figures of her friends. Kinkajou stumbled to the ground in front of Moon, her wings turning crisp and black as flames ate them away. Carnelian's voice howled in pain from inside. Tamarin and Umber lay half in, half out of the cave, gasping as dark smoke filled their lungs.

Moon! Moon! Darkstalker pulled her out again. *Close your eyes. I can take your mind to a safe place where you won't see any of this.*

"No!" Moon shouted. "Don't do that!" She pushed herself up and started running toward the history cave.

What are you doing? Darkstalker asked.

I have to stop it.

There isn't time. Can't you tell? The explosion is only a few minutes away.

Then I have to warn them. Someone might be in there already.

A half-second pause, then: *Is that wise? Don't you want to keep your power a secret?*

"Not if it means my friends will all die!" Moon cried.

The vision slammed into her again, stamping her to the ground like a giant talon. More fire. Another burning dragon, maybe Pike or Bigtail. Umber lying in a charred heap on the ground, Sora sobbing beside him. Qibli with his wings in flames, screaming for help.

"What is wrong with you?" a cool, arrogant voice asked from above her. *Is she all right?* his brain worried, more sympathetically.

"Winter." Moon shook her head, trying to clear it. The IceWing was really there, standing in front of her, really not on fire, not dead. His scales were smooth, pale blue, unburnt. His eyes were arctic pools.

"Some kind of NightWing seizure?" he asked, looking down his snout at her. His tail flicked and he took a step back, toward the history cave. She could see the archway only a few paces ahead of them, quiet and flame-free.

"You can't go in there." Moon lunged forward and grabbed his forearm in her talons.

We're touching — she's — I'm — her scales against mine — I can't want this — his mind whirled.

"What are you doing?" he barked, but didn't pull away.

"Please don't go in there," she managed. The vision was storming back. "Something terrible is going to —"

Qibli burning. Tamarin burning. Winter safe, Icicle safe, Kinkajou burning —

Winter was holding her up; she'd fallen against him and he was trying to lift her back upright, his wings supporting hers. "What something terrible?" he said, his voice rising. He shook her. "How do you know?"

"Hey, leave her alone," Qibli's voice interjected.

"Stop!" Moon cried, pulling away from Winter and throwing herself in front of Qibli and Turtle. "Don't go in! No one can go in!"

"Whoa, calm down," Turtle said gently. "You're having some kind of panic attack."

"No, please listen." Moon couldn't catch her breath, not with the visions coming faster and the intensity of the thoughts around her. Tamarin dead, Kinkajou sobbing, Carnelian burning. *She's losing her mind.* "Please, please, don't let anyone go in there."

Deep breaths, Darkstalker said softly. **You'll be all right.**

"I'm listening," Qibli said, crouching to look into her eyes. "We're here, don't worry." *Must be something serious. Look at her eyes, she's terrified. Did Winter do this to her? No, he doesn't know what's going on either. What can I do for her? Find the threat, neutralize it.*

She grabbed Turtle's talons and tried to wrap his muffled mind around hers. "Kinkajou. I have to stop Kinkajou." The image of the RainWing burning kept coming back, over and over, like a knife plunging repeatedly into her heart.

"She's right behind us," Qibli said. He put one wing around her. "Moon, what is happening?"

"Yes," Winter said. "What do you know?"

Moon could feel the footsteps of other dragons through the floor. Dragons were coming for class. How could she stop them? How could she stop all of them?

She let out a cry of pain and closed her eyes. Another vision, and this time Peril was there, engulfed in flames, clutching someone in her talons. Was she the cause of the fire? If Moon could stop Peril, could she save everyone?

She couldn't think straight, couldn't focus long enough to come up with a convincing lie or a plan or anything.

"Moon, it's all right! Moon, breathe, here, lean on me." Warm rainbow wings wrapped around her. "We have to take her to Clay and Sunny, they'll know what to do."

Good idea, Qibli thought. *I should have thought of that.*

"Kinkajou," Moon sighed, leaning into her friend. The walls were fading in and out, the torchlight flaring and then disappearing and flickering back. She took a few stumbling steps as Kinkajou tried to guide her up the tunnel.

"I don't know," Winter was saying to someone. "She just collapsed."

"Hey, Carnelian," Qibli called. "Don't go in there."

"Why not?" the SkyWing's voice demanded.

"Uh," he said. "One of the torches got all smoky, the whole cave smells. Needs to air out."

"Smells fine to me," Carnelian growled.

"Come on, Moon," Kinkajou said, tugging her along. "We'll go find help."

"But the cave —" Moon said. She shook her head, trying to clear it. Kinkajou's worried thoughts were scattered all through hers, loud and sweet and muddling. Kinkajou wanted so badly to take Moon away from there that Moon couldn't find her way back to what *she* needed to do. "I have to —"

"Don't worry," Kinkajou said. "We can miss class today. Tamarin will get us any notes we need."

"Is she in there?" Moon froze. Qibli and Turtle were still beside her; Winter was a step away, watching her intently. "Did she go in the history cave?"

"Sure, but —"

"No, she can't —" Moon turned, in time to see Carnelian at the cave entrance, tossing her head.

"You're an idiot, SandWing," Carnelian said. "It's perfectly fine in there." She stepped into the classroom.

"No!" Moon cried. Farther along the tunnel, Icicle was coming from the other direction. The IceWing stopped and arched her brows as Moon dove for the doorway where Carnelian had disappeared.

With a *whoosh* and a *boom*, the cave exploded in a huge fireball.

CHAPTER 14

Moon was blown backward, slamming into the cave wall behind her. She wasn't sure if she lost consciousness for a moment or if her eyes were full of smoke. She couldn't hear anything. She could see Kinkajou screaming at the edge of the flames, but there was no sound.

Everything was coming through loud and clear inside her head, though. Most of it was panicked, wordless images and fear, cascading faster and faster until Moon felt as if she couldn't *be* any more afraid or it would kill her.

Listen to me, Darkstalker said commandingly. *I'm the calmest voice you can hear. Use me as your anchor. I'll keep talking until you calm down. Think about your heart beating. Remember that you are safe. Look around you.*

Moon blinked at the billowing black smoke that was pouring out of the history cave. A burning scroll rolled out, stopping just before her talons. Shards of glass from the broken light globes were scattered all over the floor. Winter and Qibli were running toward her. Turtle was pressed to the tunnel wall beyond them; behind him, two dragons were approaching. Only a few seconds had passed.

Kinkajou is safe, Darkstalker reminded her. *Qibli is safe. The IceWing and the SeaWing, regrettably, are safe.*

Why regrettably? Moon asked.

Ah, you are listening. Keep listening. Focus on me; don't let anyone else in, just for now.

"Moon!" Winter skidded to a stop in front of her, reaching for her shoulders and then pulling back as she flinched away. "What was that?"

"We have to get her out of here," Qibli said, sliding his wing under one of Moon's and helping her up. "The smoke —" He broke off in a fit of coughing.

"But Tamarin — Carnelian —" Moon gasped.

"What do we do?" Kinkajou yelled. "What do we do?"

Qibli and Moon staggered a few steps forward and the two approaching dragons came into focus: Sora and Umber. Sora's eyes were wild and terrified, and her mind was a mess of mud and battle flashbacks.

Focus on my voice, Darkstalker reminded Moon. *Don't let yourself fall in.* She steadied herself against his constant murmuring.

"I'm going to get help!" Umber shouted. He tore off up the tunnel.

"Is anyone hurt?" Sora squeaked. "Where's Icicle?"

"She's all right, she wasn't inside," Moon said. She twisted around, but she couldn't see Sora's clawmate anymore. Even through the thick smoke, Icicle's gleaming white scales should have been visible, but there was no sign of the IceWing where Moon had seen her before the blast.

"At least two dragons were in there," Winter said. Moon felt sick. Tamarin. Carnelian.

"Stand clear," a voice shouted, footsteps thumping toward them. Moon flinched back against Qibli as the ferocious heat of Peril's mind swept through her head, a moment before Peril herself came charging through the smoke. She didn't stop to look at them; she ran straight into the burning cave.

"Three moons," Kinkajou whispered frantically, clutching her talons together.

A minute later, Peril's smoking wings appeared, and she backed out of the cave, dragging someone behind her. She pulled the burned dragonet level with Moon and the others, then laid her on the stone floor and ran back into the cave.

Kinkajou gasped and buried her face in her talons.

"Oh, no," Moon said softly. She let go of Qibli and crouched beside the body. She could see patches of unburnt red scales, but so much of Carnelian was burned that she looked more like a NightWing than a SkyWing.

"Maybe I can —" Winter hesitated, then crouched and breathed a small amount of frostbreath on Carnelian's neck. The scales stopped smoking, but stayed black. He shook his head in frustration. *That could make it worse. I don't know,* he worried. Moon couldn't tell if Carnelian was even still breathing or not.

Moon's heart jumped as she heard more dragons running toward them; she could hear that one of them was a desperately worried Clay. He stopped briefly beside Carnelian, grief flooding through him, and looked across at Sora.

"How many are still in there?" he asked.

Sora opened and closed her mouth, unable to speak.

"We don't know for sure," Kinkajou jumped in. "At least Tamarin. Peril went back in, too."

Clay didn't ask any more questions. He ran into the fire, limping on his scarred leg, flames licking hungrily across his fireproof scales. Moon could hear how much it hurt him — his power meant he healed quickly, but the fire still burned him, even just for a moment — but he didn't hesitate.

Sora let out a choked sob and fled.

"What's happening?" Onyx demanded from behind Moon. She and Pike stared in bewilderment at the roaring flames.

"Tamarin —" Kinkajou whispered.

Onyx narrowed her dark eyes at the fire. Pike flared his wings, his mind flooding with images of the attack on the Summer Palace. Moon could see burning logs falling from the sky, crashing into a pavilion — the palace Albatross had built. She could see SeaWings desperately trying to escape through a narrow tunnel. She saw small explosions going off as some of the flaming projectiles smashed into panicking dragons.

"We shouldn't be breathing this," Qibli said, trying to steer Moon away from the fire. "This smoke is as bad as the fire, if we breathe too much."

"I'm not leaving until I know Tamarin's all right," Kinkajou said.

Moon shook her head in agreement and Qibli gave up.

A movement in the smoke, and then Clay emerged, carrying a dragonet slung across his back. Behind him was Peril with another dragonet.

Moon tried to breathe, tried to focus on Darkstalker's voice, still whispering calming things in the background. But who was the third dragonet?

"Is it all clear?" Winter asked Clay.

Clay nodded tiredly. "We swept the entire space. No one else in there."

Winter ran toward the cave, opened his mouth, and poured out a blast of icy air. He advanced on the fire, putting it out with his frostbreath as he stepped through the smoke, into the cave.

I hope he's safe, Moon thought, and then all her thoughts were crowded out by the sight of the dragonet Clay was sliding gently to the ground.

"Tamarin!" Kinkajou cried.

The blind RainWing was not as badly burned as Carnelian. She was unconscious — but she was still breathing. Kinkajou bent over her, white and green patches pummeling each other across her scales, and carefully lifted one of her friend's talons.

"I think she might have smelled something, maybe smoke, right before the explosion happened," Clay said. "She was behind one of the scroll racks, as though she'd tipped it over in front of her. It might have saved her life." *If she lives,* he thought despairingly.

"Tamarin, you're all right," Kinkajou said, biting back a sob. "You'd better be all right or I will tie you to a tree and cover you with hallucinogenic frogs. Tamarin, please wake up."

"We should get her some of those RainWing tranquilizing darts before she does wake up," Clay said, touching Kinkajou's wing with his own. "Those burns are going to hurt a lot." He crouched to study the third dragonet, lying on the ground in front of Peril.

For a moment, Moon thought whoever it was must have been burned beyond recognition, and then she realized his scales were black. It was Bigtail, the other NightWing. He was clearly dead.

Clay turned to Carnelian for a moment, touching her neck, and then shook his head. Carnelian was dead, too.

Tamarin was the only survivor, if she survived her burns.

"The underground lake," Pike said suddenly. "Let's put her in the lake. It's not far. Submerging her in water will help. I've seen — I saw this work — after the attack." He cut himself off, darted forward, and tried to lift Tamarin, but he was thin, and she was a little bigger than he was. He staggered, and Clay stopped him.

"I'll carry her. Show me the way."

"I'll come, too," Onyx said, studying her clawmate with apparent concern.

"Go to Sunny," Clay said to Peril. "Tell her to bring tranq darts and meet us at the lake." Peril nodded, glanced back at the smoking cave, and hurried away.

Qibli helped lift Tamarin onto Clay's back. Pike scurried away, running full tilt, with Clay and Onyx right behind him.

Kinkajou took a step after them, then wavered, looking back at Moon and Carnelian. By the time her mind said, *Go with Tamarin, Moon will be fine,* they were gone, and she didn't know where the lake was.

"Moon, you're bleeding," Qibli said. Moon finally noticed the trail of blood down her left shoulder and the sharp pain at the back of her head.

"I'm all right," she said, touching her skull gingerly. She could hear a lot more dragons coming their way — Tsunami and Sunny among them.

You have a lot of explaining to do, Darkstalker said quietly. *Start thinking of a good lie now.*

"Let's get you to the infirmary," Kinkajou said.

"Wait," Winter said, emerging from the cave. Behind him, the fire was hissing out. The wrecked cave was covered in ice crystals, a gleaming layer of silver over black, frost over soot. Scraps of burnt scrolls littered the ground, and the ashes of the maps on the walls were still drifting down.

At least it wasn't the library, Moon thought. How had everything burned so fast? Even with the scrolls and maps, there shouldn't have been such a big fire, surely. And how did it start?

It wasn't a normal fire. She knew that. Something had *exploded.* But did that mean . . . that someone had set it on purpose?

Winter suddenly clamped his claws around her uninjured forearm. Moon let out a yelp as the freezing shock of his scales met hers.

"Hey!" Kinkajou protested.

"Don't —" Qibli started.

But Winter didn't stop. He dragged Moon down the tunnel, away from the smoke. She could hear Qibli and Kinkajou and another pair of claws scrambling to follow them.

"What are you doing?" Moon asked him. His grip was like being trapped in ice; trying to pull away did no good. And where most dragons' minds became clearer when she touched them, his became too bright and painfully dazzling, reflecting back at her like sun off a field of snow. All she could get were flashes of sharp anger, which she really could have figured out on her own from his expression.

"Here," Winter said, pushing her into a tall, narrow cave where the air was clear enough to breathe. They were out of sight of the fire damage, but close enough that Moon could still sense the dragons gathering there. Her claws scraped against squat stalagmites jutting from the floor. The sound of water dripping somewhere slowly, drop by drop, echoed against the looming walls and distant ceiling.

Qibli, Kinkajou, and Turtle burst into the cavern behind them, bristling with outraged thoughts. Qibli had grabbed a torch along the way and shoved it into a crack in the wall, adding another circle of firelight to the space.

"You can't just push your friends around like that," Kinkajou said, hurrying over to Moon. "Especially when she's hurt. Moon, there's something in this wound." She reached out but didn't touch it. Moon twisted her neck and saw that there was something sticking out of the cut in her shoulder, like a collection of tiny, sharp splinters.

Qibli lifted his venomous tail and glared at Winter. But before he could say anything, Winter took a menacing step toward Moon and pointed one silver claw at her.

"You *knew*," he snarled. "That's why you tried to stop us from going in. You knew about the explosion and the fire before it happened." He took another step, until all she could see was the bright orange reflection of the torchlight in his eyes.

"So," he hissed. "Exactly *how* did you know?"

── CHAPTER 15 ──

Winter's words had an instant effect on the other three dragonets.

He's right, Kinkajou realized. *How — what —*

Turtle's mind was as opaque as ever, but he shifted on his talons and gave Moon a curious frown.

Worst of all was Qibli. *How did she know? She couldn't have done this — could she? She's a dragon with secrets, and Thorn said not to trust the NightWings — but why would she? I know I haven't figured her out yet, but I don't see violence in her. And yet, how did she know? But if she set the fire, why would she try to stop us from going in? But surely she wouldn't — she couldn't have — I can't even believe I'm thinking this —*

"You didn't — sorry, but — you didn't have anything to do with —" he started.

"No!" Moon cried. "Of course not!" She brushed away tears, trying to keep her voice steady. Trying not to think about Carnelian. Or how everything was now falling apart. "I would never hurt anyone."

"I know," Qibli said, but not convincingly. *She was better at hunting than anyone expected. There is strength beneath those scales. In the right circumstances, wouldn't any dragon be capable of hurting another? Even her? But why?*

"If you *didn't* do it, then do you know who did?" Turtle asked. He hadn't spoken since the blast; he hadn't moved from his spot by the wall until he came chasing after them. He looked shaken, but not destroyed. Moon wished she knew what he was thinking. Did he suspect her, too?

"Or maybe you saw something?" Kinkajou suggested hopefully. "Something that warned you?"

That might work, Darkstalker said. **At least two of them want to believe that; start with that lie and build from there.**

I don't want to tell them any lies, Moon pointed out. *Even ones they want to believe.*

She pressed her front claws together, feeling a wrenching fear all through her chest. Her mother was echoing through her head: *Never never tell anyone about your curse. Never let anyone find out. It will be the end of everything.*

"There's only one explanation," Winter hissed through his teeth, looking down his snout at her. "You did this. You set that fire. I don't know why yet, but I will find out."

The other explanation was there, hovering at the edge of his mind, but he couldn't bring himself to believe it yet. He'd been so sure — so *sure* — that the NightWings were lying about their powers all along.

"I swear I didn't," Moon said. She spread her wings helplessly. "Please believe me."

"Can't you tell us how you knew?" Kinkajou pleaded.

Moon couldn't speak. She felt as if there were claws clamped around her throat, as though her worst fear was trying to choke her so she wouldn't reveal her secrets.

Winter stared at her for a long minute, and then he lashed his tail, spikes clattering against the stubby pillars dotting the floor. "I will give you one chance, NightWing. You have until midnight tomorrow to tell me the truth — or I'm going to tell everyone what you did." He took a step toward her and she flinched back. "I knew NightWings couldn't be trusted, but I was starting to think maybe you were different. Clearly I was wrong." He stalked out of the cave.

Moon buried her face in her talons, shaking. Kinkajou reached for her hesitantly. The doubt in Kinkajou's mind — of all dragons — made Moon want to disappear completely.

I don't understand, Qibli was thinking, and that was clearly an unfamiliar and uncomfortable experience for him. His brain kept circling all the possibilities . . . including the truth, but he kept shying away from it. Moon knew it wouldn't be long before he came to it, though.

But he wasn't the first one there.

"Three moons," Turtle said. Glowing lines lit up along his wings and neck, making him shimmer eerily in the dark cave. He took a deep breath, staring at her with wide eyes. "It was a vision, wasn't it? You can see the future."

Kinkajou gasped. "No way," she whispered.

Admit nothing, Darkstalker advised.

Stay secret, stay hidden, stay safe, her mother's mantra echoed in her head.

There didn't seem to be any chance of that now.

Moon looked down at her talons and nodded.

"What?" Kinkajou cried. "What else have you seen? Anything about me?"

"When did you know?" Qibli asked, taking a step back, away from Moon. *But all those powers are supposed to be gone! So who's lying to us — the prophecy dragonets, the NightWings, or Moon? Or all of them?* "About the explosion — how long did you know without telling anyone?"

"I just saw it," Moon said. "It was right before class — sometimes the visions come months before something happens, sometimes only a few minutes. I never know. . . . It's not like it's a *helpful* power."

"But it is," Kinkajou said, bewildered. *Monkeys and mangoes, I'd love to be able to see the future!* "You saved us."

Maybe she could have saved the others, too, Qibli thought, *if she'd told us it was a vision. If we'd* known *what was going to happen, we could have stopped them. If she'd told the truth — if we'd known about her power beforehand —*

She saw Carnelian in his head, tangled up in his guilt that he should have tried harder to stop her from going in.

"Would you have believed me?" she asked him. "If I told you I'd had a vision?"

"*I* would have," Kinkajou said, wounded, and Moon realized with a wrench of guilt that that was true.

"Who else knows you can do this?" Qibli asked. "Can all the NightWings see the future?"

"No one knows," she said, wincing as a flash of pain from her injury suddenly zigzagged from her head down to her spine. "And as far as I know, no one else in the tribe can do this." *Apart from my secret friend, the legendary monster Darkstalker, of course.*

"Is that it?" Turtle asked. "Or is there anything else we should know?" He inhaled sharply, looking suddenly more awake than he ever did. "Can you read our minds?"

Kinkajou and Qibli stared at her, their eyes wide.

This is the last moment they'll like me.

This is how I lose them.

Moon felt as though she was standing at the edge of a precipice, with howling winds below her waiting to smash her into the mountains. All of her mother's great fears, the whole parade of nightmares she'd been watching her entire life, went marching through her head: dragons shunning her, dragons screaming at her, dragons setting her on fire, dragons locking her up and forcing her to use her powers for them . . . but mostly dragons hating her, everybody hating her forever.

Just lie, Darkstalker whispered. **Hold on to your one advantage.**

Secret. Hidden. SAFE.

But Moon could hear what her friends were thinking, too.

Qibli. *Won't she just lie to us? How can I trust her? How will I ever know if she's lying?*

And Kinkajou, the dragon who wanted to be her best friend: *I believe in Moon. She'll tell us the truth.*

How could she be the deceitful NightWing Winter thought she was, when she had the choice to be the dragon Kinkajou saw?

"Yes," Moon confessed. "I can read your minds. I'm sorry." She turned to Kinkajou. "I'm really sorry. I can't help it. It just happens; it's always happening. I can't turn it off. Please, please don't tell anyone."

Is she hearing my thoughts right now? Qibli wondered. He clearly saw the answer on her face, because he took another step back. *What has she heard?* The pace of his thoughts, incredibly, sped up, as he seemed to flash through all the possible things she might have seen. *All my plans to get other dragons to like me? My nightmares about my family? My thoughts about* her? *How many embarrassing — she must know — I can't — has she been laughing at me this whole time?*

"No!" Moon cried. "I really like you."

He grabbed his head, as if he was trying to keep his thoughts inside, and then flared his wings. *What if I accidentally think about one of Thorn's secrets, or one of the hidden dens of the Outclaws?* Secrets she didn't understand started spilling through his head. *Or what if she hears some of the terrible things I think about other dragons? Who would ever like me if they knew what I thought about everyone?* "Talons and tails," he mumbled. "This is not OK. I have to get out of here." He turned and bolted through the cave entrance, disappearing beyond the torchlight.

But I don't understand, Moon thought, half to herself and half to Darkstalker. *He never thought anything more terrible than any other dragon. He's more interesting and kinder and more insightful on the inside than almost anyone else I've met.*

He doesn't know that, Darkstalker pointed out. **He's never seen inside anyone else, the way you have. After a few years of reading minds, you'll see — it's often the most brilliant dragons who are the most insecure. And the ones who are most afraid of having their minds read — because they think they must have the worst, lowest thoughts of anyone — are nowhere near as bad as the ones who complacently don't care because they assume everyone else is as terrible as they are. Mostly everyone *is* terrible, by the way.**

"I wish you'd told me," Kinkajou said. Her head was spinning: *I thought she was going to be my best friend, but all along she was hiding this huge secret from me. And now Carnelian is dead, and Tamarin is hurt, and someone tried to blow us up, and there are all these grumpy dragons here, and school is nothing like I expected. I wish it was yesterday. I wish none of this had happened. I wish someone who could SEE THE FUTURE had maybe STOPPED ALL OF THIS FROM HAPPENING.*

"I'm sorry," Moon said again, hunching her shoulders miserably. "I was afraid. It's not exactly the first thing I tell other dragons."

"Well, it *should* be!" Kinkajou said, fiercely enough to make Moon flinch. "If you're going to be in our heads hearing everything, then you should at least warn your friends. And if you're seeing the future, and it's *bad*, then you *really* have to tell someone. I don't understand you."

"I didn't want you to hate me," Moon said.

"Well, did you want me to trust you?" Kinkajou demanded. "Because this is the opposite of how to do that." Orange and red were starting to flicker through her scales. *Why am I even bothering? She knows what I think. She can hear it all herself.* "I have to go check on Tamarin. I need to think. The kind of thinking that's just between me and me," she added sternly.

And then she was gone, too, leaving Moon with Turtle.

That's what happens, Darkstalker said with a sigh. ***But don't worry. They'll come crawling back when they need you.***

I don't want them to crawl, Moon thought with a shudder. *And now what do I do about Winter? If Qibli and Kinkajou reacted that badly — won't he hate me even more than they do? But if I don't tell him something by tomorrow, everyone will think I set that fire. That I killed Carnelian and Bigtail.*

She sank to the floor, wrapped her wings around herself, and started to cry.

After a moment, she felt a wing gently brush her back.

Even when he was touching her, she couldn't sense anything but that quiet fuzz from Turtle. He looked down at her with his dark green eyes.

"Come with me."

CHAPTER 16

It occurred to Moon, somewhere deep inside the mountain, that perhaps following Turtle off to a dark secluded spot might not be the best idea.

Between the vision she'd had of him and Anemone, and the fact that she had no idea what he was thinking, she suspected she probably ought to be more nervous.

But his mind was so quiet and — well, *cozy* seemed like a strange way to describe someone's brain, but it was the best word for his. Trying to listen to it was like sinking into soft moss, muffling all the voices of the other dragons in the school. Or like being underwater, she guessed.

The voices got quieter anyway as they walked, putting layers of rock and space between her and the thinking going on up above. Neither of them spoke, although she could think of a million things she thought she should tell him. There were few torches down this far, but Moon's eyes adjusted to the dark, and Turtle's scales glowed just enough for them to see the floor beneath their talons.

Here and there she saw slick, glowing trails along the

rocks, and after a while she realized they were left by luminescent snails as long as her claws.

Soon after that, she noticed a faint dripping sound up ahead, and then all at once, the passage opened up into a huge cavern studded with stalactites, shimmering with glowworms — and surrounding an enormous underground lake.

"Oh," Moon whispered. At first she thought there were glowworms in the water, too, and then she realized she was seeing the reflections of stars. Far above them was a hole in the roof, big enough for a dragon to fly through with her wings outstretched. Big enough for the moons to shine through, casting broken silvery-green light across the still water. Two of the moons were visible through the hole, half full and swathed with clouds in the growing twilight.

Moon looked around for Pike and Tamarin, but although a faint burnt smell still hung in the air, there was no sign of the injured RainWing or the dragons taking care of her. They must have immersed her and then taken her to the healing cave.

Turtle nodded at the lake. "You should wash your shoulder. I'd take you to the infirmary, but I imagine Clay is busy with Tamarin right now."

It had started to hurt in earnest while they were walking. Moon peered at it again, then slowly edged into the lake. The water was colder than she'd expected, sliding around and under her scales, and when it hit her wound, she yelped with shock.

There was a small splash as Turtle dove into the lake beside her. He surfaced and studied her shoulder as she gingerly dipped it under, washing off the dried blood. It started to bleed again, but after a minute it stopped, and she could see the prickly thing stuck in it more clearly.

"This might hurt," Turtle said, and without any more warning than that, he pincered his claws around the object and yanked it out of the wound.

"Ow!" Moon cried. Turtle pressed his talons to her shoulder as another spurt of blood fountained out. She felt a little faint, and caught herself wondering what he would do if she collapsed here in the lake. Would he leave her to drown?

He lifted his claws, checked that the blood had stopped, and then dipped his talons in the lake to wash them off. He was still holding the strange object, and now he rinsed it off and peered at it.

"What is that?" Moon asked, scooping water over her shoulder. She could see that it was a blackish-brown misshapen sphere, about the size of a rainforest frog, and covered in those sharp thorns.

"I think I know," he said, "but I should look at it in better light, and maybe check the library. How's your shoulder? Can you fly?"

"Probably," Moon said. She glanced up at the moons shining through the hole in the roof and caught herself wishing she could fly all the way to one of them and just stay there, surrounded by silver and silence.

"Go ahead and try," he suggested. She knew he meant "try flying," but she looked into his unreadable eyes and wondered if he was offering her the chance to escape. She could be out that hole and on her way to the rainforest in no time. Or even farther; she could run to somewhere where Winter wouldn't be able to track her down and scrape out all her secrets.

But then he'd really believe I did it. And so would everyone — why else would I run away?

Moon hesitated for a moment, then took to the air, soaring over the lake and circling in the moonlight. Her shoulder hurt, but she could still move her wings. The silvery touch of the moons on her scales calmed her a little, but then she remembered Winter's furious expression and felt sick all over again.

She swooped around in an arc, watching Turtle swim below her.

Will they tell everyone my secret? I guess there's nothing I can do to stop them, if they decide to do that.

Do I wish I didn't have this power?

If I couldn't read minds, everyone I met would be like Turtle — completely unreadable. Strange and blank. I'd have no way to know if they were kind or cruel. I'd never understand why they act the way they do. Everyone would be all surface.

I'd think Winter was just mean; I wouldn't know about his dead brother and how he hates himself more than anyone else.

I might think Qibli was just goofy and ordinary, if I didn't know about his layers and his amazing mind and his childhood. I'd have stayed away from Kinkajou, because I wouldn't have known or believed that she really liked me.

I guess that's how other dragons live . . . never knowing how complicated everyone else is.

That's what it would be like, to be normal.

But if I could choose, would I want that?

And since I can't choose . . . should I run away from what I can do, or risk revealing it to dragons who won't understand?

Moon tilted her wings and sailed down until she landed on a craggy boulder that jutted out of the lake. Spongy, bluish moss clung to its sides and squelched under her claws. Turtle swam over and clambered up beside her.

"How did you find this place?" Moon asked.

He shrugged. "I went exploring. There are a couple of underground lakes, but this is the biggest, and the only one with a view of the sky."

He leaned back to look up at the visible moons. Moon studied him for a minute. *I don't know him at all.*

"So," he said slowly, without meeting her eyes. "I guess you must know my secret."

"No," she said, stopping him before he could say too much. She was desperately curious, but she didn't want to trick him. "Turtle, I — I don't know why, but I can't read *your* mind. With a few dragons, I just don't hear anything."

He gave her a startled expression. "Like there's nothing in there?" His snout crinkled, amused. "That's alarming. *What* are you saying about me?"

"I'm saying you're safe," Moon said. "Your secrets are safe. I can't hear your thoughts." She hesitated, wondering if she should mention the vision about Anemone. Something made her hold back.

"Oh," Turtle said. "Awesome? I think?" He thought for a moment, then shook his head. "I'm not very interesting anyway."

I'm sure that's not true, Moon thought.

"Thanks for letting me keep my secrets, then," he said, giving her an easy smile. "So what are you going to do about Winter?"

Moon dug her talons into the rock. Her stomach hurt and she had this horrible, prickling, tense feeling everywhere, as if she might erupt out of her scales. She made herself lie down on the boulder and reached to drag one claw through the pool below her. "I guess I have to tell him the truth," she said finally.

"Not if you don't want to," Turtle said. "Why don't you figure out who really caused the explosion, and tell him that instead?"

Moon gave him a bemused look. "Oh, all right, I'll just go solve that mystery by midnight tomorrow. No problem."

He shoved her off the rock and she landed with a splash, coming back up startled and sputtering.

"What was that for?" she cried.

"You're a *mind reader*," he reminded her. "All you have to do is walk around the school until you hear someone's mind going, 'Well done, me; tip-top explosion I caused today; aren't I a clever arsonist.'"

"It's not exactly that easy," Moon said, spreading her wings to stay afloat and shivering in the chilly lake. "It's really noisy out there; you have no idea. And you're not the only dragon who can shield his thoughts from me. What if it was someone like that — someone like you?"

"Well, it wasn't me," he said, not sounding the slightest bit offended. "So anyone else you can't hear, put them on your list of suspects and keep listening to everyone else in the meanwhile. Why wouldn't you? You could figure this out in an hour if you just hear the right dragon."

"And if they're thinking about it when I do hear them," Moon said. She climbed back onto the boulder and shook the water off her wings. "But if it were that easy, I should have heard them planning it. I should have heard *something* from *someone*. . . ." She stopped, realizing she had.

The conversation with the dreamvisitor. Planning to kill someone — multiple someones. She couldn't believe she'd forgotten about that, even in the chaos of the explosion. Was the fire in the history cave the plan she'd overheard?

And if so . . . then perhaps the dragon with the dream-visitor (Queen Scarlet?) would return tonight to find out if it worked. Maybe there'd be another conversation between killers in the dark, under the cover of dreams.

And if Moon was listening at the right time, maybe she'd have a chance to catch them.

～ CHAPTER 17 ～

"I have to get back to my sleeping cave," Moon said, leaping to her feet and slipping on the wet stone.

"Oh," Turtle said, "uh, sure. Did you figure something out?"

"I hope so," she said. "Can you lead me back?"

As they hurried up the tunnel, leaving wet footprints behind them, she told him about the conversation she'd heard two nights ago. "I wonder if I should tell someone," she said nervously. "Like Starflight or Sunny? Or — Tsunami?" She shivered all the way to her toes at the thought of trying to tell the ferocious SeaWing something like this.

"I don't think so," he said. "I say keep it to yourself until you know more. You never know how someone will —"

"Shh." Moon put out her tail to stop him from moving. They were near the history cave again; the lingering smell of smoke filled the air, along with a deep chill from all the frostbreath Winter had sprayed. The corpses of Bigtail and Carnelian were gone, leaving dark imprints on the ash-covered floor, surrounded by the marks of several talons.

Someone was in the cave, poking through the ashes. . . .
She could sense two dragons arguing. She motioned to Turtle
to stay quiet, and they crept forward until they could hear
the voices clearly.

"We'll use the dreamvisitor to tell Glory tonight. She
needs to know about Bigtail, at least — but maybe she can
also tell us what to do." It was Sunny, all her thoughts twisted
in a knot of guilt and grief and distress.

"*I'm* the Head of School," Tsunami said. "*I* can tell you
what to do. That's my job *and* my favorite thing in life, I
mean, seriously."

She was trying to break the tension, but Sunny was barely
listening. "Should we shut down the school? Send everyone home?"

"That's what *she* wants," Tsunami said fiercely, her mind
bristling like it was full of spears. Moon heard her pick up
a piece of debris and throw it at the wall. "Sunny, you
know Queen Scarlet must have been behind this. She's trying to destroy this great thing we're building, and we *won't
let her.*"

"But what if she hurts more students? And who's working with her? And how can we stop her if we can't find her?
And how can we keep them all safe?" Sunny's voice broke.

"We'll catch the dragon who did this," Tsunami said. "I
promise, Sunny. I will rip them apart myself."

"I should send a message to Queen Ruby about Carnelian,"

Sunny said, watching the ashes of a map crumble under her claws. "Maybe we should notify all the queens, in case any of them want to withdraw their students."

Tsunami groaned. "That means my mother will be here by sunrise, and Anemone will be gone twenty seconds later."

"How did it start?" Sunny wondered. There was a shuffling noise as she came closer to the entrance. "Umber said there was an explosion . . . and it must have been something near the doorway, where Carnelian was . . . Tsunami, what's this?"

Out in the tunnel, Moon and Turtle exchanged glances.

"I don't know," Tsunami said. "But I know I hate them. There are others all over the floor, buried in the ash. I've already been stabbed a few times and it's like they have TEETH. I practically have to dig them out of my scales. No, don't give it to me; it'll just attack me like the others did."

Turtle held out the little ball of thorns and gave Moon a look. She nodded, guessing it was the same kind of thing Sunny and Tsunami had found.

Apparently that wasn't quite what the look meant, though, because he nodded back and then stepped right into the history cave. Moon jumped back, startled, and then hurried after him. *That would have been a useful moment for mind reading,* she thought to herself. *She* would have voted for staying hidden, but it was too late for that.

Tsunami and Sunny whirled around and blinked at them.

"Turtle!" Tsunami said. "You shouldn't —"

"Hey, sorry," he said. "We heard what you were saying and — I might know what this is." Turtle held up the thorn ball, which matched the one in Sunny's palm.

Moon tried to take shallow breaths. The air in here smelled worse than smoke; it smelled like scorched dragon flesh. It was colder, too, this close to the melting film of frostbreath. The ashes drifting over her claws were heavy and damp; they got in between her scales and stuck to her wings like insidious gray cobwebs. It was horrible, in every way.

Horrible, too, to hear the instant flare of suspicion from Tsunami's mind. *What is Moon doing here? Why was she listening to us?* Sunny's reaction was less suspicious, but perhaps only because she was too tired and worried to think of it.

"Yeah? What are those?" Tsunami asked her brother. "And where'd you get that one?"

"Moon got hit by it when the explosion went off," he said, pointing to the wound on her shoulder. "I'm pretty sure I've seen these before. After the attack on the Summer Palace, we found things like it on several of the surviving SeaWings." He turned the ball over and cut into it with one of his claws, revealing a bright green interior. "It's a seed pod. It comes from something called a dragonflame cactus, which grows only in high altitudes, in the mountains."

"How did you figure that out?" Sunny asked.

"My mother tortured a SkyWing prisoner until he told us," Turtle said matter-of-factly. Sunny and Tsunami both winced. "He said the SkyWings use the cacti as bombs, because when they come into contact with fire, they explode, sending fiery bits of cactus and seed pods everywhere. I think the idea is that if you tried to exterminate them by burning them all, they'd first of all attack you back, and second of all release all these seeds so that a hundred more cacti would grow from the ashes. Kind of a cool evolutionary thing that makes sense if you're a plant trying to survive on a mountain full of fire-breathing dragons, right?"

He looked up and caught the expressions on their faces. "But, uh, horrible, obviously."

"So it's a SkyWing weapon," Tsunami said. She studied the floor. "Probably set with some kind of long fuse, slowly burning until it reached the cactus. Hidden somehow. Hmmm."

"You think one of our SkyWing students did this?" Sunny said, running through the list in her head. *Flame is pretty angry at the whole world — Fatespeaker and Glory were both worried about his aggression problems. But he's more the type to lose his temper and start a fight over prey, not plan to set a fire from a distance.*

"Or someone who was told what to do by a SkyWing," Tsunami pointed out. "A SkyWing like Queen Scarlet, for instance." She paused, then added, "Or . . . there is another SkyWing here. One who's betrayed us before."

Sunny was already shaking her head. "It couldn't be Peril."

"Why not?" Tsunami said. "We don't know what she's capable of."

"No, I mean, it *couldn't* be," Sunny said. "She couldn't touch a cactus like that without it blowing up. Think about it."

Tsunami frowned, then snorted grudgingly. "I hate it when you're smarter than me."

Sunny suddenly seemed to remember that Moon and Turtle were there. "You should go back to your sleeping caves," she said. "We've told everyone to stay there until we figure out what to do next." *Oh, I shouldn't have let them hear me speculate. What if they tell everyone? I keep forgetting to act like I'm in charge instead of one of them.* "Please don't say anything about this for now, all right?"

Moon nodded, and Turtle handed the seed pod over to Sunny.

"I'm sorry about all this," Sunny said. "It's so awful. It shouldn't have happened here."

"But we'll get to the bottom of it," Tsunami promised. "We'll find the dragon who set that bomb, and then I will tear off his wings and hang him from the eastern peak of Jade Mountain."

Sunny winced. "Tsunami, yuck."

"Can we check on Tamarin before we go back to our caves?" Moon asked softly.

Tsunami shook her head. "Clay is taking care of her. We'll let you know soon how she's doing."

Moon nodded, and then followed Turtle out into the tunnel again.

The sleeping corridor was quiet to dragon ears, but Moon could hear the churning fear and rumors and guesses rolling through everyone's minds. Very few of them were actually asleep, although by now it was fully dark outside.

She hesitated before they reached her cave, thinking of Carnelian and Kinkajou, and how different everything had been this morning.

"It'll be all right," Turtle said. "You'll find out who did this. Let me know if I can help."

Moon watched him disappear into his sleeping cave, where Umber was worrying about Marsh and Sora. She closed her eyes and found Sora in a deep sleep, somewhere farther away . . . the infirmary, Moon guessed. She must have been given tranquilizer darts, too.

She listened to the minds around her for a long moment, but no one was chuckling gleefully over their arson today. Icicle, Pike, and Mightyclaws were asleep. She could feel the strange fuzz of Onyx's brain but couldn't tell whether she was asleep or awake. Flame was not in his sleeping cave at all; he was somewhere else in the mountain, and she could only hear a distant echo of his bitter, angry thoughts.

What can you hear? she asked Darkstalker. *Do you know who did it?*

You could leave, you know, he answered without answering. **You don't need these dragons. Your friends are furious with you and that IceWing is dangerous. But you have me. If you**

leave now, I could help you find my talisman, and then you could free me. Who would care about a small fire then? We could change the world, Moon. No more war. No more killing. We could do that together, you and I.

Moon didn't know what to say to that. She could hear Kinkajou, Qibli, and Winter all thinking about her, and Darkstalker was right. It would be safer to get out of here. But she didn't want to leave them. She didn't want to lose them from her life if there was any chance of keeping them.

She folded in her wings and ducked into her sleeping cave.

Kinkajou was curled in her hammock with her eyes closed.

Moon slid over to her nest, trying not to look at Carnelian's ledge. It felt empty in here without her fuming and muttering in the background.

"All right," Kinkajou said suddenly, without opening her eyes. "I know this is silly. Of course you know perfectly well that I'm awake and pretending to be asleep. But can you do me a favor and pretend you believe it, please?"

"I will," Moon agreed.

She lay down and wrapped her tail close around her. She wished there were a way to shut out Kinkajou's thoughts, which were bouncing and tumbling all over the place like monkeys that had eaten the wrong berries: *I wouldn't have lied to her like that. I can't believe Carnelian's dead. What would it be like to hear what everyone is thinking? Who would*

I want to listen to? Maybe Winter, he seems very mysterious, but I guess he isn't to Moon. I hope Tamarin is all right. I wish they'd let me see her. Maybe I can sneak out and see her tonight. Is Moon listening to all this? Does she know anyone else who can read minds? Would she tell us if we asked? What if all the NightWings have these powers? But Bigtail obviously didn't, or he wouldn't have gotten blown up. Is she asleep yet? I wonder if I should tell someone about her. Maybe Glory. Glory would know what to do.

You could always kill her, Darkstalker suggested. **I'm kidding! Ha ha, evil nightmare dragon, right?**

That's not funny, Moon said.

Too soon? he asked. **All right, I'll wait another two thousand years to make jokes about my evilness.**

Moon tried to focus on the dreams of the dragons along the corridor. Pike was dreaming about swimming with whales, except he kept seeing Tamarin's burnt face on all of them. Someone else's dreams were of a battle, grappling with dragons in a blue sky with a waterfall down below. Others were deeper, in a sleep without dreams, and Winter was just sliding into sleep. From the jittery, speeding feeling of Qibli's brain, Moon guessed he wouldn't be able to sleep tonight.

She didn't think she'd be able to either, but as the hours passed she felt her wings getting heavier, and her eyelids kept trying to close. *Need to stay awake. I have to catch Scarlet if she comes with the dreamvisitor.*

More dragons were asleep now, close to midnight, and it

was harder to tell whose dream was whose as muddled images overlapped and swam together.

Moon wasn't sure if she was dreaming herself when she finally heard the slithery voice from two nights ago.

Is it done?

No. It was . . . an eventful day. We've had a few deaths, but not the ones you want.

I am not a patient dragon. Your time is running out.

Oh my, do you have a scroll for those? Ominous Clichés for Aspiring Villains?

I wouldn't recommend mocking me. It hasn't ended well for anyone.

You sound pretty menacing for a dragon who has to make others do her killing for her.

Tomorrow, said the slithery voice. *Just one of them, think you can manage that? Kill one of them by the end of tomorrow . . . or you know what will happen.*

I'll do it, came the response. *Don't worry, they'll be dead soon. And if you touch him, I'll kill you, too.*

A rumbling laugh. *Good luck.*

The connection was severed, tossing Moon away and into her own dreams, which echoed with deadly dragons, falling mountains, and clouds of fire for the rest of the night.

PART THREE

THE DARKNESS OF DRAGONS

—— CHAPTER 18 ——

Kinkajou was gone when Moon woke up. Moon could hear her distantly, in the infirmary, watching over a sleeping Tamarin.

She tried to stretch her wings and flinched at the pain in her shoulder. Her head, too, still throbbed from hitting the cave wall. Everything seemed to hurt more than it had the day before.

I couldn't tell who that was last night, she thought. *Darkstalker? Your power is so much stronger than mine. Could you see who was talking to Scarlet? Was that Scarlet?*

He was quiet for so long she wondered if he was asleep, or if that was even a thing he did.

I know some things, he said at last. *But everything I could tell you leads to futures that end badly, for you and for me. For instance, I can see clearly that if I tell you right now who has been speaking with the fallen SkyWing queen, you will seek out that dragon, and you will end up dead. Which would be unfortunate, both because I quite like you, and because then I might have to wait another thousand years to be rescued.*

Moon was shaken. She straightened the leaves around her bed, noticing the way her talons trembled. *You can really see a future where I die today?*

Quite clearly. Also a few where you die tomorrow. Actually the next couple of months are quite perilous for you altogether.

She stared at the moss of her bed, wondering if there was enough to bury herself in it and never come out. *You're not exactly helping with my afraid-of-everything problem*, she pointed out.

I think you're braver than you think you are. But maybe that's a future version of you. One that may never exist, if we're not careful.

But I have to find out who set the fire, she thought. *I have to tell Winter something by midnight tonight.*

Believe me, I will do my best to keep you alive, Moonwatcher.

She remembered Sora's calming ritual and tried to imitate it. Mud didn't feel soothing to her, so she thought of the rainforest, and imagined that her bones were as strong as the giant mahogany trees. She imagined that her wings were as vast and wide as the treetop canopy, and she imagined all the creatures of the rainforest — sloths, lizards, frogs, dragonflies, jaguars, tapirs, toucans, monkeys — all responding to her talons, spreading out through the trees and then galloping back to her with news, like the scurrying thoughts of the dragons all around her.

She folded her wings, made a determined face, and headed for the door, where she collided with Qibli coming in.

"Don't say anything," he said quickly as she stumbled back. He spoke fast, as if hoping his spoken words would drown out his thoughts, but those were only a mirror of his speech, as though he'd practiced what he was going to say a few times over. "Not yet, give me a chance. Listen, I'm sorry about anything you've heard in my head. I wish I could shut it off or that I was a nicer dragon on the inside, but I guess it's too late and you already know how I am. I don't know what it's like for you — I would think confusing — but at least you must know I'm not the one who caused the explosion yesterday. And I think that's the most important thing, and you're the dragon who has the best chance of figuring it out, so I'm here to help you, is what I wanted to say."

He took a deep breath, and now she could hear the struggle he was going through: Run away from her, or stay? Find a way to be friends, or warn the world about her? Trust her . . . or not?

"Why do you think I can figure it out?" she asked, although she could guess.

"Isn't that what your powers are for?" he said. "If I could read minds and see the future, that's what I would do — stop bad dragons before they hurt anyone — or, in this case, hurt anyone else, I suppose. Why else would you be able to do what you can do? Don't you think that's why you have them?"

Moon had never thought of her powers quite that way.

All she'd ever heard from her mother was that they were a curse, a dangerous condition, and she should hide them. Or, according to Darkstalker, they were a gift that destined her for power and made her better than other dragons.

But they were something entirely new in Qibli's shimmering mind: a tool she could use to help and protect other dragons. *If* she used them wisely.

This was a kind of test, she realized, although he didn't consciously know that. If she helped catch the dragon who killed Carnelian and Bigtail, Qibli would be able to believe her powers could be used for good. He'd be able to believe that *she* was good.

"Of course," she said. "Yes. I was thinking the same thing — I want to help. But I don't know where to start."

"How does it work?" he asked. "Can you just dig around in a dragon's brain and find out anything you want?"

She shook her head. "It's more like walking into a room and hearing a conversation; I think I pick up whatever is going through a dragon's brain when I'm near them. Sometimes it's clear, linear thoughts, and sometimes it's a jumble of words, and sometimes it's pictures, and I get a lot of emotions, too. Sometimes it's so strong that it's hard to tell what I'm feeling myself. And it's always louder and stronger when I'm touching someone." She reached out unconsciously to demonstrate, and he shied away from her.

She dropped her talons. "Sorry, I didn't mean to —"

"It's all right, sorry," he said, shifting guiltily at the hurt look on her face. "I have to get used to this."

"I know."

"So the bad guy would have to be thinking about what he's done in order for you to catch him," Qibli said. "But they must be, right? After killing two dragons, wouldn't that be all you could think about?"

Moon rearranged the scrolls in the rack by the door, scanning the thoughts along the hall. "Apparently not. I haven't heard anything clear like that yet." She hesitated. "But there are a couple of dragons here whose thoughts I can't hear, and I don't know why. Onyx. Peril — sometimes a thought gets through, but it's all fire in there. And . . . Turtle."

"Turtle?" Qibli echoed. "He can shield his thoughts from you?" *That's hardly fair. How did he figure out how to do that? He doesn't seem clever enough for* — Qibli cut his own thoughts off. "If you heard that, don't listen to it. I like Turtle. I don't mean to be mean. He can't be the one who did this, right? Peril, maybe. Onyx . . . I don't know anything about her. I don't think she was in the Scorpion Den, or I'd at least have heard of her."

"I'm not sure it's one of them," she said. "But if it is, I wouldn't be able to hear them, that's all."

He nodded. "All right. See if anyone else thinks anything suspicious at the assembly, and if not, we'll focus on those three."

"Assembly?" she said.

Qibli stepped into the hallway and lifted a small message off the wall. In subdued letters, it read: GATHER IN THE GREAT HALL AT THE BELLS.

"Poor Sunny," he said, rubbing chalk dust off the edges of the tablet. "She must be so upset."

"She is," Moon said.

Three gongs echoed through the tunnels. Dragonets began to emerge from their caves in silence, a flowing mass of scales and wings all heading in the same direction. Qibli studied the ones going past, momentarily forgetting to worry about Moon reading his mind.

Who did it? The answer is in the motive; that's what Thorn would say. So why? The Outclaws never used anything like bombs, because Thorn didn't want collateral damage. Targeted killing if necessary, open challenges if possible. A picture of his mother flashed through his mind, but Moon didn't catch why; she was sure from his earlier memories that his mother was still alive. *Blowing up innocent dragons while you're far away — it's a coward's choice. Were they trying to kill someone in particular, or as many dragons as possible?*

And did they succeed? Trying to kill Tamarin makes no sense; she must have been an accident. But Carnelian and Bigtail — they were fairly unfriendly dragons. They could have made enemies quickly. Or . . . one enemy.

He turned to Moon with his tail raised, an expression like lightning striking on his face.

"Pike?" she said. "I didn't think of that."

Qibli's eyes widened.

"I'm sorry," Moon said immediately. "I'm really sorry, I couldn't help hearing it."

"It's fine," he said, shifting uncomfortably. "I suppose it makes for faster conversations. Pike fought with both Carnelian and Bigtail before the explosion. I can't think of anyone else who might want *both* of those dragons dead."

"But do you think it could have been that specific?" she asked. "How could anyone know who'd be in there when the cactus exploded?"

"Cactus?" he said.

Two gongs sounded. They started toward the Great Hall, staying well behind the other dragons so no one could overhear them. Keeping her voice low, Moon explained about the dragonflame cactus and the seed pods, watching his brain spiral out into all the possibilities that meant. She also told him about Queen Scarlet and the dreamvisitor conversations.

"Oh," she said, stopping suddenly in the tunnel. "I wasn't supposed to tell anyone about the cactus! I totally forgot! Sunny asked us to keep it a secret."

"But you had to tell me," he reassured her. "I need all the clues if we're going to figure this out together. Don't feel bad; I won't tell anyone else." He shrugged. "And I bet you can see in my brain that I'm telling the truth."

He was, and he was also trying to be funny to hide how

freaked out he was, and then feeling stupid for trying to hide anything from her.

"So you think it was probably a SkyWing," he said, "or at least someone working for Scarlet. And perhaps they were just trying to disrupt the school and didn't care who they killed. That makes sense. But it is possible they were after someone in particular . . . and we all heard Pike threaten Bigtail in the prey center."

"That's true," said Moon. "He's really angry on the inside."

"How surprising. He's so mellow on the outside," Qibli said wryly.

"I think he nearly died in the Summer Palace attack," Moon said, then stopped with a gasp. "Oh — so he must know about the dragonflame bombs, too!"

The last gong sounded, and they had to hurry; even so, they were the last ones to enter the Great Hall. The other dragons of Jade Mountain were all gathered, with the five teachers and Fatespeaker on a raised ledge facing them. Moon could feel their surging emotions clearly, but she thought she could have read them just as well by the looks on their faces, the way Qibli was doing.

Sunny: devastated. Tsunami: furious. Clay: grieving. Starflight: anxious, and trying desperately to puzzle out what had happened. Fatespeaker: scared for Starflight, and a little unsure about whether this school was worth it. And Webs, who was mostly relieved that he'd been late to class and had therefore survived.

The students, on the other talon, were a mess of jumbled mental energy. Moon stumbled as she approached the crowd; it felt like stepping into a hurricane. It was worse than the fear set off by Peril's arrival. This was an avalanche of terror, everyone convinced they'd be the next to die. Moon thought she'd been scared before; now she felt as though her claws were melted to the ground, all her nerves screaming, "Run!" while her frozen body disobeyed.

Qibli must have seen something in her face. He stepped closer, until she could feel the warmth of his scales, and whispered, "Remember you're feeling everyone else's fear; it's not all yours."

Find an anchor, Darkstalker reminded her. ***Don't let yourself be overwhelmed.***

Easy for you to say, Moon shot back. But she reached out and latched on to Tsunami's thoughts. The SeaWing was loud and angry, but at least she wasn't petrified.

"Hi, everyone," Sunny said somberly. "I know you're all worried about the awful fire that happened yesterday. The first thing we want you to know is that the school is not closing, at least, not right now, *but* we understand if you want to leave. There are dragons on their way here now who can escort you safely home." Her mind flashed quickly past Glory, Deathbringer, a six-clawed SandWing, and a big MudWing who looked like Clay.

"We understand if you want to go, but we're hoping you'll choose to stay," Clay added. "We'd ask you all to give us two days before you decide. Give us two days to find out what happened and who did this. If we can't — if we think it's too dangerous to stay here — we'll consider shutting down the school."

Moon was surprised to realize how sad that made her. Three days ago, she would have been thrilled if the school was closed and she could go home with no guilt. Now, even with all the trouble with her friends, she wanted to stay. She wanted the school to go on, and she didn't want to give up.

Moon. Startled, Moon looked around and found Qibli staring intently at her. He tipped his head. *See if you can edge this way. Pike's over here.*

Only half listening to Clay's speech, she sidled through the crowd until she was directly behind the SeaWing. Carefully she disengaged from Tsunami's mind and opened up to the swarm of thoughts around her.

Maybe I should go home. But is it any safer there?

It must have been someone in this cave. It could be the dragon right next to me. She does look kind of smug. That worm; I should bite her.

I heard the whole cave exploded and then collapsed. Maybe the whole mountain will collapse next. I knew it was stupid to live somewhere with rock over your head all the time.

What would Queen Glory do? She'd know how to protect us. At least the princess was nowhere near the fire.

There, that was Pike. She narrowed her focus onto him.

He had a confusing mind. His thoughts rampaged around like wild rhinoceroses; half of them began and then trailed off as he jumped to another. *If Anemone had been hurt — maybe Queen Coral is right — can't protect her if I'm dead — dare to kill me, I'll rip off their — that poor little RainWing — I miss the Deep Palace, nothing catches on fire there — wish I'd had a chance to fight that NightWing — would've given him a tail whack he'd never forget — never even got to fill his bed with slugs — so pointless, having dead enemies, nobody to yell at — there's Anemone; that IceWing is standing too close to her; maybe I'll go bite him — wonder which of these idiots set the fire — that'd give me someone to snarl at —*

Moon pivoted to meet Qibli's eyes and shook her head. Pike was an odd, bad-tempered dragon — and might be secretly protecting Anemone for Queen Coral — but he wasn't their killer.

Frowning, Qibli scanned the crowd, choosing and discarding suspects at lightning speed. He crossed off all the RainWings right away, which Moon agreed with; none of them ever had an aggressive thought, as far as she'd seen. He paused on Umber and thought, *Too loyal to Clay*, then Marsh: *Too nervous*. Moon agreed with that as well; from the frantic terror spiking out of Marsh's head, she rather thought he belonged in the infirmary, too, tranquilized in the bed next to Sora's.

Winter and Icicle? he wondered, studying the two haughty IceWings, who stood a few paces away from the rest of the crowd, with the other four IceWing students forming a sort of barricade between them and everyone else. *Not Winter,* he mused. *He was with me or near me most of the day, especially right before class. But maybe Icicle?*

Moon knew she wouldn't be able to get very close, but she edged toward the IceWings anyway. Winter stretched his wings and twisted his neck to search the crowd — for her, Moon realized, ducking out of sight behind a large MudWing. *Midnight tonight,* she thought. *Either I figure out who did it by then . . . or I come up with a really great lie . . . or he exposes me to everyone.*

All of the IceWings had sharp, glittering minds, and clumped together like they were, it was even harder to distinguish Icicle's thoughts and read them clearly. They seemed to bounce off the others and be reflected several times over. But after a minute of concentrating, Moon found herself balanced on the sword's edge that was Icicle's brain.

By the teeth of the Great Ice Dragon, this is boring as sand, Icicle grumbled internally. *I shall certainly tell Mother and Father and Aunt Glacier what a waste of time this entire school is. What have I learned so far? Even dragons who have been to war can be pitiful emotional wrecks. IceWings are superior to every other tribe — of course we knew that already. And don't set any dragons on fire, or else a bunch of sentimental soft-talons will cry and moralize and lecture you about it end-lessly afterward. YAWN.*

Moon tipped her head. Was that an admission of guilt? It was hard to tell.

I should also tell her this place has done something fright-ful to Winter. Clearly he's too weak to associate with dragons from other tribes — he's talking like he might almost find them interesting. I wonder if I should tell him about Hailstorm. He wouldn't try to stop me, I don't think, but it would be too tire-some if he did.

Moon wished she could circle back and hear that again. Who was Hailstorm?

Icicle made an impatient movement, and Winter shot her a warning glance. His sister rolled her eyes. *Why are they STILL GOING ON ABOUT THIS? Two dragons died, so what? I've killed nine times that in almost every battle I've been in. We don't need to HEAR about it ENDLESSLY. They should just find the dragon who did it and give them a slow, horrible death. Perhaps by making them listen to Starflight talk for the next hundred years.*

Up on the dais, Starflight was earnestly trying to explain something about psychological trauma. Moon slid quietly away from the MudWing's shadow and searched until she found Qibli's eyes on her, then shook her head. It didn't sound as though Icicle had done it either, although she had a deeply cold, unpleasant mind.

Qibli beckoned surreptitiously, flicking one of his wings at the far wall. Moon followed his gaze to Flame, who was brooding in a shadow by one of the torches.

He is a SkyWing, Qibli thought, and looked at Moon. *Perhaps?*

She lifted her wings in a "maybe" gesture and started working her way over to the scarred dragon. Tsunami was speaking now, explaining that they would catch the culprit and asking for anyone with information to come forward.

Moon could just imagine that conversation: "Hello, I have information about the bomb, which I gathered by listening in on my classmates' thoughts and dreams. That's OK, right? I didn't see 'no telepathic spying on your friends' in the student handbook. . . ."

Although she was trying to move subtly, one step every thirty seconds or so, Flame swung his head around to glare at her when she was still several paces away. She froze in place and kept her eyes on Tsunami, checking his mind. Did he know she was deliberately getting closer to him?

If he did, she couldn't tell. It seemed as if he was just projecting hostility at everyone indiscriminately, and she'd wandered across his field of hatred.

Darkness filled his head like a torrent of inky bile. She found herself glancing down at her talons, half expecting to see black stains left there from even brushing the surface of Flame's thoughts.

But will this convince her to come get me no of course not she'd rather leave me with fools and killers than take care of me herself even after what the NightWings did to me even after what Viper did to me even after what the Talons of Peace did to me she's the one who's supposed to care about me but she doesn't no one does will she even worry about me when she hears probably not she hates my face as much as I hate my face I wish I could rip off every SandWing's venom barb and then use them to stab all the NightWings in their smug snouts —

Moon's stomach hurt as though she'd eaten a tree full of rotting fruit. Flame's fury sucked her in and trapped her like a beetle in slime; she couldn't climb out, and she couldn't get clean, and she felt as if all the light was being slurped right out of her.

He could be the one. His mind went right past Carnelian and Bigtail — *stupid half-baked, or all-baked ha ha, idiot dragons they're lucky they're dead or else they'd be shambling scarred monsters like me* — without a flicker of pity, sadness, or remorse. His loathing was so unrelenting that he barely seemed to have room to think about the fire itself, either that he'd set it or not.

Moon forced herself to turn toward Qibli, but he was studying the other dragonets again and didn't notice her anguished expression.

And then, wound into the tangled gloom in Flame's head, she heard: *I wish I'd done it everyone would take me seriously then but I wouldn't hide it I'd roar it to the world —*

So it wasn't him. And she needed to get out of his brain, before she drowned here.

Help me, she whispered.

See his thoughts as a boulder, not a wall or a river, Darkstalker said, instantly there when she called. *Believe they are movable first, wrap them into a ball shape, and then imagine a slope below them, and push them away downhill.*

Moon tried, dragging the sticky dark webs off her mind and rolling them up. But as she pushed against them, out of the corner of her eye she saw Flame's head shoot up.

Who's there? he demanded. *WHO'S THERE?*

And with a ferocious blast of fury, she was thrown forcibly out of his mind.

— CHAPTER 19 —

Don't react, Darkstalker cautioned. Moon kept herself still, although she felt as if she had been kicked in the face and she wanted to bolt out of the hall as fast as she could. Flame was glaring about even more viciously now, eyeing all the NightWings with particular suspicion.

How did he know? she cried frantically to Darkstalker. *I've never seen anyone do that. How could he notice that I was there?*

I don't think he knew exactly what was happening, Darkstalker said. **I don't want to risk probing deeper while he's on the defensive like that. But I suspect he just felt . . . a presence, let's say. He can't be sure it was a mind reader. Especially if you stay calm.**

Moon wasn't quite sure how to accomplish that; no one in this entire cave was calm.

But to her relief, a moment later, Sunny announced, "That's all we had to say. Please come see us if you feel like you want to leave, or if you have any questions. There are no classes today, but we're all here to take groups out hunting or swimming or flying, and the art and music caves are both open. We'll let you know what we decide about tomorrow."

She turned to Clay, and the students became a milling mob of whispers and flashing teeth. Moon was able to slip away from Flame and find Qibli.

"Are you all right?" he asked immediately, ducking his head to study her face. He steered her into a corner, carefully not touching her, and spread his wings to shield her from the other dragons. It didn't stop the stampede of worries, rumors, and complaints from trampling through her head, though. She couldn't focus, couldn't block anything out; she was too shaken by Flame's attack.

Qibli's own mind was already speeding forward. *I wonder if reading minds is tiring. Is it an infinite resource, or is it a power that drains as she uses it? Or is it more like a muscle that gets stronger the more she exercises it? Sure wish I'd had a skill like that when I was living at home; could have dodged a few more attacks from Sirocco and Rattlesnake. Maybe could have figured out how to make Mum like me. Moon looks like she's been slammed into a mountain.* "You look . . . tired," he said diplomatically.

"I just had a weird experience in Flame's head," she said in a low voice. "It's horrible in there."

"So he did it?" Qibli asked. His tail flicked up into a stabbing position and his brain went, *Did he bring the cactus from the Sky Kingdom or find it somewhere near Jade Mountain and how long has he been planning this and how did Scarlet choose him and —*

"No, no, stop," Moon said. "I don't think it was him. I don't think it was any of them. Pike, Icicle, Flame — they were all thinking about the fire like someone else did it."

"Camel farts," Qibli cursed. "They all seemed like perfect suspects."

"Yes," Moon agreed. "They may all still do something terrible, just not this particular thing."

He squinted at her. "Was that a prophecy? Did you have visions of them?"

She shook her head. "Just guessing."

Qibli swiveled his head around to watch Icicle parading out of the hall with the other IceWings trailing behind her. "If you know that . . ." he said thoughtfully. "If you had a list of the dragons with the darkest thoughts, you could keep track of them. You could check their minds every day and catch them if they're planning something. You'd know who to keep an eye on." *Like Thorn's potential enemies list, but even more targeted, with more inside information,* he mused.

"That, um," Moon started, then hesitated. She didn't want to argue with him, when he was starting to see her power in a positive light. But — "That seems kind of wrong, doesn't it?" she admitted. "I mean, judging dragons by their dark thoughts, and using that to justify spying on them? Lots of dragons think dark things sometimes; it doesn't mean they'll ever actually do them. Almost half the

NightWings in the rainforest had an occasional fantasy about killing Glory and stealing the throne, but most of the time they're just grateful to be alive and fed. I don't know, I guess I don't like to think of myself as sneaking around in dragons' heads. I can't help what I hear, but it doesn't seem fair to do it on purpose. I mean, unless we're catching a murderer, like now."

"Hmmm," he said, but before his thoughts could swoop off on that tangent, he shook his head and stepped back. "Let's go find Onyx. She seems like the best suspect we have left."

"But I won't be able to hear her thoughts," Moon said. "How will we learn anything from her?"

He grinned. "The old-fashioned way. With our eyes and ears."

That sounded alarming and inefficient to Moon, but she followed him warily to the cave opening, where most of the dragonets had gone. Everyone seemed to want to be out in the light. It felt sort of inappropriate how gorgeous and sunny it was outside, an early morning full of whistling birdsong and humming bumblebees among the purple mountain flowers.

Moon noticed that most of the dragonets were staying in clumps with others from their own tribes. Flame had slithered back into the mountain, but the other three SkyWings took to the air together, beating their huge wings and soaring as high as they could. She saw Coconut and two subdued

RainWings find a large swathe of sunlit grass and lie down, spreading their wings. Umber and Marsh had gone to check on Sora, but the other two MudWings were tramping down the mountain together, looking for a cool, muddy spot.

She wondered where all the NightWings had disappeared to so quickly. They wouldn't want her with them anyway — but did they have a secret place in the mountain where they all went together, somewhere she didn't know about?

"So much for our winglets," Qibli said.

"It's only been a couple of days," Moon said. It was true — she felt as though she'd been here for months, but really she'd stood right here with her mother barely four days ago. "Maybe the winglets will stick together more once we all know each other better."

Anemone pushed past them, leading Turtle, Pike, and the other SeaWings. She cast an arch look around at the other dragonets.

I could find out who did it in two shakes of my tail, she thought indignantly. *But Tsunami won't let me. Shouldn't use my powers! When it's something important like this?* She shook out her wings and tossed her head. *Maybe she'll change her mind by the time we get back.*

"Are you sure this is safe?" Pike asked her. "Going to the lake? You could be attacked —"

"Not with all of you strapping dragons along to defend me," Anemone said, shooting him a smile. *Ha,* she thought to herself. *I'm more dangerous than any of you, if I have to be.*

Her mind flashed to an image of her own claws holding a spear, then a dragon disappearing in a cloud of bubbles and slithering green shapes. She shuddered and forced her thoughts back to the mountain skies. "Come on, let's go."

Moon watched them soar away and wondered what Anemone was capable of.

Beside her, Qibli was thinking the same thing about Turtle. But he turned instead toward the clump of SandWings who had found a stretch of flat gray boulders and were baking their scales in the sun. Sprawled comfortably in the middle of them was Onyx, whose black forked tongue kept flicking in and out. Seeing her with all the others, it was clear how much older — and bigger — she was. She was no dragonet; Moon couldn't understand why she was here.

The littlest SandWing, Anemone's clawmate, saw Qibli and Moon approaching and her whole face lit up. Moon realized she was the one Qibli had been talking to on the first day.

"Qibli!" she cried. "Are you going home? I might go home. Do you think Father or Thorn would be mad if I went home?"

"They'd be happy to see you, Ostrich," Qibli said with extra gentleness in his voice. "They want you to feel safe. But I promised to protect you, and I will, so remember you are safe here, too. It's up to you."

"I do feel better now that you're here," she said. He reached one of his wings around her, and she leaned into his shoulder.

"Why've you got a NightWing stuck to your tail?" one of the other SandWings asked. The question didn't sound friendly, but his mind was more curious than hostile. The primary impression Moon got from all of them was that if Qibli decided to do something, it was probably a good idea. They all had him closely linked to Queen Thorn in their minds, and even the two that hadn't been Outclaws before were deeply respectful of her and anyone associated with her.

"She's in my winglet," Qibli said, as if that made this normal. "Everyone, this is Moon."

They all nodded, even Onyx, and Ostrich said, "I like the silver scales by your eyes. They're not diamonds, are they? I wish I had some treasure, or scales that looked like treasure. They're pretty."

Moon managed a smile, wishing she could pull ferns over her head and hide from all their dark stares. But after a minute, the SandWings mostly stopped thinking about her. Their thoughts were all *What's going to happen to me?* and *What's everyone else going to do?* and *If I leave, will the others think I'm a coward? If I stay, will they think I'm an idiot?* Moon curled herself as small as she could on one of the boulders, feeling the heat from the SandWings' scales in addition to the sun.

"Will you go back to the stronghold, Qibli?" one of them asked.

"No," he said. "Thorn sent me here to learn, and I know she'd want me to stay."

Just a few words, and instantly the others were all think-ing, *Yes, stay, I should stay, he's right, Thorn would want that.* Moon wished she could have even a quarter of that effect on other dragons.

"What about you, Onyx?" Qibli asked her. "Where would you be going back to, if you left?"

She narrowed her black eyes at him. That quiet fuzzy hum surrounded her, like what listening to fog would be like if it were turned into sound. Moon folded her front talons together, unsettled. What was going on in Onyx's head? How was she blocking Moon so completely?

And me, Darkstalker reminded her quietly.

"I didn't grow up in one of the big oases, if that's what you're asking," Onyx said. "It was just me and my mother, roaming the desert, and she's dead now. Which is why I applied to come here — I have nowhere else to go. But it doesn't matter, because I'm staying."

Just her and her mother? Moon thought. *Kind of like me. Except she had her mother all the time, not just in snatches here and there. She was never alone.*

"Did you fight in the war?" Qibli asked.

"Did you?" Onyx shot back.

"In a way," he said. "For Thorn and the Outclaws."

She flicked her tongue: out, in. "I chose not to choose a side. None of those dragons were fit to be queen."

The two non-Outclaw dragons both had unhappy rip-pling reactions to that comment: *Blaze wasn't so bad* and

Perhaps not a good queen, but Burn would have been a strong queen. Then both thought, *Thank the moons it's Thorn instead*.

"Wow," Qibli said. "I'm amazed you were able to avoid Burn's soldiers for so long — what are you, twenty years old? And without hiding in the Scorpion Den either; at least, I don't remember you being there."

"Nineteen," Onyx said. "And no, we stayed away from the Scorpion Den, too."

"Your mother wasn't a fan of other dragons?" Qibli joked lightly. He was trying to figure out whether to ask if they'd had help, perhaps from Queen Scarlet, but in a way that wouldn't make her even more suspicious. But he could tell that she was already displeased. Questions in general clearly weren't her favorite thing.

"That's right," Onyx said.

"Your diamonds are so cool," Ostrich said. "Did it hurt to get them set between your scales like that?"

Onyx blinked, and Moon saw that Ostrich was deliberately disarming her. The little SandWing was young, but smart, and although she wasn't sure what Qibli was fishing for, she instinctively knew how to help him get past the surly older dragon's defenses.

"Yes," Onyx said, stretching out one wing so the small black diamonds could catch the sun, winking and sparkling between her yellow scales. "But that is half the point. If I could endure that much pain just for a little beauty, imagine how much I could handle in a battle, or for my own survival. I think the most beautiful things should also be frightening."

Qibli shot Moon a look, but before he could say anything, Ostrich leaned forward and peered at Onyx's amulet.

"And what's that?" she asked, genuinely curious now. "Does it mean something?"

"Yes." Onyx wrapped her claws around the amulet, paused, and then flipped a catch to reveal that it opened up. Inside was a twisted hunk of black rock, bound to the amulet with copper wires. "This is a piece of the rock that killed my mother."

The other SandWings gasped, and Onyx smirked at their expressions.

"Oh, I didn't do it," she said. None of the other dragons had had that thought, but now they all did. "No," Onyx went on, "this rock just fell from the sky one night. It went straight through her head, leaving a burning hole behind, and over she went. That's when I thought, *Well, time to join the world*." She snapped the locket shut, making Ostrich jump. "Beautiful *and* frightening, don't you agree?"

"Can I see it?" Ostrich whispered.

Onyx turned the amulet between her claws for a moment, then lifted it off her neck. "Just for a moment," she said. "I think it came from the comet — you remember the one in the sky when the war ended? The false brightest night? It was up there when the rock fell. So I call it skyfire."

She dropped the amulet into Ostrich's talons.

And suddenly, out of the blue, there was a new voice in Moon's head.

That's right, admire me, fear me, wonder about me. You all have no idea who I am or what I'll be one day. One day soon. No more hiding, Mother. I make the decisions now.

At the same moment, Ostrich's thoughts vanished; the only thing Moon could hear from the little SandWing was that quiet, shimmering hum.

Moon stared at Onyx, then at the amulet, which lay open in Ostrich's talons. The black rock glittered at her like the dark heart of a faraway star.

That was it.

That was why she couldn't read Onyx.

It was the skyfire.

── CHAPTER 20 ──

Moon had no time to react before Darkstalker was there in her mind, louder and fiercer than he'd ever been before.

Do not tell anyone about this. You understand? A stone from the sky that can block a mind reader's powers? If other dragons find out, we'll be ruined. Everyone will get one, and then we'll be deaf, Moon, do you understand? If this gets out, it'll be like ripping our claws off. Promise me you won't tell anyone.

We wouldn't be deaf, she thought back. *We'd be no worse off than all the normal dragons out there.*

If you could give up this gift so easily, then you shouldn't be allowed to have it.

Moon was flustered by his intensity. *Shush for a minute, will you? This is my one chance to hear what Onyx is thinking.*

Darkstalker subsided, muttering. Ostrich was still holding the amulet, all her thoughts fuzzed out as she gently poked the rock inside. If they wanted to find out whether Onyx had set the bomb, they had to make her think about it right now.

Of course, Qibli had no way of knowing that. He was busy contemplating Onyx's dragonethood with her mother and trying to figure out why she was here. He didn't even look up when Moon subtly tried to catch his attention. She'd have to do this herself.

"Um," Moon blurted. "What do — who do — have you, uh —"

The SandWings all swiveled their heads to stare at her.

What is she trying to say?

Weird crazy NightWing.

I heard that she can barely form sentences; guess that's true.

She tried not to listen; she tried not to think about running away. And then the right question came to her.

"How's Tamarin?" she managed at last. "Have — have — have you been to see her?"

"Oh, my poor little clawmate," Onyx said with a sigh. At the same time, her mind went: *I don't see why I have to care about dragons from other tribes, but it seems to be expected, for some reason. At least Tamarin was a quiet, agreeable dragon to share a cave with; she didn't snore like Mother or tell weepy stories and expect me to care — like Mother. Uch, I hope they don't give me another clawmate. Perhaps if I act totally shattered, they'll let me keep the cave all to myself.* "It's absolutely devastating," she said. "I'm just devastated."

She reached to take the amulet from Ostrich. *But I haven't heard anything useful yet!* Moon thought.

"Um," she said quickly. "Can I see it?"

Onyx looked as if she wanted to say no, but Ostrich was already passing the amulet into Moon's talons.

"D-do you, um . . ."

Moon froze in shock.

The world had gone silent. Not the outside world; her inner world. The constantly seething, twittering background noise of all the minds around her had abruptly vanished. It felt as though she'd just been plunged into the deepest trench in the sea.

Darkstalker? she called, staring down at the skyfire between her claws.

There was no answer. He was gone. Everyone was gone.

It was *worse* than going underwater; it was like being yanked from a three-dimensional world into a two-dimensional one. The dragons around her might as well have been pictures in a scroll, flat and empty and unknowable.

Terrified, Moon thrust the amulet into Qibli's talons and jumped back.

"Hey, careful with that," Onyx snapped.

Everyone's minds came rushing back at once, and Moon, who had always thought she wanted more silence, found herself unbelievably glad to hear them — even the ones who were thinking she was extremely peculiar.

MOON! Darkstalker was yelling. *MOON!*

I'm here, she said.

Three moons, you scared me, he said. *You vanished so completely. I thought you were dead.*

"What am I —" Qibli began, bewildered.

"It's really cool, look at it," Moon said. She wanted to close her eyes and settle into the noise around her; she needed a moment to calm down. But Onyx was full of irritable thoughts about her amulet and not thinking about the bomb at all. In a minute she would demand it back. Moon didn't have time to recover — she needed to get an answer right now.

"Onyx, do you think they'll catch the dragon who set the fire?" she asked her. Too direct, but the only thing she could do.

Does she suspect me? Onyx thought. *How odd.* "Of course," the SandWing said aloud. "They're the great 'dragonets of destiny' after all." *By all the serpents, I hope they do catch whoever did it so we can stop blithering about it. This a tiresome distraction from my plans. Perhaps I should go back to the desert and try another approach. Or . . .* She tipped her head and gave Qibli a speculative look. *They say this one is practically Thorn's third wing. If I —*

Her train of thought abruptly cut off as Onyx snatched the amulet out of Qibli's claws. "That's enough ogling," she said.

Moon wished she could hear what Onyx's mysterious plans were, and how they involved Qibli, but at least she knew one thing: Onyx was not the one who set the fire.

So who did?

She sat thoughtfully, staring at her talons, as Qibli chatted with the other SandWings and occasionally shot more probing questions at Onyx.

Pike, Icicle, Flame, Onyx . . . if it wasn't one of them, who could it be?

Had she misinterpreted one of the minds she'd read? Was it really one of them after all? Or who else could she be forgetting?

Are you sure you can't help me? she asked Darkstalker.

Seems like the same question I've been asking you, he said quietly.

She hooked her claws into a crevice in the rock and started digging out some embedded moss. *Does that mean you'll tell me who did it if I agree to free you?*

No, he said. **Because then you'll resent me and then you'll start thinking I'm manipulating you and then you won't trust me and then you'll decide you'll never free me.** He sighed. **You don't realize how badly I need you, Moon. It's harder than you can imagine, figuring out what I should say to you and trying to help without getting you killed.**

Moon felt guilty. She'd been focusing on the fire and her friends and all the problems that came with being a secret mind reader. And meanwhile the only dragon who accepted her completely this way was trapped in a stone prison, desperately clinging to the one hope he had: that she would take pity on him and find a way to set him free.

Tell me more about your talisman, she suggested.

A pause. **Really?** he asked.

Well. If I do decide to search for it, I need to know what it looks like, don't I?

He hesitated again.

Finally: *Can I trust you, Moon?*

She found a tiny green caterpillar inching through the crack in the boulder. Carefully she let it crawl onto her claw and then lifted it safely to the ground, away from the dragons. *You tell me,* she said to him. *You can see every single one of my thoughts. You must know more about me than any other dragon in the world. So . . . do you trust me?*

After another moment, Darkstalker suddenly barked a laugh that echoed in her skull. *I guess I don't have any choice, do I?*

You could wait for the next NightWing mind reader, she pointed out. *Now that they're living in the rainforest, having eggs under the moons again, there will probably be more, right?*

On the one talon, it was reassuring to think there would be others — she didn't have to bear *all* the responsibility of being Darkstalker's *only* hope forever. On the other talon, thinking about another mind reader making friends with Darkstalker and being the one to rescue him . . . it gave her a strange protective feeling that she couldn't even explain.

But on the third talon, maybe somebody else would have a better chance of figuring out how to rescue him. And then she wouldn't be blamed if it all went horribly wrong.

But then on the fourth talon, she liked the idea of being somebody's hero, doing something brave and dangerous and changing the world.

All right, all right, Darkstalker said. *I can't listen to you think in circles about it anymore. But Moon, this is the most important thing: You must never forget that my talisman is the most dangerous animus-touched object in all of Pyrrhia. If it fell into the wrong claws, it would be a disaster like you can't imagine. You need to promise me: If it looks even for a moment like someone else might take it — someone like Flame, for instance — you'll have to destroy it.*

Destroy it? Moon thought back. *But then you'd be trapped forever.*

Yes, probably. I can't bear to think about it. But even that would be better than the alternative: a weapon of that kind of power in dangerous talons. I'm very serious, do you understand?

I do, Moon thought. *I promise.*

All right, he said slowly. *It's a scroll.*

A picture came into her head of a scroll wrapped in a black leather casing. The casing opened and the scroll unrolled. A pen appeared, writing words that blazed for a moment like fire before sinking into the page and turning into dark purple ink.

As with all animus-touched objects, it can be used by any dragon who comes across it, Darkstalker said. *You simply write your command — for instance, "Give this necklace the power to make me invisible when I wear it." Or "Enchant this mirror to spy on whichever dragons I choose." You must be as*

*specific as possible, or the magic is liable to go awry and rein-
terpret your request in some odd way.*

Are you sure it still exists? Moon asked, studying the scroll
in her mind. It looked like it was made of thicker paper than
most scrolls, but still, scrolls could burn so easily. *If it's out
there somewhere, why hasn't anyone figured out its power and
used it in the last two thousand years? Or what if the NightWings
took it with them when they ran away and it was destroyed in
the volcano?*

I don't know, Darkstalker said in a half-choked voice. *If no
one knew what it was — and I carefully kept its power a secret
from everyone but Clearsight — then I don't think anyone
would guess how to use it. It's true, though, that I don't know
if it has survived all this time. But I have to believe that it has,
or else all hope for me is lost.*

Moon sighed, and Qibli looked across at her curiously.

Even if I do find it, she thought, *how could I possibly get it
to you? Neither of us know where you are. Maybe we should
figure that out first. Maybe it would be easier to dig you out
than to find one lost scroll in all of Pyrrhia — and then what,
stuff it through ten layers of rock?*

I suspect it's not a matter of a little digging, Darkstalker
said. *But there is a small hole near me, which must reach
through all the way to the open air, because every once in a
while I can smell a breeze, and sometimes, even more rarely, a
mouse or insect blunders into it and I get to eat.*

Moon hadn't even thought of that. *You're surviving on just the occasional clumsy mouse? How can you live without eating?*

My own foolish enchantment was designed to keep me alive through anything, he said ruefully. *Not starvation, nor cold, nor old age, nor stabbing or fire or frostbreath can kill me. I can still feel hungry, though. Extremely, enormously hungry. Turns out it is quite the curse I've put on myself.* He made a semiamused noise, as if trying to brush aside any self-pity.

And . . . there's no way to undo it? Moon asked. *I mean, whatever you enchanted to make you immortal — it's not, like, a necklace you can take off?*

You mean if I decide I want to die? Darkstalker thought for a moment. *No. It's not a necklace. I don't think I could undo this enchantment, not unless I had my talisman back. In any case, I have not quite reached that level of despair yet. I still — I would like to see the sun, at least once more, for instance.*

Moon looked up at the sun, shining brightly over the mountain landscape, and thought how easily she took it for granted. Over the mountains to the north she could see heavy gray storm clouds gathering, but on Jade Mountain it was still a beautiful day. Sort of an unfairly beautiful day, if you thought about Carnelian and Bigtail and Tamarin.

There is another option, Darkstalker said. *If you found my scroll, you could use its power to find me and free me yourself. You wouldn't need to bring it to me.*

Oh, Moon thought. It hadn't occurred to her to use it herself. Animus magic — it sounded so much more dangerous than her own little powers. *You mean, if I wrote something like, "Please enchant this map to show me Darkstalker's exact location"?*

He laughed. **Well, I must admit I never said "please" to my talisman, but you certainly could.**

The dragons around Moon all suddenly began to get up. She blinked at them, startled, and Qibli grinned.

"I suspected you were a million miles away," he said. "We're going to the prey center. A few dragons just came back with food, so we're hoping there'll be enough for everyone."

"I just need a lizard," Ostrich said. "I couldn't eat yesterday, after everything, so I'm hungry now, although I feel bad admitting that."

"Oh — here," Moon said. She'd been absently watching a fat brownish-green lizard for the last few minutes; it had been inching slowly out into the sun below the boulders, looking for insects to eat. With a quick stab, Moon impaled it on her claws, then presented it to Ostrich.

"Talons and tails," Ostrich said, regarding her with awe. "I didn't see that coming. You're really fast."

"True," Qibli said. "She's an amazing hunter. Got another one hidden somewhere for me?" Moon shook her head, although she knew he was kidding.

"You can have this one," Ostrich said immediately.

"No, thank you, you have it," he said. "I'd like to stop by the prey center anyway. Moon? Coming, too?"

She nodded. The other SandWings had already gone on ahead; Ostrich bounded after them. Moon and Qibli followed more slowly, and Moon said in a low voice, "It wasn't Onyx."

"Really?" he said. "How do you know?"

Don't tell him, Darkstalker warned.

She hesitated. "I just — do."

He frowned, and she felt all the progress of the last few hours spiraling backward. *She's lying to me again, I'm sure of it. But about what, and why? If she can hear Onyx after all, why not admit to that? Unless this is all a trick to make me suspect Turtle — she could be lying about everything, about all the others being innocent — she could be trying to steer me to someone for her own agenda — what do I really know about her, after all, and why would I think she'd want to help me find the dragon who killed Carnelian; perhaps she doesn't even care —*

"Stop, please stop," Moon said, futilely pressing her talons to her ears. "I'm not lying, and I *do* want to figure out who did this. Please trust me, Qibli."

He flicked his tail and took a step away from her. "I'm sorry," he said. "I'm not sure I can do that yet. It's too — You know what, let's split up for a while and try again later." Without waiting for her answer — and now worrying about what else she'd see in his head — he took to the sky, flying down to the prey center cave opening.

Moon's wings drooped. *I ruined it,* she said to Darkstalker. *He was almost willing to trust me again. I should have just told him the truth.*

You can't tell anyone about the skyfire. You must see that.

You may be back to being my only friend, she said. *Possibly forever.*

Well, if you're only going to have one, I'm not such a bad one to have, he joked. Or at least, she thought he was joking.

There were more dragons in the prey center than she'd expected; all the SeaWings were back, along with all the SkyWings, a few IceWings, and a couple of NightWings. It was easier now to use the raindrop trick, though; she slipped them all quickly into background pitter-pattering, and her oncoming headache faded away again.

Then she spotted Umber, Marsh, and Sora across the cave and felt her wings lift. For one thing, Sora must be feeling better if they'd let her come down here, and for another thing, Umber and Sora didn't completely hate her yet. They would probably let her sit with them to eat anyway, which would be better than trying to sit with that ferocious expression Mightyclaws was wearing.

As she moved toward the siblings, she caught a glimpse of Qibli watching her. He was wondering whether he should warn the MudWings about her mind reading, especially Umber.

So I'd better enjoy them now, she thought ruefully, *since they won't be my friends for much longer.*

"Hey," Umber said as she approached. Sora and Marsh both kind of flinched and nodded at the same time.

"Hi," Moon said softly. "Sora, how are you? Are you all right?"

Nothing is all right, nothing, she caught from Sora's brain. There were fragments of terror and memories of battles and fire jolting through the mud pool in Sora's mind, and she could tell Sora really would have preferred to be tranquilized again, but she'd forced herself to come down here. *Icicle*, Moon heard, and guessed that Sora wanted to prove herself to be tougher than her clawmate thought she was.

She slid the rest of Sora's restless thoughts into a raindrop, conscious of Qibli's eyes on her back and feeling like an intruder in Sora's fear. She did the same with Marsh and Umber, although Marsh was mostly surveying the cave and nervously wondering what to eat, while Umber was preoccupied with worrying about his brother and sister.

"She's doing better," Umber answered for Sora. "Clay said she even got up and went for a walk for a little while last night."

"Really?" Moon said, looking at her. *Why would she wander around the mountain in the middle of the night?* She wondered for a split second whether Sora could be the dragon who'd been scheming with Scarlet, but then she remembered the first night she'd heard the dreamvisitor conversation.

Sora had been one of the few dragons still awake at that hour; Moon definitely remembered noticing her mental mud ritual. She hadn't been asleep and dreaming, so she couldn't have been the one talking to Scarlet.

Sora glanced anxiously around the cave. Following her gaze, Moon saw Winter and Icicle stalking in from one of the tunnels. She felt like bolting, but she made herself stay put as Winter rapidly scanned the cave and spotted her. His eyes narrowed, and he thought, *Only half a day left, NightWing.*

She ducked her head. What was she going to tell him at midnight? She couldn't point to anyone as the culprit yet.

Icicle snatched a fish from the central pile and stormed toward her usual ledge. Winter picked up a fish, too, but hesitated. Moon could hear him debating whether to come over and talk to her.

Please don't, please don't, please don't, she prayed.

"Do you want to go talk to Icicle?" Umber asked Sora, who was still staring at her clawmate. "I'm sure she's been worried about you."

Sora didn't answer, but a flash of contemptuous disbelief broke through Moon's raindrops, so sharp and fierce that it took her a moment to realize it had come from the quiet MudWing.

She turned and saw Icicle climbing into the alcove. With a disdainful flick of her wings, Icicle turned to look down at the crowd. One of her wings lightly brushed the stalactites over her head.

There was a loud *crack*, then a splintering sound, and suddenly the sharpest, most wicked-looking stalactite broke off from the ceiling and plummeted down toward Icicle.

──── CHAPTER 21 ────

Moon shrieked, sure the rock spear would impale the IceWing through the head or neck. The raindrops all vanished in a scream of terror from everyone in the cave.

Then she'll be dead, dead, dead, sang one voice in the rising tumult in Moon's head.

But Icicle twisted out of the way at the last moment, and the stalactite shattered against the ground.

There was a frozen minute of shock.

Oh, that's interesting, Darkstalker mused. *In most of the futures I saw, that worked and she died. This changes . . . many things.*

Moon didn't have time to respond to that; the whole cave had erupted in chaos.

"Icicle!" Winter shouted. He spread his wings and sprang toward her, fighting past the dragons who were all stampeding the other way. Icicle was staring at the spot where it had fallen, her heart pounding. Even above everyone else, Moon could hear her fury and disbelief.

Who DARED attack me?

Still reeling, Moon turned and found that Umber, Marsh, and Sora had fled with most of the other dragons. A few moments later, no one was left in the prey center except the two IceWings, Qibli, Moon, and Clay, who had also rushed to Icicle's side.

"By all the moons," Clay cried. "How did that happen? Are you all right?"

"No!" Icicle roared, lashing her tail. "Someone tried to *kill me*!"

The niece of Queen Glacier! Qibli thought, and then reprimanded himself. *Not the time, Qibli.*

"What?" Clay looked up at the other stalactites in the alcove. "But — no — surely that was an accident. How — and who —"

"That was no accident," Winter said, pointing grimly at the spot where the fallen stalactite had hung. Claw marks were clearly visible in the rock, as if someone had scraped painstakingly through the spire until it had been barely suspended, ready to fall at the lightest touch.

"But *who* —" Clay said again, searching his brain. *She's unfriendly, but not bad enough to kill. . . .*

"I'll tell you what else," Icicle spat. "That bomb yesterday was probably meant for me, too. *I'm* the target. Someone was trying to kill *me*, and I'm going to find whoever it is and turn them into a glittering ice statue, which I will then beat to smithereens with my tail."

Icicle was the target all along? Qibli and Moon exchanged

looks. If she was right, what did that mean? Qibli's brain was rapidly organizing the students into possible categories of IceWing enemies — but Moon had an awful, awful sinking feeling that she already knew who this pointed to.

"You can't do that, and that's impossible anyway," Clay said again. "No one could have known who'd be in the cave when the cactus exploded. We think it was set to happen before class started — so there was no guarantee that you'd be in there then. If it was an assassination attempt against you, wouldn't they have made sure you were there?"

"I was supposed to be," Icicle hissed. "I'd planned to go early because I needed one of the scrolls. Just by luck, I decided to go by the underground lake first. Otherwise, I *would* have been in the history cave and I *would now be dead*."

"So who knew that?" Winter asked. "That would narrow it down. Did you tell anyone you were planning to go early?"

Icicle snapped her jaw shut and stared at him and Clay, her pale blue eyes glittering.

Only one dragon, she thought. *I only told one dragon that. So I know exactly who to kill.*

A freezing shiver rattled down Moon's spine.

Sora.

Moon turned and bolted out of the cave. *I have to find her first.*

She didn't know exactly what she was going to do, but she had very clearly seen what Icicle planned for her claw-mate, and Moon knew she couldn't let that happen.

Even though Sora killed Carnelian and Bigtail. Even though she could have killed any of us. Didn't she care? What about Umber? She must have delayed him. . . . She would never hurt him.

Sora, where are you?

Moon raced through the tunnels, checking the library first. Starflight was in there, alone. He lifted his head, startled, as she sprinted through, but she didn't stop. She didn't have time to explain or ask for help; she knew Icicle would be on Sora's trail any second.

In the Great Hall she stopped to catch her breath and reached out with her mind. The music cave? The underground lake? The art cave? What was Sora thinking about?

An image of Tamarin came through. Sora had gone back to the infirmary.

Moon whirled and dashed toward that corridor. At the mouth of the tunnel, she collided hard with a small brown dragon, and for a confused moment she thought she'd found Sora already.

"You're not safe —" she started to gasp, and then realized it wasn't Sora. It was Umber.

"I'm not? What?" he said.

"Sorry, not you, I have to —" She stepped around him.

"Wait," Umber said. "What's wrong?"

"Moon, you have to tell him." Moon turned and saw Qibli hurrying across the Great Hall. He'd seen her run; he knew that she'd figured it out, and one of the three guesses in his head was even right.

But if I tell Umber what his sister did, it'll destroy him, she thought. *If he even believes me.*

If Qibli hadn't been there, she would have kept running — she would have dealt with Sora herself. In his mind, though, she found a lightning-fast list of reasons to tell Umber that she would never have thought of herself. He wasn't consciously sending them to her, but they were all there on the surface as he struggled with what to do.

He may not understand, but he'll want to protect her. He can do that better than you can. You need someone to help you if you're planning to stand in Icicle's way. He needs to know the truth about her, the way you'd want to know if someone in your family did this. He's good and loyal; he's the only one who can help her. And if Sora is still dangerous, he may also be the only one who can stop her.

Moon met Qibli's eyes. He was right about all of that. "Umber," she said, "I'm sorry, I have to tell you something awful."

"Oh, no," Umber said. His face twisted and it was almost like his heart spoke rather than his mind. *Sora? Marsh? Clay?*

"We know who set the bomb yesterday," Qibli said.

"And she just tried to kill Icicle," Moon said.

Umber took a step back, shaking his head. "No. It's not true." But he saw the pieces falling into place and knew it was. *Pheasant thought this would be too much for her. But I thought she was stronger than this — I thought we were all better now.*

"It was Sora," Moon said gently. "And Icicle knows it, too. We have to get to her before Icicle finds her, or she's dead."

He didn't argue anymore. He didn't ask how they knew. He just turned and ran, and they followed.

Up the winding stone tunnel, their claws scraping against the rock, their wings pulled in, their tails hitting the walls as they ran.

Why? Why would she do this? Umber kept thinking, over and over in a jagged rhythm.

Moon didn't know. All the things she'd learned and all the thoughts she'd read, and she'd still missed it. Quiet Sora had taught herself to bury her thoughts so she couldn't even hear them herself. So many things scared her that the only way to deal with them was to push them under and stop them from entering her brain in the first place. Whatever she felt about Icicle, it was hidden under all the mud, buried deep along with her nightmares and memories of the war.

They burst into the healing cave. Sora was crouched by Tamarin's bedside, crying. Kinkajou was not there — *but she just left,* Moon realized. *Sora asked her to leave — so she could apologize to Tamarin.* The RainWing was still unconscious, wrapped in white bandages from wings to tail.

Sora looked up and saw it in their eyes. "I'm sorry,

Umber," she sobbed, collapsing forward. "I didn't mean for anyone else to get hurt."

"Oh, Sora," Umber said. He went over and put his wings around her. "Sora. Sora, I love you anyway. But why did you do it?"

She covered her face with her claws. "Don't you know who she is?" Her words came in gasps, between hiccups and sobs.

The flood of images from Sora's mind was inescapable. Moon felt them like a waterfall, pounding along her wings; a waterfall she could suddenly see, over an open plain with rivers running through it to the ocean. A battle was raging. Brown dragons and white dragons grappled in the air, shooting fire and frostbreath, roaring with fury and pain.

And there was Sora, darting through the melee. Her face was set grimly; behind her, Marsh was close on her tail, his features wracked with fear. A pair of IceWings lashed out at them with their serrated claws and Sora just managed to pull Marsh out of the way in time. They swooped around to try again.

"Reed!" Sora yelled. "Help us!"

A big MudWing dove toward them, swatting IceWings aside with his tail as he flew. But another MudWing got there first — a thin brown female that Moon had seen in Sora's mind before. She slashed one IceWing through the neck and then twisted to set the other IceWing on fire. He flapped away, shrieking and batting at the flames along his wings.

"Thank you, Crane," Marsh called.

Their sister turned to smile at Marsh and Sora. And then an IceWing plummeted out of the sky, out of nowhere, seized Crane in her talons, and slit her throat.

"No!" Sora screamed.

The IceWing turned to give her a malicious, triumphant grin.

It was Icicle.

The memory faded, but the destroyed feeling hung heavily in Moon's chest.

"She killed Crane," Sora sobbed into Umber's shoulder. "I saw her. I *saw* her. She's the one who killed our sister."

"Sora, how can you be sure?" he asked, pulling her close. "It was a terrible battle. There were a hundred IceWings there, and we were all fighting for our lives. Your memory could be playing tricks on you." *She could be finding the enemy of her nightmares in the first IceWing face she saw here,* he thought. *Or else, if she's right, we have the worst luck in the world. Ending up in the same cave as Crane's murderer? I would have lost my mind, too.*

Moon didn't think that was true. Umber's mind was a lot more resilient than Sora's. She could see that — and now she could also see that she was not as much like Sora as she'd thought. Perhaps they were both shy, but Sora was also fragile — too fragile for the awful things she'd been through.

I'm afraid there may be awful things ahead for you, too, little Moon, Darkstalker whispered.

But I'm not fragile, Moon said. *I won't* be *fragile. I refuse.*

I think you're right about that, he agreed.

"I'm sure it was her," Sora said. "I'm not crazy, Umber. I got a scroll to look up IceWing physiognomy; I made sure she'd been on the front lines. I couldn't ask more specific questions without making her suspicious. But I knew what she did, and I couldn't let her live."

"The war is over, Sora," Umber protested.

"This had nothing to do with the war," she said.

"But what about everyone else?" Qibli asked. "Didn't you care if the rest of us died?"

Sora couldn't meet his eyes. "I thought she'd be the only one in there. I've never used a dragonflame cactus before — I expected it to go off sooner. And she should have been in there. I can't believe I failed *twice*." She gave Tamarin an anguished look. "And then the other two dragons — and poor Tamarin — but it's just collateral damage, isn't it, Umber? We learned about that from the SkyWing generals."

He shook his head, unable to speak.

"And then everyone was looking at me," Sora whispered. "Everyone was thinking about me and how awful I am and how much they hate me. They could see right through me, I know they could."

"No, Sora," Moon said, "they weren't, truly. Dragons think mostly about themselves. Everyone is so worried about what other dragons think of them, they hardly stop to decide what they think of everyone else. Believe me, no one is thinking about you as much as you think they are." She'd finally realized how reassuring that was. All her self-doubt and nerves and feeling like an outsider — once she paid attention to what she could hear around her, it turned out those were the things that made her the most normal. It turned out that was how *everyone* felt. "And certainly no one is thinking about you as much as *you* are thinking about you."

"Except maybe Icicle," Qibli said abruptly. "Who is coming to kill you right now." Moon jumped; she'd almost forgotten about that. "We need to get you to Sunny and Tsunami so you can confess and they can keep you safe."

"We can't," Umber said. "I'm sorry, but if we do that, Sora ends up dead. Either Icicle will find a way to kill her, or Queen Ruby will demand an eye for an eye for Carnelian."

He's right, Darkstalker said. *Handing her over leads to very few paths where Sora is alive two months from now. But otherwise you're letting a killer go free.*

You hinted at this once, didn't you? Moon thought, remembering. *Send a friend to her death, or help a killer escape. You meant Sora.*

"We'll leave now," Umber said. "I'll go with her. I'll keep her safe." *And keep everyone else safe from her,* his mind finished the thought.

"But then you'll be a fugitive, too," Sora said. "And what about Marsh?"

"Clay will get him back to Reed and Pheasant," Umber said. He turned to Qibli. "Please tell Clay everything — tell him we're sorry — I know he'll understand. But if we involve him, the queens will shut down the school. We have to leave without saying good-bye." Umber blinked back tears.

Should we stop them? Qibli was thinking. *What's the right thing to do? What would Thorn do? Sora's not well and I don't want her to be killed — but she did kill Carnelian and Bigtail — and tried to kill Icicle. But she needs to be taken care of — and where does the cycle end? If Icicle kills Sora, wouldn't Umber or Marsh be justified in killing her? And then wouldn't Winter want to kill them? Isn't the whole point that the war is supposed to be over? Replacing it with a series of vengeance killings is not going to make the world any better or safer.*

And then Moon heard Icicle's thoughts, coming closer and closer.

She made up her mind. "Go," she said, stepping toward the window, a tall open hole big enough for a dragonet Sora's size to squeeze through. "As fast and as far as you can."

"Thank you," Sora whispered. She squeezed Umber's talons and darted toward the window. At the edge, she turned to look back at Moon. "It was self-defense, too. Beware of Icicle, Moon. She talks about killing all the time, even in her sleep."

"What does she say?" Moon asked.

"Our very first night here," Sora said, "when I still wasn't sure — I was almost sure it was her, but I thought I must be mad, and I couldn't let myself sleep because what if she did the same thing to me that she did to Crane? And then in her sleep, she muttered, 'Killing is easy enough.' That's when I knew. She's a murderer and she won't stop until someone does what I failed to do."

"Let's go, Sora," Umber said sadly.

Qibli stepped forward and twined his tail around Umber's for a moment. Moon felt Umber's longing and heartbreak and loyalty like a physical pain in her chest. He leaned forward to give Qibli a quick hug, and then Moon, and then he scrambled up after his sister.

A heartbeat later, they were gone, two small shapes winging away into the dark clouds.

Moon turned to Qibli, realization dawning.

"Icicle is the one conspiring with Queen Scarlet," she said.

Killing is easy enough. Moon had heard those exact words in the first dreamvisitor conversation.

She noticed that the violent blizzard of Icicle's mind had veered off; she wasn't thinking about just Sora anymore. She was thinking about the caves where Sunny, Clay, Tsunami, and Starflight lived.

"We have to hurry," Moon said. "She may not get to kill Sora — but that's not the only dragon she promised to kill today."

— CHAPTER 22 —

Moon and Qibli ran through the winding tunnels of Jade Mountain. Dragons jumped out of the way and stared at them as they shot past; Moon caught flashes of *What's happening?* and *Was there another fire?* and *Should I be running, too?* and *Oi, SandWing, watch it with that tail.* She thought she saw Winter looking out of one of the caves they passed but didn't slow down to check.

Moon, stop. You can't do this. I have to stop you, Darkstalker said. *This is not wise. It's not safe. I can't let you confront Icicle. There are so many ways in which it goes horribly wrong —*

Like she kills me? Moon asked. *Are there possibilities where she doesn't kill me?*

Ye-es, but they're faint — Moon, I can't lose you —

I can't sit by and do nothing, she answered back. *While Icicle kills somebody? Somebody who might change the future of this world? Look into those futures, Darkstalker. Without Sunny or Starflight, Clay or Tsunami, isn't the world a darker place? If this school fails, how soon are the tribes back at war?*

He was silent for a long moment. *I see your point. But the world without you in it is also much diminished, Moon.*

Really? She couldn't imagine that was true.

Let Qibli go stop her on his own, Darkstalker suggested.

Can he do that and survive? she asked. *Honestly?*

Hmmm, he said. *Maybe a one in three hundred chance.*

Not good enough, she said. *I need to be there.*

For him to survive? Darkstalker sighed. *Yes. You do.*

She tried not to be terrified by this reminder that she was running toward her own death; she tried to just focus on the distant echo of Icicle. Where was the IceWing going? The rage was clear enough, but her surroundings were not. Moon concentrated and heard *Not here . . . not here . . .*

"They're not in their sleeping quarters," she said between gasping breaths. "She has to look for them somewhere else."

"She could have killed Clay in the prey center," Qibli pointed out. "So why didn't she?"

"I think — I think she didn't want to do it in front of Winter," Moon said, stopping and pressing on her temples. "And Clay is the biggest. Maybe she wants to kill off the easiest ones first. Sunny?"

"Sunny's not that easy to kill," said Qibli.

"Starflight," they both said at the same time, and whirled to race to the library.

Icicle got there first.

Moon and Qibli burst in to find her silently creeping up on Starflight. Her lethally sharp claws were outstretched and her jaw was moving, calling up the deadly IceWing frostbreath. When she saw them, her eyes widened and flicked from them to Starflight and back. The blind NightWing was crouched in a corner, sorting scrolls by touching the stamps on the edges, but he raised his head in Moon's direction.

"Starflight, look out!" Qibli shouted.

Icicle leapt forward and landed on Starflight's back. He yelled with pain, and she wrenched him around so his body was between her and the others. Her talons wrapped around his throat and her wings pinned his to his sides.

"Don't do anything stupid," she hissed.

There's a window right behind her, Qibli thought. *If she realizes that, she could kill him and jump out before we could stop her. But right now she thinks she needs him as leverage so we'll let her go. We'll have to distract her so I can attack. Too dangerous this way; I might hit Starflight with my tail instead of her. Search for weaknesses. Get closer if I can.*

"Please don't kill him," Moon said, holding out her claws. "Just let him live and we won't stop you — you can leave, go wherever you want."

"I promise," Starflight said, his voice hoarse with fear. "You won't have done anything wrong, Icicle. You can still go home now, but if you kill me, Queen Glacier might not take you back."

Is he right? Icicle wondered. *She might appreciate a reason to get rid of me so I'm not a threat to her or her daughters. But if I succeed and Scarlet gives me what I've been promised, I'll return home a hero, no matter who I kill along the way.*

"You can't trust Queen Scarlet," Moon said. Icicle jerked her head around to stare at Moon. "Listen, please. Set him free, and I promise we won't tell anyone you were conspiring with her."

Icicle's wings flared. "How did you know that?" she snarled.

"Queen *Scarlet*?" said a voice behind them. "Icicle, what are you doing?"

It had been Winter they'd run past, and of course he had followed them. The dazzling confusion of his mind was brighter than ever. He couldn't even process what he was seeing — his sister, about to kill Starflight.

"Stay out of this," Icicle warned him. "Unless you'd like to be helpful, in which case, go find Sunny and kill her."

"What are you talking about?" Winter shouted. "Why would we do that?"

He's a weak fool, Icicle thought, cold and clear. "Mother always said you weren't as strong or smart as Hailstorm," she spat.

Winter flinched as if he'd been struck.

"I see you edging closer, SandWing," Icicle said, glaring at Qibli. He stopped moving. "Listen. I'll just take this librarian with me to make sure no one follows. I'll release him once I'm a safe distance away. That's the best deal you're going to get."

"She's lying," Moon said. "She'll kill him as soon as she gets a chance."

And Moon would know, Qibli thought.

Icicle shot a poisonous look at Moon. *Very well, Plan B,* the IceWing thought. *Multiple kills, escape in the chaos. That SandWing is just within range of my frostbreath, and then I slit Starflight's throat, break the little NightWing's neck, and go after Sunny and the others. Winter can stay and whimper over their bones if he wants to.*

She seemed to be focused on Moon, but her mind was waiting for Qibli to try sneaking forward again.

One step closer, SandWing. One . . . step . . . now —

"Qibli!" Moon yelled, leaping at him. She shoved him out of the way as a blast of freezing air shot out of Icicle's mouth.

Get down! Darkstalker roared in her brain.

Moon felt as if he'd slammed great talons into her back and thrown her to the ground. The frostbreath went over her head and caught just the edge of Moon's wing; she screamed at the sudden pain.

Everything happened at once, along with a deafening thunderclap of fury and adrenaline that surged into Moon from all the dragons in the room. Winter roared and charged toward them. Starflight jabbed Icicle hard in the chest and she let go of his neck with a grunt, but as he staggered away she grabbed him again and smashed him into the cave wall. He crumpled to the ground with his eyes closed.

Moon let out a cry and ran forward to crouch beside him. She reached out and felt the flicker of his brain dropping into unconsciousness. He was still alive.

In the same moment, Qibli threw himself at Icicle and knocked her off her feet. The IceWing and the SandWing struggled, rolling across the floor, kicking scrolls in all directions. Qibli stabbed his tail at her but missed. She flung him away so he crashed hard on top of the main desk and slid over behind it.

Seconds later, Moon was seized by cruel, cold talons and pinned to the ground. Icicle's claws wrapped around her neck.

"Icicle, don't!" Winter yelled. He grabbed his sister and tried to drag her off Moon, but she was bigger than he was and too heavy to move.

"You never won when we fought in the hatchery," she snarled at him. "Don't bother trying now. And for what? A couple of NightWings? Don't you remember that we hate them? Don't you remember what they did to our tribe? To Hailstorm?"

Winter froze, still clutching her shoulders.

His mind slipped into the well-worn tracks Moon had heard on the first day she met him. *The NightWings killed him. And all of them. All of Scarlet's IceWing prisoners.*

"The NightWings came right out of the sky and killed every last IceWing in Scarlet's mountain prison," Icicle said. "While the IceWings were still bound and chained. Remember?

And do you remember why? To make Queen Scarlet free *that* one." She let go of Moon's neck with one talon to point at Starflight. "He's the reason they're all dead."

Winter did remember. Moon could see it all flooding through his head. This was the heart of his guilt. He'd gotten his brother captured by SkyWing soldiers when they went looking for scavenger dens in the mountains. So his brother had been in Queen Scarlet's prison when the NightWings arrived to save Starflight, and they'd killed all the IceWings in a show of strength. Every last one.

That was why Winter hated NightWings.

"But Starflight's not to blame," Moon choked out wretchedly. "He's the kind of dragon who will stop the killing, Winter, not cause any more. He's good inside — just like you are."

His eyes, blue as arctic oceans, stared into hers.

"Good, pfft. Would you rather be good or strong?" Icicle spat at him.

In response, Winter smashed his sister across the head with his tail.

Icicle fell back, roaring, and Moon gasped for air.

"Starflight and Moon didn't kill Hailstorm!" Winter shouted. "Queen Scarlet did! She's the one who took him prisoner! He would have died in her arena sooner or later. How can you work with her? How can you work *for* her? How can you do anything she says?"

He advanced and Icicle retreated, back toward the bank

of leaf-covered windows. A trickle of dark blue blood was running down the side of her head from a gash near one of her horns. The same dark blue was smeared across her white shoulders, bleeding from a dozen cuts left by Qibli's claws. She was panting heavily.

"You are the worst kind of dirt-covered whale chum," Icicle growled at Winter. "You've ruined everything."

"It seems to me like you're the one who's done that," he said.

"You don't understand," she said. "You *idiot*."

Winter stopped, his wings spread menacingly. "So explain it to me," he said.

"Our brother is alive, you fool," she snarled. "Queen Scarlet told me. She kept the most important prisoners in a secret, separate prison. He wasn't killed by the NightWings, although twelve of our fellow dragons were."

Moon clutched her head as agonizing spears of shock ricocheted through Winter's brain, like flying shards of a broken mirror.

"Hailstorm is *alive*?" Winter cried.

"Yes — and if I had succeeded in killing the prophecy dragonets for Queen Scarlet, she would have given him back to me. To us," Icicle hissed. "But instead you've killed him all over again. And now you have to live with that forever."

CHAPTER 23

Winter turned to Moon, agony written across his face. She knew what he was asking, even though his mind couldn't put it into clear thoughts yet.

"It's true," Moon said, scanning Icicle's thoughts. "At least, that's what Scarlet has told her. Scarlet could be lying, but Icicle believes her."

"Why didn't you tell me?" Winter said to his sister.

"Because you're worthless," she spat. "And I didn't want to waste time arguing with your sensitive moral sensibilities."

"She means she didn't want to be talked out of it," Moon said fiercely. "And she knew you would try, and you might even have succeeded, because you're *not* worthless; you're smart and brave and capable of caring about other dragons."

"Is it really true, though?" he said, a question not quite for either Moon or Icicle. "Hailstorm isn't dead?"

Icicle narrowed her eyes and flicked her tail, weighing the possibilities. "There's still time," she hissed at him. "We could still kill the dragonets and get him back."

Winter hesitated, wavering. The memories of his brother were warm and tense, loving and terrible at the same time. He missed him desperately. And he needed to atone for the guilt of losing him in the first place.

But he shook his head. "Not with more killing. Not for Queen Scarlet. It won't work."

"Fine," Icicle snarled. "I hope you choke on a walrus and die."

She whirled and dove out the nearest window, tearing straight through the leaf pane and letting in a burst of too-bright sunlight.

"Icicle! Stop!" Winter yelled. He ran to the window and leaned out. "Come back! We can find him together!"

There was no response. In the fading echoes Moon could hear as Icicle flew away, she saw that the IceWing was planning to find Queen Scarlet and complete her mission somehow. The dragonets were far from safe.

Behind the desk, Qibli groaned, and Moon darted over to him as he sat up gingerly. His pale yellow scales were dented and bruised and his amber earring had been nearly torn out of his ear, making a small ragged tear where the hole had been.

Six-Claws said it was idiotic to get this, he thought, touching his earring with a wince. *I can't believe I let an IceWing knock me out. Thorn would be unimpressed. I should have started with a fireburst to her face, but I thought she was going to attack Moon and I just jumped in without thinking. Stupid, impulsive, everything Thorn says I need to learn to fix.*

Moon reached toward him and then hesitated. "Can I —?" she asked.

He met her eyes and nodded. She took one of his warm talons in hers and gently felt his head. There was a sizable bump over one eye and a couple of claw marks slashed across his chest, but nothing as bad as she'd feared, considering Icicle's formidable claws.

"That's right," Qibli said. He tried to stand up, flinched, and sat down again. "She'd better run. I was just resting for part two: the crushening! Where I do some — crushing — and it's — very impressive — I think I'd better lie down."

"Looks like you'll live," she said to him, relieved.

As will you, said Darkstalker, sounding pleased. **At least for now. Tomorrow —**

Let's not think about tomorrow right this second, Moon suggested. *And by the way . . . thank you.*

Moon sat with Sunny as night fell, on the tallest peak of Jade Mountain, watching a storm approach. A wall of rain was visible to the south, sweeping slowly toward them; patches of blue sky still peeked through the building banks of dark gray clouds. The wind seemed to carry the faraway scent of dragon fire, ocean spray, and the rainforest. Moon wrapped her wings around herself, shivering as the breeze picked up and small raindrops began to fall.

Sunny had her tail tucked around her back talons and was pressing her front talons together. Her strange green-gray eyes were fixed on the line of desert they could still faintly see to the west.

"Poor Sora," she said. "Queen Moorhen and Queen Ruby will be looking for her. Poor everybody, really, even Icicle. I mean, if Queen Scarlet had Clay — I don't know what I'd do."

"There's one more thing I have to tell you," Moon said.

I'm not sure this is wise, Darkstalker interjected.

I'm not going to hide anymore, she answered. *Even if that means giving up a little safety. Or, all right, a lot of safety, you've made your point.*

She took a deep breath. "I can read minds. And see the future."

Oh dear, Sunny thought immediately, her face creasing with skepticism. *Another Fatespeaker.*

"It's true," Moon said. She explained about the full moons, and about how she'd hidden her powers from everyone, and about how she'd used them to overhear Icicle and Scarlet and foresee the fire.

When she finished, Sunny's thoughts were a lot less skeptical. "That's kind of a huge secret to have kept for so long," she said, studying Moon's eyes. "It must have been hard."

Moon nodded.

There was a pause, and then Sunny said, "Can you tell what I'm thinking right now?"

"Sure." Moon shook out her wings, tilting her head at Sunny. "You're wondering how Tsunami will react to this — you don't think she'll believe me. And part of you is worrying about Starflight and hoping Fatespeaker will take care of him properly." Sunny arched her brows, startled. "But mostly," Moon hurried on, "you're thinking about the school and wondering if it's already failed. You're thinking about giving up and sending everyone home, because it's only the first week and all these terrible things have happened. You're wondering if bringing peace to all the tribes is too hard, and if you're not the right dragon for the job."

"Wow," Sunny said faintly.

"But you are," Moon blurted. "You can't give up. Of course it's hard; the whole point is that you're trying to fix something that's nearly impossible to fix. But if no one ever even tries, then it will always be terrible. You and Clay and the others . . . dragons believe in you. You have to take that gift and do something with it, not run away from it."

Hmmmm, Darkstalker said significantly.

I know, I hear myself, she said.

"Was that a prophecy?" Sunny said hopefully. "Did you see us changing the world? Like, five eggs to hatch on brightest night, five dragons born to teach history and art and get everyone to calm down and be nice to each other?"

Moon laughed. "When the school has lasted twenty years, the tribes will be at peace?" She shook her head. "No, it's not a prophecy. It's just faith."

Sunny nodded. "I know all about that." *And if we make our own destiny, that's what I want mine to be,* she thought. "Let's go back inside before those clouds really open up on us." She reached out and touched Moon's shoulder. "Thank you for telling me all that, Moon. I mean, about your powers and everything."

They flew down to the Great Hall, where Moon found Kinkajou and Qibli waiting for her. Kinkajou ran over and threw her wings around Moon. Her frantic relieved thoughts seemed to bounce wildly along Moon's scales. *Alive! Friends! Heroes! Averting tragedy and saving the day!*

"Qibli told me what happened," she said. "I can't believe I missed it all! I can't believe I wasn't there to protect you! You're totally heroes, saving us all from bad guys! Although I'm kind of confused about who's the bad guy and who I should be mad at, because SORA WHAT but also Icicle was totally scary but then SAVING HER BROTHER ACK so I get it but still, attacking my winglet! My best friend! Not OK!"

Best friend. After everything? "I thought you were mad at me," Moon said. Out of the corner of her eye, she saw Sunny slipping away with a wave.

"I was, but that was yesterday," Kinkajou said. She released Moon and stepped back, gleaming gold and pink with blue all along her spine. "I mean, I realized it's not that big a deal; I kind of say everything I'm thinking anyway, right?" She grinned. "Or if you hear something you shouldn't, that's kind of worse for you than for me, I figure. And I was thinking if *you* promise to tell me all *your* secrets from now on, then it won't matter if you know all of mine. Right?"

Moon smiled back, but thought uncomfortably of Darkstalker.

Stop, stop, he said. *I see all the bad decisions you're about to make. Don't do it, Moon.*

"Where's Turtle?" Moon asked, ignoring him.

"Here," he said, stepping out of the shadows. She hadn't noticed the quiet fuzz of his mind beyond the clamor of Kinkajou's thoughts.

"Can I see your armband?" she asked.

Inside her head, Darkstalker sighed. *I literally can't see any future where I can talk you out of this.*

Oh, good, Moon thought. *Then take a break and don't try.*

Turtle slid the golden band down and over his talons and handed it to her. The silence instantly fell over everything and Moon shivered. It was such a *lonely* feeling. How did other dragons live like this all the time?

She studied the black rocks studded around the band. There were six of them, smaller than Onyx's stone, but they were all the same scorched-looking black with flecks of silver and otherworldly metals.

"Where did these stones come from?" she asked Turtle.

"Oh, it's kind of a cool story," he said. "I was out swimming at night with a few of my brothers a while ago — it's great, the sea at night with all the stars — and we were watching the comet that was so bright, remember? And then I saw something like a trail of fire fall from the sky into the ocean. No one else wanted to come search for it with me, so I figured I could keep what I found, which was this big chunk of black rock that had fallen all the way to the sea floor. It wasn't hard to find, actually; it turned the water all around it a whole lot hotter. Anyway I took a few bits that had broken off and had them made into that armband."

"Skyfire," Moon said, passing it back to him. She had a brief, intensely curious impulse to give the armband to Qibli for a minute, so she could hear what Turtle was thinking and maybe find out his secret. But that was exactly the kind of thing she needed them to trust her *not* to do. "That's what Onyx calls it. She has a piece of it, too."

Qibli went still, looking at her. He was already figuring out what she was going to say.

She turned to include Kinkajou as well. "It turns out that skyfire can block mind reading. I discovered that today, while we were talking to Onyx. That's why I can't read her, or Turtle — if you're wearing this rock, I can't hear your thoughts at all." She faced Turtle again. "I was hoping — if it's all right with you, Turtle, I wondered if Kinkajou and Qibli and Winter could each have one of these rocks. You're all my friends — my winglet — and I want you to have a way to keep your thoughts private."

Kinkajou leaped up and hugged her again.

"Very cool," Qibli said, giving her a smile.

"That explains a lot," Turtle said. He started picking at the stones in the band. "Of course they can have them."

"I'll take Winter his and explain everything," Moon said with a deep breath.

"Actually," Qibli said, "I have bad news."

Moon saw it in his mind; she couldn't believe she hadn't picked it out of the torrent of his thoughts before.

"Oh, no, really?" she said.

"What?" Kinkajou asked. "What? What? WHAT?"

"It's Winter," Qibli said. "I checked our cave for him an hour ago. He's gone."

— CHAPTER 24 —

"Gone?" Kinkajou cried with dismay. "Why? Where'd he go?"

"I don't know, but Bandit's cage is missing, too," Qibli said. "So I don't think he's coming back."

"Oh," Turtle said. "I saw him leaving, but I thought he was just going hunting. I should have stopped him." He managed to pry two rocks free and handed one to Qibli, then another to Kinkajou. Their thoughts fuzzed out into that quiet hum as they slipped the rocks into the library card pouches around their necks. Moon could still hear dragons elsewhere in the school, but she knew she'd miss listening to Qibli and Kinkajou.

I'll just have to listen better to what they actually say, she promised herself.

"Which way was he going?" Moon asked Turtle.

"Northwest, toward the forest that's between the mountains and the desert," he said. "Uh. Where are *you* going?"

Moon was heading for the mouth of the cave, where they could see sheets of rain pouring down.

"I'm going to find him," she said.

"In this weather?" Turtle protested.

"Oh yay!" Kinkajou cried. "Me too!"

"Are you sure?" Moon said to her, waving one wing at the storm outside. "I understand if you don't —"

"I'm a *Rain*Wing," Kinkajou said. "It rains all the *time* in the *rain*forest. Trust me, I can handle it."

"I'm not sure I can," Qibli said, rubbing the back of his head. "But I'm coming with you anyway."

Kinkajou looked expectantly at Turtle.

He shuffled his feet, flickering his glow-in-the-dark scales nervously. "In this *weather*?" he said again.

"Come on, Turtle!" she said. "We're a winglet! We're all that's left of the Jade Winglet! We should stick together! Also, how can you be bothered by a little water? You *live* in it. You can actually breathe it. You'll be fine." She bumped his hip hard enough to overbalance him and he took a staggering step sideways.

"It's *different*," he objected. "Swimming is not the same as trying to fly while getting blown about and whacked in the face with little balls of water and also lightning — have we talked about the lightning?"

"He's coming, too," Kinkajou said to Moon. Turtle sighed in defeat.

"None of you have to do this," Moon said. "I just — I feel like I owe it to him."

"He's my clawmate," Qibli pointed out. "Also, I am a total expert on evil brothers and sisters."

"And I am coming to keep you safe," Kinkajou said. "Don't argue with me, I'm very menacing." She turned her wings black and bared her teeth, but the pink scales that remained rather undercut the effect.

Moon smiled at them. "All right," she said. "Let's go."

It seemed as though they flew for hours before they reached the outskirts of the forest, and then they spent forever circling over the trees. Moon kept thinking she heard a distant whisper that sounded like Winter, but the force and fury of the storm drowned out even the noise in her head.

"M-m-maybe we should go back," Turtle shouted to her as they did another pass over a clearing she was sure they'd flown over three times. "Maybe he's halfway to the Ice Kingdom already."

"I don't think so," Qibli called back. "Not with Bandit. He wouldn't fly too far with that cage — scavengers don't handle this kind of weather as well as we do."

Turtle made a "would rather not handle this weather either myself" face and tried to shake some of the rain off his waterlogged wings.

"Wait!" Moon cried, grabbing Kinkajou's tail. "I heard him! This way!"

She swooped toward the trees, half blinded by the downpour. A gust of wind blew her sideways at the wrong moment and she collided with the top of a tree, but she righted herself and dropped down through the branches to the forest floor.

The others followed, one by one, as she led the way through the dark forest. Suddenly she stopped to listen to a voice up ahead.

"Go on, get out of here. I know it's raining, but it's better than the Ice Kingdom, trust me."

"Winter!" Kinkajou yelped. "That's him!"

Moon breathed a plume of fire and it reflected off silvery scales in a clearing to their right. They hurried over and found Winter crouched beside his scavenger cage. The door was open and Bandit stood at the edge, staring bleakly out at the huge, dark forest and the storm.

"By all the snow monsters, what are you doing here?" Winter demanded, flapping his wet wings.

"Looking for you," Moon said.

"And we found you!" Kinkajou added. "We're amazing!"

He turned his head to look back at Bandit, avoiding their eyes. "I'm not going back to Jade Mountain," he said. "I'm going to look for my brother."

"I thought so," Moon said. "We want to help you."

"We *do*?" Turtle said, sounding alarmed.

"Yes!" Kinkajou said. "I didn't know we did, but now I totally do!"

Wait, came the voice of Darkstalker, faint and whispery. *Moon. Please don't leave me.*

She hadn't thought of that — that if she went with

Winter, wherever he meant to go, she'd be flying out of Darkstalker's range. He wouldn't be able to communicate with her anymore. He'd be all alone.

I'm afraid I'll go mad, he said. **With no one to talk to — no way to know if you're all right . . .** For the first time ever, his surface cracked and she saw past what he wanted her to see. Beneath the funny, confident, commanding voice she knew, she felt a deep hole, and all the way down the hole reverberated with infinite loneliness. A moment later, Darkstalker pulled his guard back up, and she was left skating on his conversational thoughts again.

I'll come back, she promised, feeling hugely sorry for him. *And listen, while I'm out there . . . I can look for your talisman.*

Will you? he asked. **Really?**

I will try.

Winter was shaking his head. "You can't come with me," he said. "I'm going to Queen Glacier. I need to explain it all to her and get her to help me find Hailstorm."

"Wouldn't it make more sense to go to the Sky Kingdom?" Kinkajou asked. "Your brother must be imprisoned there somewhere, right? We could look for him in, like, all the mountain caves, or something."

"Or you could go after Icicle," Qibli said. "Try to find out more about what Scarlet told her."

"I don't know where she's gone," Winter said bitterly.

"I have a guess," Qibli said with a glance at Kinkajou. "You won't like it, though. I think she's gone to the rainforest. She knows the one Scarlet hates the most is Glory — everyone knows that, if they know the story of what Glory did to her face. So I think Icicle might think that if she kills Glory, Scarlet will forgive her for failing to kill the others."

There was a hushed silence, broken by the patter of raindrops and a roll of thunder overhead.

"Then *I'm* going to the rainforest," Kinkajou said fiercely. "I'm not letting her kill *my* awesome queen."

Which is the right way? Moon wondered. *Where should we go?* If only Darkstalker could tell them. This seemed like exactly the right time for a vision of the future.

Are you sure? he asked.

Yes — can you tell us how to find her? Moon asked.

No, he said, **but I've been trying to protect you from this . . . and if you're leaving my range, then I won't be able to anymore.**

What —? Moon started to ask, but then suddenly a headache hit her like nothing she'd ever felt before, like an entire tribe of dragons descending on her head with their claws out. She staggered back with a cry, and the others whirled toward her.

"Moon?" Kinkajou leaped over, colliding wetly with her in the dark. Her scales were slick with raindrops as she tried to hold Moon up.

But Moon couldn't stand; the weight of the vision was bearing down on her. It was everything from her nightmare: the mountain falling, the dragons dying, the fire and earth cracking and destruction. Words were marching through her head and out of her mouth, inexorable and strange:

"Beware the darkness of dragons,
Beware the stalker of dreams,
Beware the talons of power and fire,
Beware one who is not what she seems.

Something is coming to shake the earth,
Something is coming to scorch the ground.
Jade Mountain will fall beneath thunder and ice
Unless the lost city of night can be found."

She choked for a moment on the last line, as though it were coming out edged with thorns. But at last it was said, and she collapsed into Kinkajou's wings, and the vision disappeared, taking the headache with it.

"By all the snakes," Qibli said. Thunder rolled across the sky again and lightning flashed, illuminating the scared faces around her. "What was that?"

"That's what you've been muttering in your sleep," Kinkajou said.

"It sounded like a prophecy," Winter said disbelievingly.

Moon forced herself to stand up, although her wings were

shaking so hard she thought they might fall off. "Turtle," she said, "please give him one of the rocks."

Winter eyed the small black stone with suspicion as Turtle dropped it in his palm. "What's this?"

"I have a lot to explain," she said. "Everything, the whole truth. I'm going to tell you everything."

Everything? Darkstalker said with a distant sigh.

"That sounds ominous," Winter said.

"No more ominous than *Jade Mountain will fall beneath thunder and ice*," Qibli said. "I hope we're all planning to talk about that, because I'm extremely unsettled right now."

"She said we have to find the lost city of night," Kinkajou said. "That's all, and then everything will be fine. Right? Isn't that what everyone else heard?"

"I'm pretty sure I heard that we're all going to die," Turtle said. "Death, death, monsters everywhere, death."

"Is that it?" Qibli asked Moon. "Is that what you saw? Jade Mountain is going to fall on us all?"

"I don't know," Moon said. "I've had visions, but none of them ever came out in words like that before. I don't know what it means."

Probably means it's important, Darkstalker offered.

Thank you, that's very helpful, she retorted. *Does it mean that what I saw is inevitable?*

No . . . there's another possible future, he said. *But it's along a very difficult and dark path.*

She closed her eyes. *Can I see that one? Is it awful, too?*

In response, she felt a slow spreading pain through her temples, and a moment later, a vision appeared. It looked like Jade Mountain Academy, but somehow different. Sunlight poured through the windows as she moved through the caves. Small dragonets she didn't know, each of them a different color, played a game of chase in the sky.

She came into the library and the dragon at the desk raised his head, listening. It was Starflight, but he was older, radiating happiness and peace. A small black dragonet raced into the cave, leaped onto the desk, kissed the side of his head, took one of the scrolls, and flew off down another tunnel, calling, "Thank you, Father!"

"No flying in the tunnels!" he called after her, but he was smiling.

Clay — older, bigger Clay — poked his head in through another entrance and said, "My class is asking for more scrolls about the War of SandWing Succession. I thought maybe you could come talk and talk and talk at them instead, and then maybe they'll go to sleep and stop asking me questions."

"Ha ha, hilarious," Starflight said, sliding out from behind the desk. "Firefly, just put that back when you're done, all right?"

Over in the window bay, a dark purple dragonet answered, "Sure," absentmindedly. She was curled up with two other dragons, one blue and one a deep orange-brown Moon had never seen before. They had a scroll spread out in front of them and were studying it together.

"Can you imagine?" the blue one said. "The tribes hated each other so much back then."

"It's a good thing we're so much smarter than all the dragons who lived before us," said the purple one importantly. "We'd never make *their* mistakes."

"I'm glad we're here, though," said the third dragonet. "At the Jade Mountain Academy. I'm glad it exists."

"Me too," the others said in unison.

The vision faded quietly away.

That's what we're fighting for, Moon thought. *Thank you, Darkstalker.*

I can help you make it real, he said. **Remember that when you can't hear me anymore.**

Moon felt the rain splattering against her wings. She looked around at her friends, all of their minds humming quietly, closed off. She wasn't a scared dragonet alone in the rainforest anymore. She was a mind reader and a prophet, and she had a prophecy to fulfill; an IceWing to rescue; a talisman to find; a possible supervillain to release, or not . . . and a world to save, even though it didn't know it needed saving yet.

No more hiding.

"Winter," she said. "There are a few things you need to know about me."

EPILOGUE

"Frog spit and goat tongues!" Queen Scarlet cursed. She shook the sapphire in her talons violently. "Why isn't it working?"

"It probably is," her companion said smoothly. "The dragon you're looking for must still be awake."

Scarlet glared at him. The vast black sky wheeled over their heads, studded with stars like diamonds. The three moons lit up the toothy peaks of the mountains all around them. "It's the middle of the night. Why wouldn't she be asleep? I gave her an ultimatum. I need to know what's happening there."

He shrugged, tapping something between his front talons. *Tap. Tap.* "So try a different dragon."

She wrapped her claws around the blue stone again, growling to herself. "Has to be someone I know," she muttered, "but I don't want those dragonets to see where I am." After a moment, she closed her eyes. "All right. An old favorite."

It only took a minute for her to drop into Peril's dream; as usual, it was tortured and weird, with several Queen Scarlets chasing her through the Sky Palace while corpses of burnt dragons lurched out of various doorways to attack her. Scarlet snorted. What was the point of being a glorious monster with talons of fire if you were going to agonize over it so much? Peril's power was absolutely wasted on her.

"Stop!" she roared, planting herself in Peril's path. Peril skidded to a halt and looked frantically around; she thought Scarlet was another one of the dream queens. She'd always had trouble figuring out when Scarlet was really visiting her, which could be useful, especially at times like this.

"Who died today?" Scarlet demanded. "Tell me! Who is dead?"

"No one!" Peril cried. "I didn't kill anyone! I swear!"

"Stop blithering," Scarlet growled. "Someone must have died today at that ludicrous school."

Peril shook her head wildly. "No. No. No one is dead. Clay is safe, that's what's important. No one is dead. Oh, a MudWing and an IceWing are gone, but they're alive, not dead, no one is dead."

Scarlet hissed. She yanked the sapphire away from her head, snapping abruptly out of Peril's dream.

"I'm going to murder that IceWing!" she yelled. "This is not thrilling at all!"

"She failed?" said the other dragon. He shifted from shadow to moonlight, his scales rippling in strange moonlit colors. *Tap. Tap. Tap.* "How surprising. Should I kill your prisoner?"

"Yes," Scarlet hissed. "Wait. No." She paced along the ledge, fuming. If she let Hailstorm live, Icicle would stop being frightened of her; her threats would mean nothing. But if she killed him, she'd have lost her only bit of leverage on a very useful pawn.

Tap. Tap. Tap.

Of course, Icicle wasn't the only dragon who wanted this particular prisoner back. There was another brother, wasn't there? But Scarlet had never seen him. How would she get into his dreams?

Was there another way to get to him?

Or someone else who could kill the dragonets?

"I should do it myself," she muttered. She knew that. She just — every time she thought about that RainWing: the jaw extending horribly, the fangs pointed straight at her and the venom flying toward her face — it gave her a sick, squashed feeling that reminded her of her melted scales. It wasn't *fear,* exactly. She would never say that.

But if she could find a way to kill them from a distance . . . or at least Glory . . . that would be preferable, certainly.

"STOP THAT INFERNAL TAPPING!" she roared. "What is it, anyhow? What are you fiddling with in your horrid, gloaty way?"

"Oh, this?" The dragon lifted the ancient scroll into the moonlight, looked up at it, and smiled. "Don't you worry. This is nothing."

WINGS
OF
FIRE

will continue . . .

An epic series takes flight!

Read them all!